# NOTRE DAME REVIEW

# Notre Dame Review

NUMBER 27

Editors
John Matthias
William O'Rourke

Senior Editor
Steve Tomasula

Founding Editor
Valerie Sayers

Managing Editor
Jaclyn Dwyer

Executive Editor
Kathleen J. Canavan

Sparks Editorial Asst.
Lindsay Starck

Editorial Assistants
Melanie Cotter
Donald Cowan
Daniel Citro
Ryan Downey
Hilary Fox
John Joseph Hess
Raúl Jara
Iris Law
Jessica Martinez
Tasha Matsumoto
Grant Osborn
Elijah Park
Justin Perry
Sami Schalk
Michael Valente
Jacqui Weeks

Advisory Editors
Francisco Aragón
Matthew Benedict
Gerald Bruns
Seamus Deane
Cornelius Eady
Stephen Fredman
Sonia Gernes
Joyelle McSweeney
Orlando Menes
James Walton
Henry Weinfield

The *Notre Dame Review* is published semi-annually. Subscriptions: $15 (individuals) or $20 (institutions) per year or $250 (sustainers). Single Copy price: $8. Distributed by Ubiquity Distributors, Brooklyn, NY, and Media Solutions, Huntsville, Alabama. We welcome manuscripts, which are accepted from September through March. Please include a SASE for reply. Please send all subscription and editorial correspondence to: *Notre Dame Review*, 840 Flanner Hall, University of Notre Dame, Notre Dame, IN 46556. *The Notre Dame Review* is indexed in *Humanities International Complete*.

*Notre Dame Review* copyright 2009 by the University of Notre Dame
ISSN: 1082-1864
*Bridges and Views* ISBN 978-1-892492-26-5

# CONTENTS

# American Bridge

*Michael O'Leary*

1.

The dead can move but not of their free will,
refusing neither ceremony nor
decomposition when the quiet earth
pulls down the flesh from limb to limb and all
eyes shrivel into raisins on a stem,
resigned instead to gestures offered by
the living to make sense of senselessness.
Decay is irreversible and like
a pile of steaming compost or the stew
of bubbly creek, life percolates with heat
from its corruption; froth and foam conspire
to float a restless bubble on a breath
of rising air, its profile glistening
with iridescence as its membrane thins
and gathers in a radiant teardrop
before it falls back to the river which
is never the same, a trickle now,
now swift and spirited away to sea.
So when Achilles staggered by the surf
after he'd twisted through another night
without sleep, neither pride nor grief made him
lash Hector to his chariot and drag
his corpse around Patroclus' tomb again;
it was the sea with its black catenary
of breakers jagging the dawn twilight
from Egypt to Achaea and beyond.

2.

A series of transmission towers pitch
a tent of low cloud cover threatening rain
above the Skyway, guyed between each by
the hyperbolic droop of power lines
undulating all along the South Shore,

over the roads and railroads and the swales
of dried-up cattail, lacing through shagbark
and stands of rank ailanthus naked yet
along the banks of the Grand Calumet
up to the muddy gray yard of the old
American Bridge fabrication shop
surrounded by pale grass and dirty sedge
where ten-ton cranes delivered freshly cut
sections which were then spliced and fitted clean
to pre-assemble the Hancock Tower
laid out completely on its side before
being trucked up piece by piece to the shores of
Lake Michigan where it was riveted
and spliced together for a second time
according to design, then braced from high
winds by ascending Xs and bedecked
in thirteen acres of aluminum
and tinted glass to face the vast pancake
of grassless prairie spreading south and west
and down the lake's great tongue back to the mills
where each of its members was first rolled out.

3.

When meteors streaked the sky, priests would comb
the desert for remains to prove the truth
of the old gods' approval; regardless
of whether Thoth or Amun bore the gift,
a dagger wrought from pure sky metal placed
at King Tut's breast would lay Aten to rest.
But the sweet savor of unctuous fat,
of marrow crackling on a burning pile
of ore was soothing, sweet, and wholly best
to offer, to atone for all that's wrong.
After the hecatomb, beneath the cake
of char, a bloom of iron burning low
was primed to be transformed into an ax
to cut more oxen for the sacrifice.
But when blacksmiths forgot about the lance
cooking long at the back of the forge

an accidental alchemy emerged:
the heat had changed the microstructure of
the iron crystal so that carbon seeped
into the new interstices, making
the metal denser and stronger fivefold.
Quenched in a bath of oil, the carbon froze,
remaining packed in that geometry,
a higher energy, resulting in
a steel which, when annealed, could cut through bronze
like tender lamb and make pulp of the skull.

4.

The young inventor Henry Bessemer,
self-taught by casting model wheelwork at
his father's type foundry, sold a new shot
the British had already pooh-poohed to
Napoleon III at the outbreak
of the Crimean War. Elongated
and cut with grooves to rotate forward through
the mark, the 30 lb. projectile proved
too heavy for an iron cannon, while
the cost of steel remained prohibitive.
With something to discover, Bessemer
began an open hearth experiment
of fusing steel in molten iron when
he realized that air could oxidize
the excess carbon from crude pig iron.
A revelation followed, spewing slags
and splashes of metal high in the air.
Tapping a molten incandescent stream
from the converter and then forming it
into an ingot, Bessemer saw that
the iron was wholly decarburized,
ready to be formed into rods and plates
which would then span the Mississippi in
the low and graceful arch of the Eads Bridge
and mount the prairie skyline steel frame by
steel frame like Monk's Mound at Cahokia.

5.

For every form there is a function or
a hierarchy of functions. Each beam,
each column of the Hancock Tower holds
the next in place—for every action there
is always an equal and opposite
reaction—channeling the flow of force
back to the earth and lifting up the bulk
of glass and steel so that someone can say,
"I see the bluff of sand across the lake
divide the water from the firmament
like a puff of smoke on a cloudless day."
The possibilities of form may be
infinite but they are constrained by law—
the center and circumference of the real—
the radius of which can only be
inferred from failure and catastrophe.
There is no urge more natural than the urge
to know, but reason fails, exactitude
remains elusive and though it may all
resolve into a single number, crude
experience most often must suffice.
Try and try again; fail; fail differently.
Try now again to petrify the blade
of light cutting across the macula,
to cut the light of day from rock, to give
light form and raise it high above the plain.

6.

Quarried in ancient Swan below the First
Cataract on the east bank of the Nile
4000 years ago, the obelisk
of reddish granite rising now above
St. Peter's square was first cut whole from rock
with hammer, chisel, fire, and water, then
polished with diamond dust, and draggled on
a buttered sledge by 50,000 men
down to a barge dry-docked until the spring

when high waters conveyed the cargo up
to Helipolis where it was raised
before the pylon to the Temple of
the Sun, remaining there 2000 years.
Then Caesar came to tango in the sheets
of Ptolemy, but when the pretty worm
of Nylus sucked its nurse asleep the dream
of the Republic ended with Pharoah's death
who proved to be one Caesar too many.
In order to transport the obelisk
to Rome where it was re-erected in
the circus Nero would eventually
adorn with Christians crucified to slake
the fire of 64, Caligula
built a ship large enough to later bear
a herd of elephants when Claudius
invaded Britain for its mines and slaves.

7.

In 1585 Sixtus V,
newly elected pope, sent out a call
for architects to find a way to move
the obelisk from Nero's erstwhile tracks
to the piazza facing St. Peter's old
basilica 800 ft. away.
Domenico Fontana's massive twin
towers designed to bear the stress and strain
of tackle which would raise the obelisk
convinced the panel to select his plan.
Rolled on logs up to the square, when time came
to raise it to the vertical the pope
restrained the crowd to absolute silence
by penalty of death so that the men
and horses cranking all 44 cranes
could hear Fontana's voice directing them.
By noon the sun had lengthened all the ropes
so that the dangling obelisk began
to sag as they slackened and no amount
of pulling made them taut again. All hope

seemed lost until a seasoned sailor broke
the silence—"Water on the ropes!"—to which
Fontana acquiesced. The water caused
the ropes to contract and thus took up slack,
allowing them to lift both obelisk
and death sentence such broken silence wrote.

8.

Things happen for a reason; strands of hemp
are twisted together to fashion rope
which can be used to drag a corpse
across the plains of Troy or pull a ship
into the slip at Gary Harbor where
some 60,000 tons of taconite
originally mined outside Hibbing
at the Hull-Rust-Mahoning Open Pit
in the Mesabi Iron Range before
being crushed, separated into ore,
rolled into pellets, hauled by coal car to
the Twin Ports and then shipped by oreboat down
Lake Michigan to U.S. Steel and now
unloaded, melted, blasted with hot air
and rolled into deep beams and columns thick
enough to bear the wide expanse of sky
and lake, the rising sun, the moon and stars,
and three crows heading south on Lake Shore Drive
zigzagging black on black between the Mies
apartment towers, west on Chestnut when
the eye at last braids a crooked path straight
up to the top, not quite to vanishing,
where parallel lines worry in the wind
about the foundation as Fazhlur Khan,
the engineer behind the simple truss
tube system, anticipated they would.

9.

Each structure is a diagram of force,
which is itself a manifestation

of energy: the bending of a beam,
the oscillation of a molecule
about its point of equilibrium.
Matter can't act alone, but only as
a seat of energy, which is itself
a temporary arrangement of parts
in the continuous descent of change:
the contours of a dune, the trace of waves
ribbing the bottom of the lake, the wind
driving them on, the pressure gradient
along the water's edge, the spinning world,
light and warmth, nuclear fusion, the shock waves
of supernovae, new geometries,
the causal singularity of space
and matter at the beginning of time,
the perfect streamline of a swallow's wing
as it banks inland to its little nest,
the mind's ability to apprehend
that journey from a drop of morning dew
come down upon the earth to the hard rain
lashing the door of a fabrication shop
in northern Indiana: even this
chain of causation sags from the pull of
intention to be here again alive.

# LORD GOD BIRD

*Colin Cheney*

*...and other possible sources of this pale blur include the pale head markings of a pileated woodpecker, light reflecting off the bird's back, or video processing artifacts.*
*—David A. Sibley,* Science, *17 March 2006*

Po, ninety, marks his canvas with charcoal
taped to a length of bamboo,
says he paints for the rare moment
when he is moved by someone outside himself. Ghosts:
a father dead of TB, an island of murdered friends.

And now he is sketching a Siberian tiger
machine-gunned fifty-years-ago
that just yesterday startled a daydreaming G.I.
who glimpsed it running through the pencil & ironbark
orchids of the Korean DMZ, of the minefield.
But this orchid he roughs in now
he dug from the peak of Huayna Picchu
& carried home on the plane in a damp paper bag.
Its flowers small & spotted as with Pollack's brush.

In Camcorder footage, following the wing's ventral
surface, Sibley must have, for a moment, known he was watching spirit
photographs, not the Civil War forgeries, but the real ghosts.

I would have lied too, I would have
said it was a common thing, accounted for, not the terror
of what the bird's apparition would then have to mean.

I love the Arkansas of the American mind
where, in some quantum trick in cells of the brain,
the lost things flare back
for a few months only to disappear again.
The Greeks had a name for this empty frame in the Camcorder
left filming in the swamp: *Aornos,* meaning *birdless.*

Looking hard at the barest outline of wing,
I hear the old chaos of the songbirds
Po gave away one by one to make room for Sylvia's memories
in their emptied cages,
Sylvia who yesterday he found asleep
beneath her sculptures—clay over chicken wire, feathers
from the birds—wearing her best jewelry & a nightgown.

# WATSON AND THE SHARK

*Colin Cheney*

1.

A young whale entered the mouth
of the Gowanus yesterday, lolling under the subway bridge
by the scrap iron yard. A gash somehow opened
in his side, he soon bobbed to the surface—
a balloon of unrecoverable oil.
Maybe they wait for the canal, in thunderstorm,
to reverse course & return the corpse
to the sea on its acres of rain.
Or haul it up Red Hook's
shore, by the grain elevator, to be hacked
into raw hunks & driven to the fields of Fresh Kills
to sleep, unable to decay, in the leachate & graves there.
Or maybe, though they didn't, someone held a match
to his blowhole's pilot light & let the sad gondola
he'd become explode, a living lamp the rain & overflow
could beat against, work toward open ocean.

2.

In the summer, whenever it rained, my mother
                                        drove us up the emerald necklace
to stand before Copley's painting of that instant before
                                        whatever happened

happened. Would they haul the glowing body
                                        free of the storm-water,
we are meant to ask, the boat-hook
                                        sink true in the fish's haunch before Watson,

the boy already raptured of his clothes,
                                        is taken? Sixteen, my mother
had been swept into a culvert pipe, jumping into a swollen crick after a neighbor

who had fallen in
& passed through & was pulled free. But she caught there,
the green hurricane water sluicing her body,
the pulse of dirt, watercress

& leaf-molt stirring in her ears. Copley, too,
was taught to hate water, barely
remaining sane during the long passage from Boston to Europe
to study the bodies

of saints, how muscle can be set aglow under the proper lacquer-work
of turpentine spirits & linen
lain like a burn-bandage across the canvas, soaked

in poppy oils, the pressings of walnuts.
And so I always thought the naked figure
was some kin to Christ, his son maybe, so washed with light, as I thought

he was adrift not in Havana's harbor
but Boston's—my home waters so green
with pollution then. Copley is said to have stolen Watson's posture from an archangel

he saw in one of the museums in Parma maybe, or Rome.
And the two sailors
reaching for their friend echo the apostles' strain to haul in their suddenly

God-laden nets in Rubens' *Miraculous Draught of Fishes*,
or perhaps Tassaert's etching
of Jonah being heaved to the sea, given to the whale for wickedness.
Yet here,

in Havana, in Boston as a child, they are pulling him back, one of their own.
Salvation is one possible theme,
so frightened she was of something those years,

our mother, propped-up in her water-bed
reading of near-death experiences, of angels
reaching to guide you through the tunnel, but you saying, no,
no, there is my body

riven on the table beneath you,
saying I want to go back. Did she hope we believed
the boy would be swallowed whole to be resurrected three days later, spat

out onto the shore as Jonah was, as she was downstream, found tangled
in yellow irises?
She held my hand tight as we watched those waves for some sign,

just as Copley did those weeks he didn't know which child his wife had left
behind, playing each of them into the grave,
first his eldest, & then his daughter,

each taking turns drowning in Boston soil burning with civil war, until
he finally lets his youngest son go
as he does the boy in his painting into the maw

of what we know could only have been a tiger shark,
though the anatomy
was all wrong. The beast has already torn free his leg below the knee, the flesh

of turpentine beginning its slow digestion
in the belly of the wrongly-rendered fish,
flesh close to, as he wrote to a friend back home, *The knee & part of the thigh*

*of the little Jesus in the Madonna's lap at Mr. Chardon's.*
Or perhaps more the dull wash
of Jonah's humid skin as he waited to be released, hearing the pulse of the blood

in the walls around him, the wash & pressure of sea. What manner of whale
was it—a blue,
humpback, the whale shark? Will you promise me, she asked

each of us in turn, driving home through the rain,
that you want to go to heaven?

3.

*Go to Kut*, people say, *you will find your son there.*
Nets hung from bridges fill with bodies that took three days
to drift downstream from the city. Untangling
the rotten limbs, matted clothes from the reeds

& trash the nets are meant to capture—*His belly*
*is cut open*, one of the gatherers says, *I can't*
*lift him free*. Leaning over the gunwale
the other asks *Does he have a head?*

Bodies left unclaimed are buried shallow in a corner
of a cemetery reserved for those dragged from the river.
Shallow—so they can be exhumed. Yes, their bones
call out for something. Under the morning stars

wheeling, we might want to say, waterbirds observed
the migration from the killing fields. Or that fish
bore them along as Pliny tells us dolphins would bring
half-drowned sailors back to shore. But they cry out

merely to be as whole as they are still in each of their mother's
minds, not the chimera of hewn parts—hands, beautiful
beaten faces, burnt legs too small for the nets
to catch—that keeps climbing the embankment

only to come undone & fall back to the river again.
A girl is being buried now. *2656, this is her number*,
the gravedigger says. Upstream, another body is let
into the olive water, & then his head after him.

4.

Forgive me for forgetting your name.
A childhood friend of my wife, your boat caught in a lightning storm—
like this one tonight in Brooklyn—off Georges Bank.
Freezing in dark waves of rain,
you soothed your mother on a cell phone, listened in the howl
& lull of the surrounding Atlantic to her voice, the nets

of haddock & cod straining for release, though they would die
with you there. Forgive me for drawing you back into the sea,
but I need to make the matter close,
as the Psalmist needed to thank the Lord for everything
before it was taken away: the sea teeming with innumerable things,
& for ships, for Leviathan even—that creature standing in
for everything unknown or barely glimpsed, or forgotten.
As you do, sometimes, when I finally go to bed
listening to rain in those pear trees in the common yard,
pears that no one picks, that hang there like bell-buoys,
that let go of their branches
like a net cut loose of its storm of silver, scattering & then gone.

# INTERVIEW WITH CIARAN CARSON

*Jenny Malmqvist*

*Ciaran Carson was born in Belfast in 1948. He was brought up bilingually, speaking Irish at home. He is the author of eleven volumes of poetry, most recently* For All We Know and Collected Poems, *which appeared in 2008. His early collections,* The Irish for No and Belfast Confetti, *introduce Belfast as the subject matter of his poetry. Present in* The Irish for No *is also his engagement with the Irish tradition of song, music and storytelling.* First Language *and* Opera Et Cetera *display Carson's preoccupation with language and translation. His prose works include two books on Irish traditional music, two works of fiction, and a memoir of Belfast. He is the translator of Dante's* Inferno, The Midnight Court, *an 18th-century Irish poem by Brian Merriman, and the Old Irish epic* The Táin. *He also has published a collection of sonnet versions of Baudelaire, Rimbaud and Mallarmé,* The Alexandrine Plan. *Due in 2009 are* On the Night Watch, *a collection of poems, and* The Pen Friend, *a novel. He has been awarded many literary prizes, including the Irish Times Irish Literature Prize, the T S Eliot Prize and the Forward Prize for Best Poetry Collection. His translation of the* Inferno *won the Oxford Weidenfeld Translation Prize. Between 1975 and 1998, Carson held positions within the Arts Council of Northern Ireland, first as Traditional Arts Officer and from 1992, as Literature Officer/Traditional Arts Officer. In 2003, he was appointed Professor of Poetry and Director of the Seamus Heaney Centre for Poetry at Queen's University, Belfast. The following interview was conducted via e-mail during spring 2008.*

**NDR**: In your essay "'Whose Woods These Are…': Some Aspects of Poetry and Translation" in the second issue of *The Yellow Nib* (2006), you recount how you as a child would lie awake at night saying the English word *horse* over and over to yourself, "savouring its strangeness". You write that the English horse was "a horse of another colour," different from the Irish *capall.* Having grown up with, or in, two languages, how has that influenced you as a writer, considering that language is your instrument? How does one relate something in one language that one has experienced in another?

**CC**: For a start, it's made me sceptical about the authority of any one language, or any one take on the world. There are as many alternative universes as there are languages. I've realised more and more over the years that my name is an emblem of some kind of fruitful linguistic ambivalence, Ciaran being ultra-Catholic and Carson ultra-Protestant. Ciaran is from Old Irish, 'little dark-headed one', and Lord Edward Carson is perceived by many unionists and loyalists as the instigator of the state of Northern Ireland. I'm a great fan of the work of Italo Calvino and I was pleased to learn that he saw his name—Italo the Italian and Calvino the Calvinist Protestant—in the same way. And his work is a series of alternative universes. I think being bilingual also alerts one to the grammar and stylistic procedures of both languages. One language illuminates the other, because one is led to ponder the comparative strangeness of the other. Finally, I'm reminded of the pronouncement of the American baseball player Yogi Berra (famous for his malapropisms): 'If you come to a fork in the road, take it.'

**NDR**: Could you describe your writing process?

**CC**: I suppose it depends if it's poetry or prose. With regard to poetry, a poem might have its beginning in a phrase that drifts into my mind: something overheard in a pub conversation, a sign on the street, an advertising jingle, a cry in the street at night, or a sequence of words appearing seemingly from nowhere. I would have no idea at that stage as to what its consequences might be. I carry a notebook with me and jot down phrases of this kind. Many of them don't get any further, and I don't know by what mysterious process a poem might evolve from them. When I get down to the business of writing a poem, I sometimes write in longhand first, and then type it on the computer; sometimes, especially for prose, I deal directly with the computer. Since becoming at least semi-computer-literate, I've tended to explore the internet for ideas or phrases that might relate to the work in hand. For instance, I might take a phrase I've just dreamed up, Google it, and see what usages, if any, might appear in the wider web of language. I'm often surprised to see that a phrase I thought original has been used before, albeit sometimes in a very different context to the one I had in mind; and this has an effect on what I write. I could say that whatever applies to poetry also applies to prose, except prose takes longer.

**NDR**: In your work, words trigger other words and narratives are sometimes driven by linguistic association. In the sequence "Letters from the Alphabet" (*Opera Et Cetera*, 1996), each poem is sparked off by the sound or shape of a letter of the alphabet and, as implied in the title, the poems themselves may be seen as letters, messages, from the alphabet. To what extent do you see language as co-author of your writings?

**CC**: Very much so. The Googling example I've just given is an illustration of that. I think of myself as an explorer of the language, which is so much more vast than its speakers and writers. I want to learn from language how I might see the world. I'm in love with the peculiar syntactical or grammatical twists and turns any language takes.

**NDR**: What draws you to a particular form, such as the haiku or the sonnet?

**CC**: Constraints, arbitrary as they are, are always useful because in my experience the first form of words that occur to me to say what I have in mind are rarely the best form of words. In labouring to make the expression fit the constraint, be it syllable-count or rhyme, one invariably comes up with a more accurate construction. One usually learns that the original idea was clumsy and ill-framed. Constraints lead one to strain for better definitions. To cleanse the doors of perception.

**NDR**: You combine different genres—one reviewer called *Fishing for Amber* (1999) a "genre-defying" book—you take liberties with poetic conventions, and you challenge the reader's expectations on, for example, a sonnet. This play with form becomes part of meaning. Do you see form as being semiotic?

**CC**: It's bound to be, isn't it? Not only the words, but their music. When I came to translating Dante, it seemed to me that the 'meaning' of what he wrote was inextricably bound up with the *terza rima* form and its music, whether mellifluous or harsh. It seemed to me that most, if not all, of the many English translations of the *Inferno* lacked that music. So I wanted to get music into my translation, if sometimes at the expense of what we might think of as the 'literal' meaning of the lines. On the other hand, the constraint of the form often led me to consider the original in ways I never would have done, just as the constraints of a sonnet forces the writer to reconsider what he first had in mind to say. Constraint leads to exploration, adventure, and surprise. I don't want to keep writing what I think I know. I want to find out.

**NDR**: Do you think of your poems in terms of sequence, in terms of collections? How does the writing of one poem influence another poem?

**CC**: My latest collection of poems, *For All We Know*, was very much conceived as a book, though I didn't realise it until I had written three or four poems in the same voice. And I think that tendency to think in terms of books or sequences of poems has been increasing over the years. As for how the writing of one poem influences another, it's often very much a case of taking a line for a walk and seeing where it takes you. It's as much an unconscious process as it is deliberate, even though one has some notion of an overall structure. The alphabet sequences are an example of that. The sequence is given, but each poem is a play with the potential of the individual letters.

**NDR**: Your work presents me with the image of the palimpsest, in the sense of something written and written again, creating layers in which narratives overlap, each narrative bearing the trace of another. For example, stories and phrases recur from one collection to another, you write poems "after Baudelaire", and your work is rich in literary allusions and etymological excavations.

**CC**: Any time I'm asked, 'If there were one word of advice you would give to an aspiring writer?' I always say, 'Read.' If I were allowed another word, I'd say, 'Listen.' I love to read and listen, and to learn from what I read and hear. Behind anything we write is a world of other writings, and behind everything we say is a world of other sayings. A couple of years ago I was commissioned by Penguin Classics to translate the Old Irish epic, *The Táin*, which was published in October 2007. When I came to the original text, I discovered that it was not so much a text as several texts, layers of successive narratives and episodes modified by the particular agendas of the writers for their particular historical times: palimpsests, in other words, or linguistic archaeological layers. I learned something from translating those sometimes contradictory points of view, and from the several different styles embodied in *The Táin*. My Introduction to the Penguin book enlarges on that.

**NDR**: I recently came across an interesting book on Borges, *Invisible Work. Borges and Translation* (2002), by Efraín Kristal. Kristal says that Borges believed that, in our age, all a writer can do is to rewrite what has already been written. For Borges, the author is "a recreator or an editor" of other works. Your work suggests that literary texts are made from recycled earlier texts. What are your thoughts on literature, literary creation and the author?

**CC**: As it happens, I've just ordered Walter Benjamin's *The Archive*, a selection from his personal manuscripts and documents—texts, commentaries, scraps, photographs, postcards, fragments. I've been fascinated by Benjamin ever since, some twenty years ago, I came across a quotation from him which I used as an epigraph for *Belfast Confetti*: 'Not to find one's way about in a city is of little interest… But to lose one's way in a city, as one loses one's way in a forest, requires practice… I learned this art late in life: it fulfilled the dreams whose first traces were the labyrinths on the blotters on my exercise books.' It occurs to me that perhaps I could glean something from Benjamin's fragments to create a text of my own—a textile using his scraps and threads. But it's very early days yet, and I have to see what happens. As you know, I've done this kind of thing in the past, especially in *Breaking News*, which embedded quotations or paraphrases from William Howard Russell's account of the Crimean War. Even though I sometimes used extensive verbatim quotation, I always felt the words were my own, since they were necessarily modified by my own experience of conflict, and by the current wars in the Middle East, which bear eerie parallels to the mess and chaos of the Crimea. I don't think that any writer has anything new to say, but then again any utterance, no matter how often it has been uttered by others or by oneself, is necessarily new, because the circumstances, and the times that are in it, are new. You'll recall Borges' story of Pierre Menard, who rewrites *Don Quixote* verbatim, yet changes its meaning because the words mean different things now than what they did in Cervantes' time, or have acquired different connotations. It's a kind of translation in the literal etymological sense of moving stuff from one place to another, whether through space or time.

**NDR**: Translations, of various kinds, occupy a central place in your work. *The Alexandrine Plan* (1998) reveals a playfulness in your translations. "Parfum Exotique" is translated as "Blue Grass", a brand which figures in your own poems, "La Géante" is turned into "The Maid of Brobdingnag", transferring Baudelaire's female giant into a citizen of Swift's fictional world, and the setting for Rimbaud's "Au Cabaret-Vert", Charleroi, is wittily transplanted to Kingstown in your version of that poem. At the same time, there is more than verbal play going on. In *The Alexandrine Plan*, translating and "Irishing" seem to become complementary concepts.

**CC**: You might say that all writing is translation: the attempt to arrive at a suitable frame of words for one has in mind, or what one thought one had in mind. And translation is a form of reading, whether of the original text, or one's understanding of it. The music of the poems of Baudelaire, Rimbaud and Mallarmé had been hovering at the back of my mind ever since I encountered them in a school anthology in 1965, when I was seventeen.

*The Alexandrine Plan* was an attempt to pay homage to that memory. I'm sure the original poems were not far from my mind in 1968, the year of the Paris *événements* and their counterpart in Belfast, the Civil Rights marches and the violence which ensued from them. It seemed to me that, for all their differences, these three poets were engaged in some kind of revolutionary re-writing of our normal perceptions of the world. Transplanting that project to Ireland seemed appropriate. At the same time I wanted to see how far one could accommodate a very French metre, the alexandrine, in English; and its rhythms didn't seem so far away from that of some eighteenth century Irish ballads, which were themselves derived from Gaelic forms. The internal assonances in my translations come largely from Gaelic song. So there's a lot of interlingual play going on. My concern with these translations was to keep as close as possible to the form of the French sonnet. The form is as much part of the meaning as the words, so I felt I could sometimes deviate somewhat from the 'literal' meaning. I was translating what the poems meant to me; if that included echoes of my experience of Ireland, so be it.

**NDR**: Translation may be a source of formal experimentation and innovation. It was for example used as such by Ezra Pound and several modernist writers. Do you see translation as a way to push the boundaries of your own style, to try out new forms and ideas? *The Twelfth of Never* (1998), modelled on the alexandrine, and published simultaneously with *The Alexandrine Plan*, suggests something along those lines.

**CC**: I've already mentioned the Irish ballad influence on the translations; and *The Twelfth of Never* contains a good many allusions to Irish ballad. The two books were part of the same project, to take a given form and see what can be made of it. The constraint is always useful. I'm a great admirer of the French OULIPO writer Georges Perec, who famously wrote a detective novel without using the letter 'e'. In one way my play with the formal aspects of translation is hardly experiment, since the forms have been around for donkey's years, as have the Irish *sean-nós* songs which lie at the back of a great deal that I write. As for ideas, the search for metre and rhyme seem to generate the ideas. Typically I would begin a sonnet in *The Twelfth of Never* without having a clue as to what I would 'say' in the poem. The saying, the message, the meaning, came with the rhyme, line by rhyme. Rhyme was the fuel, the motor, the engine, the drive. The sonnet was the vehicle, and often I felt like a passenger, being driven into some other world by a ghostly driver. Do you know Cocteau's film *Orphée*? In it there are several routes to the Underworld: through mirrors, for example, or being chauffered in a funereal limousine by the angel Heurtebise. *The Twelfth of Never* was that kind of journey. I never quite knew where I was going until I got there. Which should be the way with all writing. If you know what you are going to say, there's no fun in it. Why write what you already know?

# *FROM* ON THE NIGHT WATCH

*Ciaran Carson*

## From in Behind

the wall
hangings

watched
through slits

is what
is innermost

a voice box
wire grille

crackling on
the darkness

harrowed by
dragon's teeth

a minefield
salted with eyebright

## It Is

never
as late as

you think
you think

you know
the small hours

grow
into decades

measuring
eternity

or dawn
to the chink

chink
of the first bird

## Between

two hoots
of a factory horn

an aperture
of silence two

puffs of smoke
an afterthought

against the blue
of night

becoming morning
as you stoop

below the lintel
to step out

into the street
beware

## The Other

darkness dawns
with yet another

all-clear
over

the blossoming
whitethorns

under which we
are still

in twos
in spite of all

the great owl
uttering

its two-whit-
to-who

**Were I To Add**

the small hours
one & two

& three
& more

calculating
incremental

steps between
the cracks

en route
to school

how many
times tables

broken like
sticks of chalk

**Beware**

the saddler's awl
the slip

betwixt this
split chink

& the next
the rider suddenly

unhorsed
by a slew

of bullets
from a host

the ticker tape
punched out

in Braille
of Morse

## With My Head On a Stone

racking
my brain

examining
the synapses

for an answer
came there none

darkness
on darkness

echoing
a soundless track

from nave
to apse

the open tabernacle
empty

## As I Was Saying

in the beginning
was

whenever
the beginning

was trying to
remember

the first words
I ever read

in whatever
holy book

I find them
stolen by

this thief
in the night

**In Braille or Morse**

a thumbnail
under my palp

two dots
for eyes

a slash for where
the mouth would

be of someone
ghosted by

the radar clutter
birds or arrows

loosed unerringly
into the sweep

of blip & echo
blip & echo

**Remembering Being**

hunkered
under the sink

whatever age
I was

encloistered
in myself

listening to the drip
drip

measuring
the silence

how many times
in three score

years have I
remembered this

# The Dude

*R. D. Skillings*

If I did or didn't do it don't matter any more. I don't even have to care. Cause of three hours ago I'm acquitted. I'm innocent. I was worried for a while, I was scared. I could've spent the rest of my life in jail. Fifteen months was long enough, half a million bail, $17 to my name. Nobody came that whole time, not even Skolly and Chaz, or Skip either, just Hedrick the court lawyer. Ma wouldn't set foot up north. On the phone she said, I don't know who you are, you're not my Jimmy that I raised.

Maybe not, I said, but I'm me. I do know that. All I remember is she sat through every one of her divorces watching the soaps on tv about yelling screaming marriages coming apart. By that time all her husbands had split, my father too. Who could blame him?

But I'm out, I'm in the clear. It was all circumstantial. The jury cried, but they had to let me walk. Three days they wrang their hands, three nights I never slept. Thank you, I says. Thank you, thank you. I made the sign of the cross, I was in tears too, I couldn't hardly hear myself. The judge was always telling me to speak up—he didn't say nothing then though. Hedrick, he just looked at me. Not sad exactly. More like he pitied me, or his own self for doing a dirty deal. He knew they never had a case. He didn't feel too good, I guess. He believed me though. Said he did. Nobody knows, that's the truth.

The cops was shocked. They didn't even have another suspect, no one in reserve. You'd think they'd have a backup, in case they got beat. Cause If I didn't do it who did? They don't know. Nobody does. I'd like to know myself.

I'm going take a rest and celebrate, drink a quart of vodka, pop some pills, what kind, who cares? I'll take what comes, codeine, amphetamine, Sominex, Percoset, then I'll smoke an ounce of dope, get laid by every twenty men I meet.

This sure ain't Palmetto Lakes. I ain't never going back there, I'm staying right here. Her niece in the paper says, This isn't the quaint little fishing village it used to be, the elderly of this town are petrified now. They oughta be, they'll get their dessert too, just like everybody else.

Seventy-nine, she was old enough. What's the big deal? Some dude couldn't stand those hymns all day long, that keyboard coming through the walls. That skreaky voice. I don't blame him, I couldn't take it either. Who could? Drove me down the boiler room, I could still hear her though, like she came through the pipes. How sweet the sound. Bull-dicky.

Give her a little tap, somebody did, lotta little taps, ten at least the coroner said. Mush he made a mess. Don't bother me, death, I'm only 27. Still good-lookin. Whaaa tcha got cookin? How about? Cookin. Somethin. Still got a few years left. Then I'll pay my dues. Less I live to be a dirty old man. Can't see waiting around too long on that.

When I hear people talk about God. All that love not war crap makes me puke. There's no peace cause there's no God, less He's a frickin scumbag worsen me. That's circumstantial. Any idiot can tell you that.

I feel good, I feel great. Not a cloud. When you're young at heart. Too hot for this frickin three-piece suit though, don't even know where it came from. Never wore a vest before. Who'd ever think it was me? Not even me, less I'd been there in court watchin myself, three whole days, all the court house jackals crowding in to hear the verdict. They couldn't wait to see me take the fall, but I busted their balls, you could hear their breath go out when the foreman said Not Guilty, like a big frickin prick fizzled down to nothin.

I'm glad a that, I'm proud of it. I look a million bucks, too, all shaved and showered. Last real shower I had, no, no, never mind that. Don't go pickin your nose, pokin your hose. Then's then. Now's now, ask Skolly and Chaz to let me have their couch back till I.... If they're not home I'll. They don't lock their door, she did though, dead bolt. Yeah.

Yeah, right here. Here's just fine. Thanks. A lot. Hey, you fool around? No? Sure? Sure-sure? Too bad for you you prissy fuck, not bad looking, who the fuck's he think he is! How come he's got the BMW and I'm hitchin and hoofin, humpin this suitcase with nothin in it, everything I own, that's what I'd like to know. Won't always be this way. Maybe.

Too hot, longer walk than I thought, much longer, legs don't hardly work any more. Hey I only lived here a little while, three weeks the papers said. How'm I sposed to remember where everything is? I was fucked-up the whole frickin time. I don't remember a frickin thing. I don't even remember *not* doin it. Sometimes though. Little flashes. Naturally. Cause I've heard so much testimony, read all the transcripts till I'm brain-washed. I been taken over in my mind.

That's why the judge sequestered the jury, the newspapers was full of lies, what a laugh, they got my whole frickin rap sheet all shuffled up, Florida, South Carolina, Maryland, Long Island, they shouldn't of published any of it, I shoulda got off right there. I'm a hustler, I'm a B&E man, I'm a burglar not a murderer. Wouldn't mind if I was. What's the difference? I'd still be me. Thieving's not so bad. Livin by my mind. I'm a sharp cookie, how about cookin?

Frick, I'm not going near that house again, it's too far. Anyhow Skolly and Chaz aren't even there any more, they left town, told some reporter I ruined their lives. They shouldn't of said that. What they got to bitch about? Look at me.

Somebody killed the old lady, that's for sure. Maybe they did it, hell no, they never had time to hurt a flea. Go to work, come home, eat, suck, fuck, snore, no wonder I couldn't sleep. Add up their money all weekend, can they afford to do this, buy that? They're too nice anyway, they felt sorry for me cause I didn't have a place of my own.

I really wonder if I could of done it. But if I did who ransacked her house? Furniture all tipped over, everything smashed, blood everywhere. Her niece said she didn't know if anything was missing. Maybe she bagged the jewelry, I sure didn't. If I did they never found it. Me neither. She was going to a church potluck supper, she was looking forward to it her niece said. How would she know, she live on the frickin phone with her old biddy? Could be, could be, it rang and rang, I can still hear it. Quit it, quit it right there, Dude, don't listen.

Old ladies like little things, little bottles of perfume, little tea-sets, they keep everything neat, they love antiques, they eat cottage cheese and Campbell's soup, watch the birds and squirrels out the back window, their days are numbered. I was real nice to her, put my manners on, my charm, I was helpful. Sometimes I feel good. She might of left me in her will. I said I wouldn't charge her to fix her screen, that's how that lowdown worm got in, all those locks, what was she afraid of? How could anybody harm an old lady like that? Why? Hey! Happens all the time. Just read the papers once in a while, Dude, people get off on that shit, right? They lap it up. I don't think I probably did it. But even if I did I'm in the clear. Anyway I didn't. Didn't. Didn't. Didn't.

Yeah, yeah, I'm in the clear. Why should I have to swear everything all the time? It's over and done with. It don't even exist any more. So don't worry so much, you're in the clear. You hear? You're in the clear.

Yeah. I must've been tappy the whole time. I didn't have no meds, nothin to cool me out, I couldn't get no rest. Tonight I'll sleep like a rock down a well. First time in. Frickin life I've had, never asked for noner this. I feel like that blind wretch like me. I drank all day, I even went to the priest, I told him I'd been in prison recently, I'd just got out, I wanted to find peace with my God. All's he could say was he felt incapable of providing guidance, I should go back to my home-town and seek help. In other words, Get the frick outta here.

So I went back to the Town House Lounge. What was I spose to do? I kept going back all day, drank more beer, had some gin, plenty a gin, Skip was on the bar so it must have been night, yeah, it was dark, I remember that all right. Well, it was December, now it's spring. Right? If you say so, Dude. Who were those two frickin guys that testified I mentioned something bad I did that I was ashamed of? I never said what it was– course I wouldn't say, I got time hanging off me like Spanish moss, probation violations, assault on a police aide, things they don't even know about, no murders though. No, I'm a B&E man, Dude. I'm a con man. Whaa-tcha got cookin?

Those two guys were fucked up worsen me, the little one said a demon came out of a guy one time and threw itself into the fire, he's the one who said I seemed to be under the influence of something, he couldn't say what cause he was drinking all day himself. Yeah. More alcoholics here than I ever seen. Try and detox this population. They said we went to two, three, four other bars. They couldn't remember. Sounds like reasonable doubt to me.

Prosecutor never asked me straight out if I did it. Hedrick neither. I told the investigators I didn't do it. Four apartments in that building, anyone could of done it. I got it all out of the papers. How'd I know anyway? It's all over, I've got to get God into my life. Like a big frickin prick, whooee! And then?

Skolly and Chaz left for work. What'd I do? I felt like shit from all the stuff I did the day before. Or was that later? I was desponding, I'd been depressed, Skolly and Chaz said so too. I was fixin to put me out of my misery, do it for real.

Woke up next morning when Skolly and Chaz said there'd been an accident upstairs, the cops wanted to know if they'd heard anything. Course they didn't hear anything, they weren't even there, I know cause I called from the Lounge, I even said so in court, there was nobody there.

Could've been somebody upstairs though. Bloody bathrobe and nightgown she had on. And those bloody jeans stuffed behind the sheet-rock in the basement, Skolly said he knew they were mine from the frayed cuffs, cause he did my laundry. Whose jeans don't have frayed cuffs? Coulda been anybody's, like her blood on them, type O, mine's A, none on the hammer, no fingerprints nowhere nohow, no flies on me. Same with that strand of hair, the F.B.I. guy said it was mine, my expert really socked it to him, said the lab stuff wasn't conclusive, coulda been anybody's. No proof at all. Hedrick asked the landlord's wife, "How'd you know he just took a shower? You see soap in his hair?" He got a laugh out of that. She said I made her nervous, I talked a lot. I always talk a lot. No crime there.

I went over to Skip's, I found his stash. He kicked me out when he came home, he didn't want anything to happen in his kitchen. I asked him to call my mother, tell her I'd found my peace. I couldn't remember her number, what name she was using. I was gobbling a handful of pills, spilling all over the place, Skip crawling after them. He didn't want his dog to get them. I was convulsing when they picked me up, strapped me to a stretcher, special delivery to Cape Cod Hospital, they pumped me out, then twenty days observation, all I did was lie around, I needed a rest, just wakin up's hard work these days, dumb-ass shrink. What'd he think I was going to say? All he got out of me was I understood the charges.

Armed robbery, breaking and entering while armed with intent to commit larceny. Dismissed for lack of evidence. Where's the evidence I killed her? I don't even know myself. Because I didn't kill her. My looks, people don't suspect, they're shocked when they find out. By then I'm gone. I done a lot of time in jail. Lotta different jails for a young guy. I might have to go back some day. Live under oath. Furniture all tipped over, everything ransacked. She had her bathrobe and nightgown on. She was going to some church supper.

I been in worse fixes than this, no you ain't Dude, no you ain't. Yeah I am. I'm out. What if God starts pickin a bone with you? I got the worry wart, I got the habit, I got to kick it. I hate needles, some people don't even wash, I keep myself clean. In the sight of the Lord. Yeah.

She shouldn't of screamed. Cop that found her, he broke down, his kids played with her. What kind of grownup plays with kids? She was going to bake them a gingerbread house. I can't believe this shit. Any of it. Can you? No.

I'm not a bad guy, I don't think I'm such a bad guy, I'd never do nothin' like that. The landlord said he was grateful he never had to see it. Bet he couldn't wait to raise the rent. My trade's a thief, a damn good one when I'm straight. I got my pride like anyone else, but I never did anything like that. Never.

The whole world's a rotten filthy slimy crud of a bung shitting bellybutton mung dung. Give it up, gotta give it up, get to a church, different church. I'll burn it down. I would if I got convicted.

Cause I didn't do it, couldn't of done it. Impossible for me to be there that time, that place. All this is making me freak. Hot in this frickin suit. I couldn't a been there, I didn't have the opportunity. I mighta had a motive. The prosecutor was just trying to convince me in my own mind. Did a better job on me than he did on the damn jury, the paper said you could hear them yelling at each other every time the door opened.

I wonder what else I left down that basement, cops would have found it by now anyway, I'll go over to the station, I'll say, By the way. Whatever it was. I want it back. That'd be a hoot. Course I knew her, can't say I liked her, yer honor.

Yeah. Rigor mortis come and gone when they found her. I never knew that before. Twelve hours in, twelve out, like the tide. I could not have been in that place at that time. Hedrick says, You couldn't of done it. How's he know? How the fricks he know if I don't?

I had alibis up the ass, that's why. It was all circumstantial. Tracks in the snow, comin and goin. Bottles of milk on the porch. Milkman musta been there. What milkman? I ain't no milkman, never touch the stuff. Three times they asked the judge what reasonable doubt means. He didn't know either, he just went in circles, he says, Convict this sucker, but they wouldn't, they couldn't, they didn't have the balls. They knew I'd come give them a lead enema. Yeah. They can't touch me, they can't double my jeopardy. Next time I come I'll pack a gun.

Hedrick says, Please don't convict him on these imaginary screams and a strand of hair. Course not, when I heard them I wasn't upstairs. I was downstairs asleep, just like Skolly and Chaz said in court. Under oath. I must have been dreaming, I was certainly fucked up, I mean to the moon, Dude, like I sat bolt upright. Skolly and Chaz said it was just a phone in some other apartment, it kept ringing and ringing, I thought it was screams, I knew it was, can't tell me it wasn't screams. They couldn't hardly calm me down, I knew something bad was happening to that old lady, whitest hair I ever seen. Like a ghost. Prosecutor said I was dreaming those screams, but that was no dream.

So I couldn't a done it. Who did? Never mind, Dude, you don't even want to know. Who'd do a thing like that anyway? You wouldn't even want to meet him. Yeah, I would. I'd wring his neck. I mean I'd suck his dick and then I'd wring his neck.

Here we are. Nobody here? What the fuck I care? Hey, Skipster, whatcha got cookin? You day shift now? What's a matter? Ain't you gonna gratulate me? After all I tipped you? Just kiddin. You know what I want. A big frickin Stoli. On the house. Hey, I mean it, I got it coming.

You got an I.D.? We don't serve non-humans.

Hey, Skipster, don'tcha even know me in this frickin suit? I'm your native son. I'm on the loose like a goose. I'm cookin.

Some places you'd have fried.

They don't do that any more. It's inhumane. I wouldn't mind the needle.

Right in your eye, people looking in, ready to pop the champagne.

Hey. Gi'me my Stoli. Please.

You're barred.

What the frick for?

What the frick you think for?

Hey! I got a right. I'm out, I'm acquitted. You didn't hear? Three, four hours ago? I got off. That's all she wrote. Rod been around lately? Randy?

So you beat the rap.

Yeah. Must be on the radio by now all over everywheres. Give me my vodka. Thanks. And a beer chaser.

So what're you gonna do now you're a celebrity?

Know anybody who's got anything? Smoke? Sniff? Pop? Whatever.

I don't know anything about anybody. Except you.

I could use a job.

Town's just opening up. You oughta be a hot prospect. Put you in a shop window like a mannequin with a hammer in your hand.

Hey, come on, don't make jokes.

I wasn't joking.

I didn't do it, I didn't do it. Okay? Somebody murdered somebody, but it wasn't me.

I don't care who did it.

You don't?

Why should I? I've done worse.

Don't brag.

To you? Are you kidding? With your mouth?

You just want me to say I did it. But I won't cause I didn't.

That wasn't your bloody shirt?

What bloody shirt?

If you don't know I don't.

They never found no shirt.

What'd you do, eat it?

Come on, come on, gi'me another.

One more and you're outa here.

What's the difference, she was just an old lady, she was going to croak anyway.

So are you.

Life's lookin up, you know? It could really be beautiful. When you're young at heart. With a million bucks. I'm sicka being poor. I gotta get a job, line some things up.

Hammers?

For Chrissake, shut up. All you people tryna put me at the wrong place wrong time. Hey, that's where I live. Walk a mile in these shoes. Two miles, must've been. This frickin suit's hot.

You oughta take that tie, go hang yourself in the head. You know those pipes? You just get up on the toilet seat and step off. That's what Trixie Judd did. He never did anything to anybody but himself. It was people that did him.

What the frick I care about him? This here's about me. Me. I tried to kill myself at your house, remember? I musta been in a bad mood. I never killed no old lady, but I done plenty.

Such as?

I kicked my mother down the stairs. Nah, I didn't, I wanted to though. Not any more. Dorothy's Gift Shop, I mighta done that. Nice clean job. You'd never believe me if I told you I done that.

Did you?

Yeah, but don't tell anyone.

Why not?

I wouldn't want it to get around.

Why not?

What d'you mean, Why not?

You swear you did it?

Yeah, why not? Hey, what're you doing?

I'm calling 911.

Hey.

This is the bartender at the Town House Lounge. I want to report a guy in here who claims he did the Dorothea robbery. Yeah. No. Okay. Will do.

You didn't really do that. I can't believe you really did that. Gi'me another. And some more beer. And some of those chips.

Here you are, spiked with my special drops. Lay you out straight. You don't know what sick is till you wake up.

You wouldn't do that to me.

Yeah I would.

No you wouldn't. You're a friend right? I might be dead if it wasn't for you.

I been thinking about that. Dumbest thing I ever did. Well, here's your pals. Gentlemen! Nice to see you.

You son of a bitch. I don't believe this.

Where is he?

Right there.

Him? This here's Mr. James Pickard. Couldn't a done it, he was up in the Barnstable House of Correction.

Then he's a liar.

Tell us about it.

Well, thanks anyway. Always nice.

I can't believe you did that.

Doing my civic duty. Why'd you say you did that job if you didn't do it? You already had your fifteen, you want another?

It coulda been me. I was just tryna find out. What the frick's goin on. Where is everybody?

Won't nobody come in with you here.

Bullshit. I'll have one more for the road. Brim it up please.

You're done. I told you. You're killing my business.

What d'you mean?. I'm just sittin here mindin my own.

People see right in through the window.

Nobody know me in this frickin suit. Buncha bananas out there all rowing with one paddle.

You're shut off. I told you.

I just want to have my drink, then I'm going away.

You pass out you'll wake up in hell. That hammer be right there beside you.

That's my prick, Dude.

Okay. That's it. I told you I did something worse than you. I did plenty, nothing like that though. You gotta go, or I'm going to puke.

Why'd you lie to me? Tryna prove you're bettern me?

Get out or I'll sic the cops on you for drunk. They'd like some action. Bored outa their gourds, nothing to do. Just shining up the thumbscrews. Get the fuck out. NOW.

Hey, I thought you were my friend.

I'll make that call. I'm making that call. Nine. One. One to go.

Frick you Skip you frickin phoney. Ratting me out. What a laugh. Cops can't touch me. I busted their balls and they know it. Little Bar at the A-House be better anyway. Nicen dark, jukebox, some cute guy, some hunk, little peace and quiet. Wake up in hell. He shouldna said that. That's no way to treat a friend.

Frick is it ever hot in this frickin suit. Where'd it come from? Where'd anything come from, Dude? Where'd I come from? Yer mother's bunghole, Dude. Why couldn't I been born somebody else? Wouldna made no difference, Dude. What d'you mean, I wouldn't be me. Yeah yer would, Doood. Hah! That's not what I mean. Whad I mean? I mean I need a bottla vodka. And some pills. I need to sleep. I haven't slept in. And a place. Consistent with. A struggle. Yeah, must've been. A blunt instrument. At least ten. Multiple fractures of the skull and multiple lacerations to the brain. Consistent with. Some son-of-a-bitch, you son-of-a-bitch. Whynt you shut up, I've heard all this before.

If God's so good why the hell don't he kill the bad people? Cause he wants them to kill each other. Save Him the trouble. God don't fool around. He cool, Dude. Yeah. Hey, whatcha got cookin? How about? With me. Oh my Oh you. Can't convict dreams and a strand of hair. What the frick. Nobody here either. What's cookin, Dude?

It's pretty early. We just opened. My name's Jimmy actually. What can I get you?

Big frickin Stoli straight up. And a beer back.

Yes Sir. Seven dollars.

I may as well run a tab. I'm going to be here a while. I just got out of jail.

Oh. Ah. Well. That's good. I'm glad you're out, Sir. It's nice you got such a nice day to regain your freedom.

Too frickin hot.

Actually it always seems quite cool in here. I always bring a sweater. You could take your jacket off.

I never took this jacket off in my life. I never had it on neither. Hedrick must've got it for me. My lawyer.

Well. It's a fine looking suit, Sir.

Too frickin hot. What's with the Sir? You been here long?

I try to be courteous to the public. After all, I'm here to serve you, Sir. Actually this is my first week. I lucked into this job. One of the regulars got sick. I've only been here a month. I've been staying with a friend.

Brimmerup, please. You don't know who I am?

No Sir, not really. I don't think you should have another. Not right away. You've got quite a start on the day.

It's my day. Far's I'm concerned. All mine. Please. Have a little class. Gimme a break. I'm a nervous wreck. I just got outta the can. I don't even have a place to stay. You really don't know who I am?

No Sir. Not really.

I'm James Pickard.

Oh. Well. We're both Jameses.

No we ain't. You got nothin on me. I used to be Jimmy. Gimme nother Stoli. Preash. You really ever heard of me?

Well. All right, Sir. One last. That'll be eleven dollars. You can do without the beer.

Yeah, yeah. Here's blood in yer eye. I'm cookin. I beat the rap. I'm a pro. I'm slick as a dick. Come in the head and you can sit on it. I got a bomb on my burner I'd like to get off on.

I'll ignore that, Sir.

Okay. I know. You're too sherry for that. Cherry. Gi'me one for the road, I'll be on my merry. One more once.

No, that really was the last. I'm afraid you're getting inebriated. I can't in all conscience.

Why you think people drink? Lemme bring ya up to date, Kid. I mighta killed somebody but I got off. I'm not guilty. That don't mean I'm innocent, but I'm not guilty. As of three, four hours ago. I'm out I gotta celebrate. Brim me up.

I can't serve you any more. I'm sorry. Why...how could something...like that...happen to you? Someone you were...intimate with? Pardon my asking.

You can read it all in the paper. I was headlines fifteen months ago. I'm not proud of it. I been through hell.

I'm sure you don't want to talk about it.

Why not? What the frick! I got nothin to fear. Prosecutor's the one doin the talkin. Him and the cops. They're talkin the talk. I'm doin the walk.

Not to pry, but who did you kill? And why?

Whazit to you?

I'm interested in people.

People. What's the big deal about people? I offed some guy. Gave me a hard time. Put it this way, he wasn't hard enough. No big deal. He's dead, dead, don't bother me. Fuck I care? Hey Dude don't make it bad, sing sweet sound, swing low I sing of thee sweet peace now blind I see no flies no flies on me. Thank God Thank God Thank God I'm free.

Sir? No, no, Sir. Sir? You can't sleep here. You'll have to go. You should go home. That's eleven dollars, Sir

All I got six, change.

That's all right, Sir. You keep it. Just go.

Frick you little prick. Woozy walls and door hang on. Wo. Wham my head. Ah shit! Ow. Ow. OW. Okay. Kay. Big lump already, no blood though. Nobody saw. Woops. Hands and knees, gotta get up can't crawl Up. Up. Wo. Wish I could puke, sleep on my feet.

Cross, just get. Car better stop, sue their ass. Stare like I got two heads. Scuse, scuse me, sorry. Frickim. Who they think they are? Lean here till whirlies quit. Beach this way, path between, weeds, been here before, old rotten wharf, some guy who. Now sit down, sit, slip off, don't jump don't fall just drop. Eee Zy. Oooof. Made it, made it, all the way. Blind now free.

Hungry. Gotta puke. Some wrong with me. Skip maybe. Why'd he say that?

Hard walkin sand. Here enough far enough. Lie down tide comen take me away never get up again no sweat. Sand nicen warm in this suit. What's that? Biting me. Sit. Up. Not so easy. Nothing on my hands, nothing in my hair. Nothing.

Nice view. Here far enough. Shoe come off. Where? Don't need, don't care.

Dues all paid. Curl up. Wasn't me. Swing my song sweet chariot. Wasn't. Isn't. Couldn't been. Hedrick said. Judge and jury too, what's the fuss? Even if it was I'm different now, I'm new. Time move on.

Well, Dude it's just you and me now. I don't like you. That's you you don't like. Whynt you shut up for a change. You shut up.

That look on Hedrick's face. Still can't figure. Lookin down at me like. Like Whatchagodcookin. Why If I did I? She shouldn't of screamed. No I. Course I. Didn't. Didn't. If I don't believe my own attorney. Couldna done it. Downstairs in bed those screams no dream, no frickin phone either. Shoulda got up, gone up, saved her ass, tap that guy, eyes pop out roll under the table. Blind peace. Such white hair. Mother Mary Jesus please God let it be over all over with forgive I forgive. Didn't mean her any harm even if I did so let go cry at last let go let go warm piss ahhh long good fart too squirt ahhhhh glubblegush heavy hot love my own can't stand nobody else's who can?

Sleep stay by me. Now no more. Evermore. Safe in sand. Tomorrow I'll...

When he came to he got cleaned up, found a job, volunteered at the Soup Kitchen on weekends, never again missed early Mass, confessed his sins and sinned no more, went back to Palmetto with money in his wallet, made amends to his mother, never drank another drop, never popped a pill, allowed himself to smoke filter-tips on occasion, not more than one or two with morning coffee, worked 24/7/365, did a life of good deeds, became someone everyone looked up to, helped the young, cared for the old, stood up for the weak and poor, was credited with making peace between people of all races, all creeds, all walks of life.

It was not always easy to be James Pickard but he kept true to his Dude, and it was rewarding because men came his way with respect. He was a living miracle though nobody knew it till he died quite young of overwork and the whole congregation, let in on his former life, overflowed with amazement, love and gratitude, and scattered his ashes in some scenic spot and put up a tall monument in the church-yard in honor of his service to all mankind as a sign of his high acclamation by his fellow men and women both.

So it wasn't such a bad day after all; in fact it was a pretty good start on all the rest of the days of his life—so No, no, he really wasn't a lost cause, cause, after all, you never know.

# *FROM* SHUFFLE

*John Shoptaw*

This sequence of poems has as its epicenter the 1811 earthquake in New Mádrid, Missouri (my home county), the largest ever recorded in North America, which coincided with (among other things) the first steamboat trip down the Ohio and the Mississippi. *Shuffle* takes the form of a triple sestina, an "eighteener," a form I patterned after the sestina: 18 stanzaic poems of 18 lines each with a 9-line coda. Each poem has the same 18 end-words, permutated or shuffled in successive stanzas as with a sestina. Before writing each line, I rolled the dice. If I rolled an even number, I would leave the endword intact (e.g., in "Buster Brown": "even," "black," "hand"); if an odd, I would shuffle or change it in some way (e.g., in "Buster Brown": "casting" from *cast*, "fouled" from *fault*, "lead" from *deal*). After each stanza, I would reshuffle the endwords, written on yellow index cards. This way, I turned *Shuffle* into a game of cards and dice, and introduced chance and luck, along with predestination, into its making.

## 5th Shuffle: Buster Brown

Cast upstream, far ahead of myself, so far I forget the casting—
Like a wetfly or an angling rod or an indefinite length of line or even
All three, tail & hackle all feathered & barbed, black
& silver dragonfly reel humming away well in hand
Back there, feeding the eyelets of its pliant pole a lowtension yarn, fatally fouled
Yet looping along oblivious, soaring but sleepy, the lure dragging its lead
Sinker high over Omaha, off Council Bluffs, the Missouri dozing, a freshwater whale
Or channel cat, waiting to strike—I sink through a shopwindow's glare towards a kid
Keen (in creased bluejeans, radiant T-shirt, stiff brown Oxfords) to try out the shoe-store's
Brand new upright birchbox, size of a casket or pulpit, equipped with a fluoroscope meter,
Rheostat dials, & three viewing scopes of leathered lead & birchwood—
One for the kid, one for his mom, & one for the salesdad, dead at 43, in whose place a card
Now rests [Shoe Rite X-Ray For A Perfect Buster Brown Fit Every Time]—where I happen
To see two skeletal feet that twitch when I twitch, like pallid sturgeons, daring
Me downwards or waving me off, bound in a ghostly leather, the corrective metal
Arch supports looking, by strange coincidence,
Like sinkers firm under each flat foot, metatarsals bruised to pleasure insoles, but oddest
Of all, I watch as the brown shoestrings, damp & squirmy, interlace what I know must be
my entire family genome, where early on a limping gene or basepair develops a little snarl that pulls the wriggling future up short, while around the feetbones rock three dicey spinsters—Ada from Decatur, Little Jo from Kokomo, & Phoebe Gimme Feevuh—gossiping & chatting, spinning the dials, ratcheting the roentgens down & up, & dandling from skirt to skirt a ravenous pair of shears, against which there's next to nothing to do or mean, short of meandering, with any luck.

## 7th Shuffle: The Odds Against Us

Then again, maybe not. What if he'd landed the job? The stars'd
Wink back. She'd still of been working late, would of boarded the block
Before. Watercolored sunsets 10¢ a card—fireflies, streamers,
Premium stock.

That night's last streetcar crackled to a halt. Olive St. & 1941. He couldn't
Find a seat. Then he lit on hers. But would he feel odd?
He needed a smoke cause he wanted her number. But would
He be given the nod?

& what about us? Were we coaxed from afar? We'll
Never know better. Or were we an accident
Waiting to happen? But what if her light'd been bad? The crimson cards might well
Of been inadvertently blackened.

They'd ride their second thoughts. His sonofabitchin job'd got away. She'd lied
About her age to St. Louis & worked fer nothin: 100 mudpied

Sunsets. But wait! She wouldn't of known that yet. So what if he hadn't happened
To of had a pencil. She wouldn't of minded. The threat
To any two things not happening is monstrous. But Luck is fibrous, nebular, overriding,
    and muddiest when the stellar core fails. She'd reach inside her purse and pull out her lipstick. Handpaint her
    number all the way up his sleeve. The whole car had to of laughed. His starched & flattened
Arrow shirt. Her piecework red.

## 11th Shuffle: Group Psychology

Many things combined to make the year 1811 the Annus Mirabilis of the West. During the earlier months, the waters of many of the great rivers overflowed their banks to a vast extent, and the whole country was in many parts covered from bluff to bluff. Unprecedented sickness followed. A spirit of change and a restlessness seemed to pervade the very inhabitants of the forest. A countless multitude of squirrels, obeying some great and universal impulse, which none can know but the Spirit that gave them being, left their reckless and gambolling life, and their ancient places of retreat in the North, and were seen pressing forward by tens of thousands in a deep and sober phalanx to the South. No obstacles seemed to check this extraordinary and concerted movement: the word had been given them to go forth, and they obeyed it, though multitudes perished in the broad Ohio, which lay in their path.
– Charles Joseph LaTrobe, *Rambler in North America* (1832)

Not out of the woods.
Not even now. We have yet to arrive at our Theory of Commotion. What mute
Word came over us, some now think, what hounded
Us out of tree, was a whiff of Radon, or else a low-
Level emission of rotten egg. Some of us sensed an undertone, a locomotive
Tingling way down in our amygdala, which roused us indignant
From our lifelike sleep. But such explanations, we feel, only further our bleak
Bewilderment. What it was was an unaccountable flurry of shadowtail, a frankly worried
Dictation of innumerable plumes we'd squirreled away ages ago, like a report card,
Without reading it. Trees intertangled. Their shadows malformed disagreeably. We cast
Ourself a significant look, as though *we* knew something *we* didn't. We hoarded mast,
Chattered & chuckled, allogroomed & mated much as before. But a cold gust of coincidence
Stopped us altogether, as though we'd just noticed what we'd been up to. We fought off flight
No longer. Without looking back, we poured downtrunk &, tail
Aquiver, flooded the forest floor. All in all, it was an oddly
Moving experience—deer, even bear, fled our fuzzy determination. Navigating by stars
Or by each other, it was better together. Needy, distrustful, we were what we could never
Rightly recollect. The current changed us unrecognizably, & so we go on, as we have to,
like nothing had happened.

## 15th Shuffle: New Madrid Shakes

In the end the stars & the moon mixed with the dark & they sank into blackness.
Not blackness, exactly. Sulphurous vapor, stinging the lights both big & little,
Stuffing the nasal cavities & mouths of the earth, put an end to the moon & the stars.
Currents of electrical fluid maybe, branching like ganglia under the earth, so in darkness
Subterranean thunder, delivered hard shocks to the earth, rippling in spasms like the dumb
Flesh of beef just killed, the fluid breaking into landwaves that swelling burst black
Matter & water upwards into the heavens. Word that the river was *cut in twain* is coincident
With tales of sudden huge falls, the Mississippi itself running backwards, retreating perhaps
From greater into lesser chaos, returning to shore the laden flatboat, the unswampt
Canoe with blankets & maize, the riverbed suddenly sprouting trees, which jumped
        upright from the bed where they'd lain since their uprootings. Wholly
Unprepared for such confusion, the humans, converted into crawling things, sinners into saints on hands
& knees, trembled around campfires & flung prayers upwards in Spanish & Osage, cast
Up African French & English, or giddily babbled, though one congregated, even
Though prostrate, was heard to mutter of a lowdown trick, the Day of Judgment come,
        like a thief, in the Night. Cattle, confounded, left calves just foaled
& mingled among them, lowed or keeled right over. Fowl swarming—their thick
Trees yowling with their trunks split open—deserted the air & wildly
Took to the shoulders & heads of the humans who'd fled their dwellings. One scared
Old couple, still holed up at home, looked out at their garden on bears & panthers, foxes
        & wolves, lying or rocking together with deer & rabbits, goats & sheep. Their red tongues hanging out the
        sides of their mouths, they peered at the humans as though wondering, would they let them back on board,
        would they let there be anymore of what they called Day?

## 16th Shuffle: First Draft

Thus far into Shuffle, the fact that I've rolled a lot more odds
Than evens strikes me, despite my native bent for oddity (taking the 18 blacks
& reds on the roulette wheel that are odd over the reds
& blacks that are even, not minding the fatal unevenness of my doddering leather
Bucket chair, which serves me as both dice cup & end table) as, well, odd.
Lady Luck is a shadowy figure. Missing from pantheon group photos, her stars
Move about unconstellated. Promiscuous, forgetful, hard of hearing, the joker of the deck,
She differs from Fate, whom she otherwise resembles, in her weirdly personal regard. A card
Marked inscrutably, Lady Luck is a river goddess—shallowdraft rudder, copiously flooding
Horn, & paddlewheel in hand. We believe in Luck, nutritious as Mississippi mud,
Enough not to cross her. We delight in playing the numbers, not knowing, even
As we play, that they're playing us, that we ourselves are numbered. As Luck
Would have it, 366 plastic blue capsules, each containing a birthdate, had been cast
Randomly into a large glass well. Gazing off, by design or coincidence,
A wizened Congressman Pirnie dabbled just his fingertips in the icy pool & handed
Over the first time-release capsule, September the 14th. One registrant, haply
Awakened that morning by a gentle shake, hiked more than hitched to his draftboard in New Madrid to declare himself 1-A, having played the odds to outwit the draft. He was among the lucky, neither mangled nor deranged. But he discovered, having scaled the New Madrid Bend levee & pitched his draft card, that his student deferment did not drop. Instead, as anhingas snaked & wheeled
Overhead, it gave off a swamp air that enveloped him like steam.

## Tarkovsky's Horse

*—Andrei Rublev*

*Dennis Hinrichsen*

Not the one saved from the slaughterhouse for this.
                Gun shot
    to the chest just before the camera rolls

so the full thousand pounds of it
                can stumble down the staircase.
    Like boiling metal poured

down a throat except it is the heart that fountains.
                A jet or spray
    as thin as water,

Rublev, painter of icons,
                on his knees elsewhere,
    until the animal staggers stiff-legged

in the blindness that is death.
                Rocks on its haunches.
    Rears. *Deus equus.*

Takes a spear like mercy to the chest. No,
                not this horse.
    But the other.

The one from the prologue—
                the animal
    on its back, its fine muscular volume

working the dust into its glistening coat,
                before it rolls
    back over,

wholly alive. Kneels in that posture
                that in Rublev
    is spirit driven down into the wicker

of the hands, the little spits that atomize
    his pleading, but
  that in the horse is instinctual grace. Bounces

once, hooves flashing. Canters away.
    For it is the animals
  in the film we follow,

the metal—dual nature—
    flesh and
  sky of them, the Tartars running

their fast ponies before the burning city,
    peeling gold
  from the cathedral towers

as geese fly. Or earlier, the slaughter of swans.
    The holy fool
  in a circle

of dogs. And then that living horse,
    which is not Rublev,
  but liquid earth rising,

and then, later, a boy,
    a cooling stream
  of it, who driven past virus

and hunger, lies. Says he can fashion
    bells.
  The prince's men are looking for his father,

a maker of bells. But the father is dead—
    and so the boy
  lies. Follows them back to the city,

says this is the creative
    spirit, raw earth, clay.
  Digs it out in rain

to daub a giant cast. And the townsfolk
believe him—
render over

knives and forks, cups and plates
to the fires he builds
to feed the hollowness

its honey. For it is like a hive
Rublev wanders
around—a wet dog—through the ruts

of his faith, edge of the story,
not painting,
watching the boy.

Rublev has killed, has set his robes on fire,
let the boat
of paganism softly knock

his own wooden craft packed with monks.
Then silence,
listless gazing. So when they

haul it up—the bell— like the very
weight of
earth itself and lay the hammer

on, it is as if from inside himself
he hears
it peal—like faith, a lie, belief…

The boy falls to the mud, crying. Rublev,
too,
for they are now one thing

kneeling in birth matter, clapper
                    and lip,
      hammer and rope, air and mud.

Rublev will paint; the boy forge bells.
                    There is Christ
      now in it… It rings. It is sweet, and it rings.

# TORSO OF A DISCUSS THROWER

*Bridgette Bates*

1

One shoulder arches slightly higher than the other as if
the higher shoulder is the reflection of the other from a mirror slanting
against a closet door.

The solidity of the rotator cuff,
a shadowed indentation, a cave where a boy and a wolf have not yet slept
together.

One shoulder arches as if it were not the same body as the other. The torso,
with its external limbs, a house, a surrounding yard where the first games
were played.

2

The old men flip horseshoes in July to score the sounds of metal hitting a
stake, a sound of familiar work, of the mines they would lift their bodies
into a cart to pulley down to strike away the layers of minerals until the
mine could afford their work no longer, the men keep playing the games
beyond nightfall because motion keeps their families from bankruptcy.

3

This is not connecting different times to create a history:

4

The yard of the discuss thrower is dusty, dirt in constant flux from the landings
of afternoon practices. Did he twirl his body into a full circle to pivot into
the throw?

There is no room around his dusty ring for an audience, for faces to perplex
over the alignment of his pose. His mother cannot watch from the kitchen
window as she drops a plate into the sink and the shards do not bounce
back.

5

In marble, his clavicle creates a slant like the strap of a messenger bag across his chest. He could carry his medals in the bag, the dried flowers from victory wreaths, second mortgage papers in transit to the circuit court to preserve a house for another year, extra discs that would clink together when his statue is carted into the lower level room where the experts will balance his stance and return him to proper dignity.

## TORSO OF A WRESTLER

*Bridgette Bates*

1

He wanted to embrace me in the form of his supposed spread arms.

The starting position to fight, upright in most animals, a form where any physical interaction is still possible.

2

With the armless statue it's hard to tell if he wants to shake my hand or push me out of his corridor, but the wrestler does not want to remain standing alone forever, so I dizzy myself around him to motion for his match to countdown.

3

How many miles do you walk through the various wings
of the museum? A government's daily recommended exercise dose?

The space broken by torsos of muscled men to remind me of the indolence of the spectators who lap around them.

4

Hundreds of miles away others fought for this fighter's body, where now you know in the distance there's an island with many prized bodies because a light bulb flickers beneath the horizon. The wrestler would volunteer to climb the lighthouse like a practice wall, grip each step to prove that real discipline rests not in will but in the upper body.

5

A young woman who inadvertently shaped up by dating a rock climber was offended by a stranger who asked if she was a bodybuilder.

To lift weights is less organic to human form than to climb rocks as the difference between the rock climber and the bodybuilder being the ages to petrify their objects of resistance.

The wrestler's difference being the resistance of another body, a body of the same weight to whom he bows in victory and defeat.

6

The couple rock climbing photograph themselves at the top of the cliff clasping hands to pull each other to their finish mark, but not during the climb with their threads raveling too distanced in their ascent to touch because to photograph something is to have accomplished it intimately.

# Torso of Apollo

*Bridgette Bates*

1

Earlier, all images of naked youth were considered Apollo. Experiments of rendering the body were considered Apollo. Rendering the body was the illumination of a free-standing god.

2

How can the mother tell for which child to pray first? The oldest has endured the longest time to go awry, but the younger is not yet tainted by years in the world. The gods' marble ears are so small they can only hear the first prayer.

3

The replicated gods, polished torsos, most appropriately headless,
exist merely for practice at perfecting the human form.

If the gods represent war there are additional props of spears to contrast with the musculature of man's forearms raised in conflict.

4

The prayer of today is different from the ceremonies of the first century. No pilgrimages to the crossroads to seek the oracle for the future truth.

We, intolerant of mythical symbols, pray for the present body. Our friend's husband's cancer. The younger son's final exam. The mothers bumping into their nightstands to dim the lamps as they kneel. Tea stain bruises across the stretch marks of their hips.

Old bodies draped for sleep, young bodies in flesh to fight.

The light of the museum illuminates a hundred gods in the mirror, a single security guard yawns in his corner, probably the baby of the family.

5

How does prayer to no one particular illuminate what we want if the statues of the gods were not intended for worship? If all the statues were meant to be a single figure?

## LONG-DISTANCE RUNNER

*Ryo Yamaguchi*

A tyrant, like the mountains—I was twelve and he said he could show us a *real* one.
I have been in many houses only once,

and then I am older all thereafter,
and this is like a sweep of metallic rain down the long avenue,

or that I expect your slender appearance in the trapped dusk, the whirring balls of the cannonade

all such paths I've lost you down.

I have a cup of coffee. I tease October through the window
with a song I keep in my head, letting the tack pivot

through all kinds of inconsequence,
great yellow light that builds a summer afternoon across the floorboards,

coffee, the stitched
days. Then, from an overwhelming white, I begin to make out my shadow in the grass

and a mild clack of balls, and little boys are watching as they ride by.
*Who has died?*

*No*, I say, but I'm not even sure where I am.
There was this conversation, all through the heaviest parts of repose, in her stiff parlor

with her hands in lace all over a history,
the boxer's hard shoulders glistening in his own muck

opened up
by the rotary cartridges, the wind in the subdued leaves. And another story,

and so on, and this is how they discovered us a tangle of wisteria,
and when I woke I had been sleeping in a pond whose silver roundness was an unforgiving,

halcyon sky. I wanted to go sleepless,
where the old television pops through the night in the shifting heat.

I wanted to clear my purpose of its alluvium,
the rubble of neon

and its bolt-hole dreams: a cache of margins set loose in the circuitry,
a jar of accumulated breakages

we thump on the side for its fortune, centuries of fungus on the doll face,
and then we are born in an artillery device;

we climb toward the brilliant circle.

A tyrant—we were throwing crabapples at the wall, and he came, and we went,
and later I watched you rise up in foam and loaded splendor over the tenement roofs

and the strung wires
until I staggered to see you, and I fell down, deeply, to the bottom of the ocean

and my new life.
The air-conditioning kicks on. I walk into the pasture and all the horses regard me,

between us a horizontal drift that covers like sudden meaning,
a front of equatorial weather pelting the desert with dead birds, how we can only think

to get going to somewhere, some place buried in the musculature of our faces
caked in sun.

So we saw the hard fact; so it persists—
where else do we land but back between our selves, the refracted pump of noise

through our hollows that ring with their own booming,
through the great, long day,

where we hear each other calling from deep in the neighborhood.

# SANDY CANDY

*Joan Frank*

Doriben's a resort town on the eastern coast of Spain. You could suggest it's like Miami Beach, with its aging neo-natives, flaccid in shorts and aloha shirts, mixed in with Cubans of all walks, hungry for work and a better life. Or maybe like Reno, Nevada in August, when everything's glinting with heat, and people who live for miles in any direction, pale or leathery, fat or thin, with blank, addled faces—creep in to wander the neon streets. Not exactly what you'd first expect of Spain.

Yet Doriben was where Lorna found herself one summer, with her husband, Brad. They had scooted south by train, to what is optimistically called the white coast (it is more a dirty brown), in an effort to find sun after a cold and raining France, and to afford several more weeks in Europe than they might otherwise have, before heading home to jobs and chores so deeply ingrained that both could replay them anytime in detail in their minds—the precise heft and sheen of every pen, every gummy coffee cup, even the motes floating in tired light from their office windows.

Brad owned a sizeable hardware store, and Lorna was assistant to the vice-president of a dried-fruit company, both in the pretty orchard-town of Sebastopol, California. It was blissful to be on their own, for a time. Brad had a stepson by an earlier marriage who'd had a couple of babies, so though Lorna and Brad were only in their forties and had no children together, they were grandparents by default. Lorna had three nephews, Brad a widowed mother. He had obligations to his staff, Lorna to her colleagues' birthdays and weddings and pregnancies: a sticky web of relational duty enmeshed them the instant they were home. Lorna sometimes told Brad she felt they were not so much a marriage as a clearing house.

Lorna and Brad knew only that Doriben was inexpensive, and that for this reason British working class folk, many on the dole, came to the town in droves on cheap charter flights and buses, to *'ave their 'olidays*, as they pronounced it. The couple found a hotel, clean and comfortable, a simple square hive of five or six stories. Their room had a smidgen view, between skyscrapers, of the sea beyond and the hotel pool below, and it had a good bathroom, which made Lorna clap her hands. Brad had done the figuring, and found they could stay at least two or three weeks in Doriben without harming what remained of their travel funds. As they wandered the town it appeared that a gigantic duffel-sack had been opened and shaken upside-down, dumping every component of blue-collar British life onto an arid section of Spanish coast. Rows of shanty-cafés lined the streets like mail slots, their scribbled blackboard menus offering winter meals: bangers and mash, fish and chips, greasy breakfasts, drinks at all hours: bar after bar named things like The Dog's Bollux, fairly giving away liquor and beer. Kids were proclaimed to be welcome everywhere, and often shot pool while the adults got drunk.

These bars and cafés were filled with a population that saw the sun so little during their working lives, their bodies and faces had mustered a thick protective layer like a callous: ruddy and scored and tough, sometimes blubbery. The young people were of a paleness close to blue. All smoked without ceasing. They drank daylong, lolling in the sun like huge sea lions, occasionally shoving each other into the icy pool, shouting and screaming, crawling back out to drink and sun more. They coated themselves with oil and lay heavy and vacated, like they'd temporarily died. The older women sunned bare-breasted. The hotel's loudspeakers shrieked the same Rolling Stones album every day, so that Brad and Lorna learned to wake to the "woo-woo" chorus from "Sympathy for the Devil." The Spanish, whose economy was struggling back from the Franco years, had learned every particular of their British guests' desires. Ice cream and candy, miniature golf, soda, cigarettes, cheap beer and liquor, old rock music at top volume, tabloid newspapers and karaoke. If you circled the town from the air it might resemble a futuristic coliseum on the sea, with skyscraping hotels forming its walls and a spreading fleamarket its floor: streets flanked with barracks of worthless goods propped in neat rows: dolls, radios, plastic toys, watches, shoes, sexual novelties.

At night the town became a reckless midway, and in the beginning to Lorna it seemed at least festive, like a tawdry county fair. She watched families and couples walking the streets or sitting in the giant pubs, smoking and drinking and nattering loudly. The kids were boisterous and small-eyed—they stared slack-mouthed at Lorna across the smeared pub tables—but they seemed to want to be where they were. Glossed-up younger couples wandered the nighttime streets; packs of teenaged girls stalked on spike heels, in tube dresses spangled with glitter. The girls left a trail of rank perfume, shooting guilty, excited glances at people they passed.

Lorna and Brad walked, and watched.

The whole town's a sideshow, Brad said, running a hand through his hair.

So it seems, said Lorna. She kept her arm firmly in his.

But no one menaced them, and in fact they could finally afford to relax in one place for a while. Lorna exulted to be able to put her shirts and shorts in the drawers of the hotel room, to have naps, hours in which to read the heavy hardback novel she'd lugged. Brad discovered where the single copy of the *International Herald Tribune* was sold and loped there happily every morning. The two drank their coffee looking out to a choppy blue sea, past the boardwalk strung with lights.

Brad was a friendly man by nature; it was one reason he excelled at his work. People trusted him; kids liked him; animals rubbed at his legs. Soon enough he announced to Lorna he'd met a nice couple in the downstairs sports bar watching soccer matches. Erleen was a retired nurse, Stan a retired soccer coach: Liverpudlians both, chatty and game for any distraction. They'd invited Lorna and Brad to "do Doriben" with them that evening. They knew, they said, where the cheapest pints were, and the cheapest dinners, and all the entertainment that mattered.

Lorna had a sinking feeling about it, a feeling she often got when Brad struck up another acquaintance. It meant losing their privacy—what remained of it. It meant presenting, inquiring. The volleyed gabble of trading background information. She shoveled it forth all year, at her own job and for Brad's staff, rounds of family, friends. At home she found herself punching the erase button for each message in their answering machine as if killing scurrying roaches. Brad was a dear man, but a sort of roving, happy dog: eager for liveliness and petting. He craved others to talk to in the course of their travels. This didn't offend her, or rather, she worked to keep it from offending her. Their natures were antithetical this way; over years they'd contrived to live around it, and she had resolved this trip to try to show him more appreciation.

The four met at Churchill's, where two tall pints cost fifty cents. Erleen and Stan looked their parts—looked a good ten years older than their actual ages, which were close to Lorna's and Brad's—their skin like jerked beef, dark and creased from cold and from direct, baking sun during the few weeks each year they could escape the cold. Their beer went down in rapid, systematic draughts; Lorna saw at once she couldn't hope to keep up. She gave her undrunk glass to Brad.

The hot sun dipped behind a skyscraper, turning the late afternoon to brass.

We're taking you to Sandy Candy tonight, Erleen was saying. You can't say you've seen Doriben until you've seen Sandy Candy. Absolutely not.

What, or who, was Sandy Candy?

It has to be seen to be believed, Erleen said, leaning forward, her face a mass of grinning creases. Erleen's hair was cut short like a man's.

We can't say more, she said, glancing at her husband.

Stan laughed and shook his head. You have to see it to believe it, he repeated. Stan was missing a tooth to the right of his incisors. He had an affable smile anyway. He wore a silver chain, combed his sparse hair back with cream, puffed constantly at a cigarette. Erleen, too, kept a lit ciggy, as she called it, traveling fast between her fingers and lips. She'd been told she should stop; as a nurse she had watched people die of emphysema. She shrugged, smiling. When she laughed it became a cough, a great phlegmy threshing deep in her chest.

The four sat outside in the coppery light. Brad kept an eye on the rugby game on the TV hung outside the bar. Three more televisions hung inside, tuned to the same game. Rugby looked rougher than anything Lorna had seen before. The men shoved each other into the mud, bleeding, trampling each other like starved animals over a bit of food. People at the other tables shouted at the screen.

Let's start out showing you all the cheapest bars, Erleen said when their glasses were empty.

They walked from den to den, each with its ear-splitting sound system. One was filled with old people singing along with a miked pianist. Everyone had beers before them, swaying in unison at their tables and benches. Let Me Call You Sweetheart, It's a Long Way to Tipperary. Erleen and Stan swayed and sang on their bar stools, grinning into each other's eyes. They insisted on going behind the bar and making Brad snap their photo with their arms around the bartender, a woman with a messy ponytail and cigarette at her lips. The bartender's face grimaced for the camera, accustomed to the ritual. There seemed no law in Doriben against bartenders drinking on the job. In the swaying and singing and clouds of smoke, Lorna and Brad smiled at each other. It would make one hell of a story.

Lorna had ceased trying to keep up with the others' drinking (even Brad, who loved pints, was having trouble), and sipped soda. Both she and Brad were red-eyed with the smoke, and Lorna would have given a lot to go back to their room, bathe the stench from her, read, sleep. But the evening had only begun. Erleen and Stan steered them past ragtag groups of revellers, past barkers in the doors of lounge-acts (the barkers calling Lorna *young lady*), past comedians, karaoke singers, strip-shows: strippers named Voom-voom Vicki, Luscious Laurie. The four listened awhile to a gray-haired man sitting on a stool, who pulled hard on a cigarette between the insults he delivered to audience members seated near him, which made the rest of the audience laugh and laugh. Then he sang a song which Lorna would remember for years afterward, a popular tune in England which had become a kind of sentimental anthem. *I just wanna dance the night away . . . with a señorita who can sway*. He didn't so much sing, as croak it. The massive audience filled the big darkened tent with singing, stumbling against one another on their paths to and from the toilets. Their white tank tops glowed lavender under the black lights. Stan and Erleen sang too, gazing again into each other's faces.

Lorna thought: oh where's the harm. This was it, she thought, for these stupefied, sad workers on their holidays. This was it.

Then it was time to go find Sandy Candy. Erleen put her hand on Lorna's shoulder as they walked, her breath ashy and yeasty: Ye'll not believe this, dearie: No one could make it up. Erleen and Stan seemed pulled along by a current, a river of humankind streaming around them. Lorna longed to run away, back to the hotel, but she knew it would embarrass Brad if she insisted on that; it would puncture the symmetry of the four like a flat tire, leave the vehicle of them listing, broken. Some part of her urged her to face her own habitual dread, overcome it, live through it—*it was only a question of living through time, a period of time*—make it a dismissed nothing, relegated to the past.

They paid their cover money—surprisingly steep—and entered an area resembling a circus tent. There was a central, paved floor where spotlights played; young, drunken girlfriends danced the Marguerita with each other. The crowds were packed thick at tiny tables; many more lined the area standing. The whole room seemed to be vibrating. Stan and Brad went off to find drinks, and Erleen and Lorna managed to secure two chairs in the din, at a table near the paved central stage. The music was deafening rock that shrieked and pounded—a raw, jungle presaging of something writhing.

A secret ceremony.

It was impossible to be heard unless you screamed.

The men came back and placed drinks before the women. Lorna sat taut. She found she did not want to look at Brad, though he'd been sweetly attentive, stroking her hair, asking several times if she were all right. They waited. The young girls danced in the spotlights. *Hey, Marguerita*. The lights played all round the room and it was clear there was a tremendous waiting in the air, smoke hanging cloud-dense, smells of whiskey and beer like moldy bread and stomach acid.

They waited. At midnight a man's English voice on a loudspeaker cheerfully asked all people below the age of 18 to leave. A great deal of movement and shouting and drunken noise followed as the younger ones, mostly girls, issued slowly from the building, carrying babies and dragging children.

More waiting.

The music pounded, relentless, insistent, jungle drums amplified so that it seemed to shake Lorna by the bones and take over her heartbeat. She felt hot, near to fainting; all the air in the room seemed to have been sucked away by the bodies pressing in. She was aware of Brad's presence somewhere near but did not want to look at him, did not want to see his face. She did not want to see anyone's face or be there but she was there and the faces were all around her. She tried to look at the faces of the strangers. They were drunk, their features blurrily arranged. She wanted desperately to flee, but told herself sharply she had to face off with it, make the long-delayed crossing into becoming the kind of grownup who could allude to events like these with a laugh and turn easily, with all the others, to something else. She had seen a few porn films and magazines: the images always resembled raw pink pork and chicken parts, bound in clear shrink-wrap in supermarket bins. Something in them roused her but mostly made her sad, for she knew a little about the work—that it paid extremely well to women who'd otherwise be on welfare. She knew these women had children and lawsuits and ill-tempered husbands or boyfriends or pimps, that often they shot heroin or speed, that while splayed or hunched and making scripted noises they were most concerned for whether their stomachs were pulled flat, whether their press-on nails would hold, how much money was still needed to buy the next desire, including the drugs.

She'd lived in the world, she told herself.

After what seemed hours a big man came with deep strides through the crowd from a back hallway, and behind the man came a small woman. She wore a long cloak and carried what looked like a portable podium, with little curtained shelves behind it. This she placed before her once the big man (glowering in meaningful sweeps around the room) had cleared a space for her at the center of the crowd. Lorna and Brad and Erleen and Stan were grouped slightly to the right of the petite woman, who stepped quickly, gracefully into the center of the crowd and threw off her cape and stood naked before them all.

The loudspeaker voice screamed: *Live. Tonight. In Doriben, Spain—the world-famous—Sandy Candy.* The crowd boiled with yelling and stomping, shouting and pressing forward.

She was lovely. Her blonde hair was pulled tightly back into a chignon like a ballerina's, her face artfully made up. Lorna thought suddenly of a beautiful Mexican hostess on television commercials in Lorna's own childhood: Aquanetta, a name Lorna had thought liquid. Aquanetta had been the color of heavily-creamed coffee, dressed in brilliant *folklorico* costumes; worn her hair the way Sandy Candy did. She'd exhibited the same exotic graciousness, the same elegant bearing. Sandy Candy could have been a diplomat's wife, giving a ball for the national ballet company of Paris.

In the smooth movement of tossing away her cape—caught mid-air by the big man, who roved his eyes around the crowd with keenness—Sandy Candy flung off a scanty bra, releasing two perfect breasts shaped like full teardrops, creamy and buoyant as a twenty year old's. She was now completely nude, a single smooth form before the roaring mass. Lorna felt her heart wring violently. Sandy Candy's body was exquisite, flawless and white, a marble sculpture. Her buttocks were silken, fruity. Her pubis was shorn save for one thin vertical line of close-trimmed blondish-brown hair, which in its own way seemed modest and tasteful as a scarf. The rock music pounded so that no sound besides a continual, throbbing roar could be distinguished, though Lorna was sometimes aware of shouts from the men of *Yeah* and *All Right*, blended into the frenzied pounding. Lorna tried to watch some of the women. They seemed drunkenly pleased yet confused, wobbly; some were staggering. One or two had been dragged out by friends in the act of being sick. A riddle of nature like platypuses: how willfully, blindly, obliteratingly drunk the Brits worked to become.

Sandy Candy walked around the cleared circle, regal, her arms open and lifted like a trapeze artist's—in welcome and acclaim, in proud delight. This was (Lorna saw, dazed) the clear message: pride of skill, pride of beauty. If her witnesses were drunken leerers, if slobbering horniness beat behind the hundred pairs of eyes upon her, if men were going to fall upon their women like dogs when they returned to their beds with the image of Sandy Candy rippling in their skulls, Sandy Candy seemed not to know it. She seemed to be addressing something not present in the stinking, dustfilled arena.

*Sixty-three years old*, Erleen was shouting in Lorna's ear. Lorna could smell the yeasty beer and bourbon on Erleen's breath. *A grown daughter*, Erleen's furrowed mouth bussed her ear like a drunken lover's. Lorna nodded without looking at Erleen, wanting to swat off that wrinkled mouth, swipe at it with a free arm as you might a heavy insect. She had no idea whether Erleen's claims could be true. Either way, what did it prove? Only that Sandy Candy took excruciating care of herself; perhaps she'd had makeover surgery. The woman was beautiful as a china vase.

Sandy Candy stepped back to the center of her clearing, smiled, and suddenly made a folding movement at her middle, bending her knees, raising her pelvis slightly up-and-forward, a pose you might hold to insert a tampon, while her arm reached between her legs. There her hand retrieved an egg, whole and apparently fresh. It looked dry as bone, Lorna could not help noticing. Sandy Candy held the egg aloft, twirling it for all to see, smiling (*this woman is naked*, Lorna thought again)—then paced swiftly to her portable podium to place the egg on one of the curtained shelves behind it. Lightly she stepped again into the center of the clearing, and over the next twenty minutes, with a series of the same quick pelvis-tilts—a posture which stabbed Lorna, because it reduced the delicate ballerina to a peasant in a toilet stall—produced another egg, a feather boa, a length of multicolored silk, a string of flashing colored lights, a British flag, a toy plush rabbit, and eventually a full, capped bottle of Coca Cola, which Sandy Candy brought to an abashed young man (she trotted eagerly, feather-light, toes turned out, a *corps de ballet* princess) clasping a silver bottle opener, which must also have been removed from herself, and in ladylike miming motions requested he open the bottle for her. She looked like a small naked white doll standing before the weaving, disheveled man, a Tinkerbell. He cracked open the bottle, and she took it from him and poured a bit of soda onto the ground as evidence of the cola bottle's realness, holding her other arm aloft in an arc of weightless grace. While Sandy Candy turned in triumph to the crowd, her back to him, the young man made a show of smelling his hand. The music pounded on, a hellish anvil chorus, and the crowd surged with raucous shouts, screaming and clapping. Sandy Candy danced each new article back to the shelves behind her podium, while the big bodyguard's eyes roamed the assembly like a distempered lighthouse beam.

Lorna had wrapped her arms around herself. She talked to herself in measured phrases. *A long-honed skill.* Stretching and filling the pelvic cavity. Removal by pressure on the lower belly. Use of breath. Placement of objects, powdered for smoothness. Hours inserting the materials so they would emerge just so—so they would not injure. Hours of preparatory time, then walking to the ring of screeching humans with a womb packed so tightly that a false move might have ripped her open inside. There was no question but she believed herself an artist. *What was her name? Alessandra?*

Phrases. *A recreation by humans.* Long-practiced. The world. Other, similar recreations. No one harmed. No theft of civil liberties. Everyone goes away, sleeps it off. Makes a funny story back home. Souvenir, Christmas ornament. No different from junkshop novelties, machines that farted when you put in pennies, plastic penises, oversized inkpens shaped like fully-clad women whose clothes disappeared when you turned them upside down. Nothing more. Nothing more.

But Lorna felt as though someone had slapped her, her cheeks stinging as the four walked out the door. The pounding music faded slowly, like a towering monster in deflation. Lorna did not look at Brad or the others, but into the swirling screams of the drunken crowds pushing across the midway. People lurched in and out of shows, burger stands, chip shops. They stepped around vomit on the sidewalks and gutters.

The four said goodnight after Erleen, brushed accidentally by Lorna, spilled French fries and catsup on herself in the elevator. She gave Lorna a hate-filled look.

Lorna and Brad were silent as they walked the few paces to their room. They fit the key into the lock and entered; the weighted door fell shut behind them with echoing finality.

Brad glanced at the clock. It's late, he said.

Yes. Lorna tried to make her voice answer in a matching tone: offhand calm. *Just get into the bed. Get somehow to sleep. It might all be erased by morning. Not his fault, nothing to do with him, not his fault.*

He turned to her when the lights were out.

What is it, he said quietly.

Lorna curled fetus-like against him and sobbed, swallowing her repulsion at the touch of him, familiar as he was.

It's a horror, a nightmare, she wept.

I found it boring, he said. I wanted to leave.

Lorna did not completely believe this, and it pressed a thorn into her head with what it implied—that the act could have interested him, done correctly. But she had no heart to challenge it, and even if she could—even if she could debate him like fucking Alexander Hamilton, what would that accomplish. *Let me fucking out of here.*

It makes me not want to be in the world, she sobbed. The world, including the treacherous body of her husband, seemed to collapse and fold over her in that bed like giant bat wings, black and tented and reptilian, rubbery and sticky. Outside through the heavy curtains, the roars of the drunken revved. Shouting. Firecrackers. A car alarm went off, undulant siren squalls. Someone was rolling a metal beer keg down the sidewalk.

Somewhere in town in a dressing room, Sandy Candy was having a cigarette and a glass of papaya juice, counting her money.

I understand, he said. We'll never do it again.

You don't. You *don't* understand, Lorna cried. We were all part of it. The worst of it. We're responsible. It's like that story, she cried.

What story? Brad took a silent breath, girding for the ordeal: talking her down, talking her through. He was tired, bored, bitterly regretting his mistake. He should have known better. Lorna couldn't watch movies with the least tension in them. She got tearful at television commercials, sorry for trees when a branch was sawed off, sorry for spiders swept into the broom. Harping at him how things might go black on them at any moment, which he could only try to chide her out of. What percentage was there, thinking that way? Yes, right, so she'd lost her mother young; poor kid had to find the body in its bed, cool and blue, mouth sagging at the corners, and yes, the father'd been a tomcat, screwing his way through boredom—a common enough tactic, if not very well thought out. So the mother'd swallowed pills—never considered fighting back or getting help. Brad still shook his head at this. But after a while Lorna's slashed childhood had to sink—*had to*—into the vast lake of everyone's losses. His own dad snuffed too young in a matter of weeks, bone-marrow cancer. You lived a while, you took hits. And truth was that after a certain age, nobody gave a shit. It wasn't compelling. It wasn't some urgent, correctible transgression that had to be *addressed*. Brad wanted a cheerful pal. Lorna was a tender woman who laughed easily, but whose natural mood slipped, without his buoying her, into a kind of baffled sadness. He'd teased her all their years, but sometimes these flayed nerves of hers became a thoroughgoing pain in the ass.

Arrangements had to be made, care to be taken.

That story where the men go fishing, Lorna sobbed. And they see a beautiful naked dead woman, drowned under the cold water in the river where they're fishing. But they've come all that way and taken so much trouble to get there they decide to ignore the dead woman, to report her to the police after they go back, after their fishing is done. Do you remember? They just camp there, fish upstream of her. And then one of the men tells his wife when he gets home, and she cries and cries and runs away from him.

Brad remembered the story, sort of. Lorna read too much. He thought it fed her morbidity. Not to mention the tedium. When he came home evenings tired, his brain felt like a piece of wood. The last thing he wanted was a book review. He was silent.

Then he thought of something, and in hopefulness asked it tenderly as he could.

Is this hormonal?

Lorna shook with sobs. The top of her head pressed his chest. We're the perpetrators, she said, looking up, her face pouchy and slick. We're monsters. A mistake by God. *Big* mistake. She spat these words, rising suddenly. Hiccoughing, she went to gather toilet tissue to stanch her streaming nose. Why wasn't he lacerated, too? Why didn't owning a penis make him sick to his guts tonight? Why didn't it just smack him over the head with its dumb mystery, leave his teeth chattering?

Why do you love me, she said after she'd lain down beside him again, and they'd been quiet for some minutes.

Because you're the most interesting person I know, he said. I'd be lost without you. You know that.

He did love her, when she wasn't in one of her states like this. He enjoyed her. She had ways of describing things that amazed him. They had fine sex—when she wasn't in one of her states like this. The breakdowns happened rarely, but to live with her was to feel their potential under the surface. Like one of those people who could bleed to death from a minor cut.

Brad could feel himself arriving to that zone in a man's life where what is wanted gets simpler, but also desperately important. Not to hurt anywhere when you got up. Enough sleep, pleasant sex, decent cup of coffee, decent dinner. No complexity, no obstructions as you reached for these things.

Things ticking over.

It was also the zone in which a man understood he had worked hard a long time, and could expect plenty more: a long time of working hard. This gave any pleasures obtained en route a trickier burden. They had to count. Lorna used to tease him about it: *Frolic, damn it.*

But I'm crazy, Lorna was saying. I can't bear what most everyone else seems so well able to bear. Why? Why doesn't that freak you out? She began to cry again.

You always have good stuff to say, he reminded her. I like talking to you.

She absorbed this. She didn't entirely believe it, but she knew he wanted her to. And that he wanted her to, counted for something. Except at bottom she also knew he was too tired to make a change, to sever a pulsing network of family and history so interpenetrated it had become a hybrid creature. They were both too old, too tired to start again. Interviewing, auditioning—it exhausted them both to consider, she knew, even in fantasy. But Lorna knew something else: that if she died, Brad would make sure—furiously, ferociously sure—he did not land someone like her again. He would probably find someone younger, and—undented. Not a single, second thought in her pretty head. Lorna had to live with this.

And you don't mind that I'm crazy this way?

I don't mind. I love you.

He felt like a captain at the wheel of a huge liner, inching through razored narrows. Lorna sighed, hiccoughing a little, and lay beside him in the dark. Outside, the howls and jeering grew fainter. In the morning she would force herself to open her legs for him, though right now the thought of it made her ill. And he would remind himself never, never, never to take his wife to a skin show again; that impulse would have to play itself out in some separate room. Meantime they would go find their coffee, read the paper, have a nap. Take a bus to a train and thence to an airplane, and fly away to manageable, above-ground lives. And the days to come, in both their minds, if they resolved it—and here was another impetus for that, perhaps what ultimately made the distress useful, even necessary—if they worked at it, the days would begin clean and glowing again, new and pure as a velvet-soft baby chick.

# UNDIVIDED ACTS

*Michael Anania*

The question of time reoccurs: relative
to what?  the speaker and the questioner,
all that their shared durations shared;  imagine

April in Paris, 1922, Einstein at the podium;
in the audience, Bergson raises his hand,
"Would you admit to two kinds of time"—

*Le Coeur á Barbe* shoved into someone's
raincoat pocket,  razor,  hot air balloon,
a steamship passing by, Erik Satie

at the rail, barely visible, Eluard, Ernst,
*The Dance of Saint Guy*, all the rage
that season, Picabia's string instrument,

literature as *LIT et RATURES*—
"physical time and personal time, what is
measured and what is experienced, known?"

"No," he said, "there is only one time, over
which the time we live has no jurisdiction."
Every duration harbors others; occasions

are mere ripples in light moving outward.
Even so, light moves in time and bends inward;
however disquieting, what we know

is neither here nor there, and intuition,
the sense that there is a world that conforms
to our recurrent suppositions and that time

envelopes us like a familiar landscape,
is act of faith based as much on perception's
limitations as its furtive accuracies.

Duchamp's *Straw Hat,* by '22, an established
sedition, the Mona Lisa's moustache,
LHOOQ, she has hot pants, *chaud cul.*

"The Fig Leaf" superimposed over "Hot Eyes,"
the sun's face or a drawing of a rotary brake,
the leaf itself squeezed from a paint tube like icing,

the figure in silhouette, one foot propped
on a black circle, sun or brake eclipsed,
the layers clear now in slant light at the Tate.

Mme. Curie attended the lecture,
Einstein's first in Paris, but if she spoke,
it wasn't recorded. Later, she and Albert

were photographed taking a walk in the grey
Paris spring. *Il fait gris,* a quality of light
or of photo-plates in a moist season.

"What do you make," she might have said,
"of the nude man in black profile, his foot
resting on what seems to be a black sun

and of his apparent precision of gesture,
and all that stands out in relief behind him?
Is one picture painted so conspicuously

over another an act of obliteration
or an effort to make us notice in art
a curt form of relativity? Do these jokes,

even when they seem merely capricious
accidental or vulgar—*she has a hot ass*—
have their beginnings in the rules we have

so meticulously challenged and broken?"
"History might well say so, though it could,
just as easily, say that you and I were freed

to think as we did by the art and music
of the 80s and 90s. When did light become
as much the subject as what it illuminated?"

"Bergson thinks that radium proves that energy
is emitted by things themselves and sparkled
across the general darkness toward life,

an unseen kind of light, magical and creative.
After all this time, my fingers ache with it."
Or did they merely walk and say nothing.

## OF LIGHT AND ILLUMINATION

*—for* Niccolò Tucci *who always returns*
(1908-1999)

*Deborah Pease*

As all manner
Of light and illumination
(To the degree
They are sensibly different)
Send refracted rays
Like bent reeds
Through water onto pebbles
In riverbeds—

• • •

As sun shears itself
Into blades of air
Through clerestory windows
Piercing cathedrals or tombs
With tame mosaic fire—

• • •

As the earth-snug fawn's
Already dappled coat
Receives through leaves
More splashes of camouflage
So too does she
Receive this force of light—

• • •

He comes to her, glowing
And her life is restored, lit up
With joy, cured
Of hidden sorrow
(Grief-cavity,
Rodent in its burrow gnawing), free,
Attuned to the effortless
Pressure of light, this source
Of love allowing her
For a moment to live again
In luminosity.

• • •

He lights a candle
On the bedside table,
His face, radiant,
Emerges from shadows—
In this room they rest,
Holding each other,
Cradling silence,
Breathing in unison through the night.

## Late Days of Wreckage

*Jude Nutter*

After driving her to the airport you will,
because you are in love, have the courage
to return to your bed without her, where,
finding a purpose in her absence,
you might sleep until dawn
breaks the varnished latch of every
bird beak open. The earth will heave
out of the mist to claim her and
by the time she is beside
her mother—who will be sleeping, thin
as moist kindling under the covers—
you will be at work, in a suit perhaps,
but unshaved, feet on the table
a folder of case notes before you,
and your gun, unbreakable heart, in a holster
against your ribs. You will have left a knife,
as you always do, out on the cutting block,
the dried juice of an orange
like shellac on the blade. In their tanks your fish
will pass the day as they always
do, folding back and forth through the water
with, now and then, a single tetra
breaking loose from the crowd and drifting
upward, little morsel of colour, to place
the pale foyer of its tiny mouth
against the roof of its world, creating

perfect circles on the surface of this one.
This world is full of clues, but she will find
no story in her mother's dying, and there
will be nights she refuses to write, nights
when you become the page. *Give me the clues,*
you will say, long-distance, from Berlin.
She will give you fear. She will give
you absence. She will give you a loneliness
common as foxgloves in the hedges

blooming, as they do, from the bottom
up, each stem unzipping slowly. Wind that heckles
metal out of the grass until the lawn
becomes a carpet of knives.
She will give you daylight drumming
its fingers on the frameless window of the sea;
the yellow flags loosening their clothes
to play wanton in the fields. Hills, fully-throated
in late shades of green. She will give you
late days of wreckage. And that small rip
that appeared in the clouds—a blue
mouth carried from one horizon to the other.
Later she will tell you how lucky she was

to have found you, how lucky
to have fallen in love as her mother
was dying; but, right now,
she's telling you her mother is lost
to her the way a kite, grounded on a day
without a breeze, is lost; that the yellow flags'
only job, which they do to perfection,
is to let go of everything they were given.
And because in such telling each clue
begins to feel like a story, and because
a story is a home, however brief, you
cannot decide whether it's love or words
that form our finest argument against despair
because, right now, she is telling
you about the fish in the mountain lakes;
how, in this world, they create such perfect
circles on the water simply by drifting
up to the surface and kissing what imprisons them.

Note: yellow flag is another name for the wild yellow iris.

# LOOKING AT PHOTOGRAPHS, IMPERIAL WAR MUSEUM, LONDON

*Jude Nutter*

It's their hands I notice first—fingers
cradling the stock of a rifle, unfolding
a field map or feeding bandoliers
into the breech of a Vickers machine gun; fingers
on the rim of a helmet raised in greeting; the hands
of a whole battalion raising their helmets in greeting
on their way to the Somme front line in 1916.
But it's hands not occupied, for the moment, with war
that move me most—hands lost in pockets, cheating
at cards, lighting cigarettes. Long-fingered,
dirty, competent—some with the bright lasso
of a wedding ring, but most without. Hands
writing letters. May 17, 1917, and someone
is sending a message by pigeon from a trench
on the Western Front, and what the camera
has given us is that moment right after
the moment when the young signalman unlocked
the soft prison of his fingers
to fling the bird skyward. The truth the eye
misses, the heart never fails
to recognize, and this is not simply
one more document of history or one more
fragment of war: this is a man
standing, empty-handed,
forever. Look at the pale cradle he has made
of his fingers; think how much it could hold.
And these are the hands that would slit
a man's throat if they had to, and yet
I know the magic the hands of a man can work
on the body of a woman he loves. There is evidence
everywhere—murder and beauty. The bird's
wings are blurred like swirling
shrouds, like vestments, like skirts and the man's
arms are caught in the follow-through—easy, natural,
a gesture like the green-smooth follow-through of spring;
and his body, too, beginning to rise.

## Orpheus Among Familiar Ghosts

*Henry Hart*

Where olive leaves littered the cave mouth,
he turned back to map his path through shadows.

*Best to know who you're up against,*
his mother warned from the aura of her torch.

He heard his dead brother singing like a sibyl
on a bar stool, echoes of his father's clapping.

He, too, wanted to strum the tortoise-shell lyre,
make doves coo and bats swing from niches.

Watching his wife drag her cloak of mold from the dark,
one ankle still limp from the viper's fangs,

he pleaded: *What do you expect me to do?*
*Take you back to buried fields*

*tangled with forget-me-nots? Pole you*
*down underground streams forever?*

When she slipped from the light
like Venus at dawn, the cave was his stage.

He plucked his lyre until chaff broke
from wheat, grapes squeezed themselves

into wine, olive trees wept oil.
He wore his costume until he became it.

Still, his father clapped for his brother,
his mother snickered beneath her torch.

What else could he do but go back
down to that underground auditorium,

perfect his most scandalous chords, hope
the dead would wake and forgive him?

# THE MAPMAKER AND HIS WOMAN

*Bill Meissner*

He should be working on his maps, but instead
he spends the day thinking that she is the distance between
point A and point B. She is Germany, in black and white, Czechoslovakia,
perhaps, in brown tones, the mountains and rivers
placed just so, the land falling and rising
exactly according to scale.

The paper his fingertips touch is dry,
not like her, such fertile land rolling with meadows and ponds.
Whenever he thinks of her, he thinks of
a peak atop peaks, a valley lush with valleys.
But lately she's always somewhere else:
museums, coffee shops with hissing steam, fruit markets,
intersections he can't quite locate.
He's only sure about highways, each inch equaling exactly a hundred miles,
about the dark ink dots of towns
etched into thick parchment.

His job is to measure the world:
nothing on his map except what's actually there—
river, a bluff that causes a
highway to angle, the blue dirt roads like capillaries that wrap the earth.
She's somewhere in that world, he knows: cafes, aquariums, aviaries
where her eyes latch onto soaring birds.
And he's inside, the four plaster walls slowly gliding toward him,
flattening him so precisely
he could be the thin line between two rectangular countries.

He wishes he could just forget about his maps,
all their lines squirming crazily
as if etched by earthworms, his maps
with the black and red stars of cities
that never light up the flattened paper.

Instead he'd like to close his eyes and dream
of fish or birds, of swimming or flying.
Instead he'd like to write a poem about her
on the back of his hand,
the looping blue letters
that tattoo his skin rising and falling with each movement of his fingers.

In the evening, when she finally steps through the doorway,
he's still sitting at his desk, an acre
of blank paper spread out in front of him.
She walks close to him, an apple still in her hand, feathers on her shoulders.
She is Bohemia in color—he can sense all the miles
on the soles of her shoes.
He wants to tell her how far away he felt from her
when she was gone, but his tongue is a discarded train ticket.
The only words he can think of are awkwardly pronounced cities:
Istanbul, Mazatlan, Kuala Lumpur, Dusseldorf.

*Done with your map?* She might ask, the liquid sound
of her words startling him.
And he might answer by pointing to the window, its clear transparency
he polished with his eyes all afternoon.
At first their conversation will be circular,
like the dark blue concentric lines
that indicate the depth of an ocean.
He wants to tell her she is that body of water, but his cracked lips
are caught on Budapest, Mayapan, Monongahela, Salamanca.

There is no ending because what they have between them
is a map that, no matter where you follow it,
leads to the same place each time:
There, in its center, you'll find two people,
waiting alone near a small road, or the stitched scar of a railroad track.
Two people, standing on uncharted ground,
staring at each other, their eyes understanding, finally,
that they are the shortest distance between two points.

## Double Portrait

*—after Frans Hals*

*Peter Robinson*

So there we are: by a garden wall's
re-pointed summer shade,
by vines encircling tree trunks, ivy
clinging to its brick
or trailed across some mildewed concrete;
thistles, spilled pots, other symbols
do their best to place us
where heart-shaped leaves lie thick, entwined,
like living necklaces.

Tendrils knocking at a window
insistently had wormed on through
gaps between aperture and frame.
Still, the blocked light came;
and though we love leaf-shadow thrown
across a bathroom floor,
in your heart of hearts you know
that this infesting mass of creeper,
it will have to go.

Far language seeps from crevices
in an August's holding truce:
the girls are playful somewhere near,
speaking other tongues.
A butterfly with red-flecked wings
rises from composted grass
beside them; only they don't notice,
lost in art works, making things,
don't see it disappear

across the distance, somewhere other,
to where a villa's peacocks
patrolling box hedge arch their necks,
shriek imprecations at a sky
with dusk tints, warmer cloud,
like choking, being sick. Your mother
mimics them alarmingly,
but the family's drawn together—
don't ask me how or why.

So there we are: a married couple
pausing in our day
to laugh out loud at contradiction,
those emblems of it on display;
and farther are the ancestors
like staffage, nymphs and shepherds
sweating through a checkered past.
They're figured down to us as myth,
there, in so many words.

# Barlach's "Floating Angel"

*Joelle Biele*

*"We have put a stop to the liberalistic carryings on of a Mecklenburg artist, who created war memorials in the worst, twisted bolshevik manner. And I hope that the last traces of his terrible works are soon removed from the places they still occupy, as has already been done in Magdeburg. He is alien to our nature and therefore we cannot exist with him in the same spiritual and thus cultural community."*

*—Friedrich Hildebrandt, Governor of Mecklenburg*
Niederdeutscher Beobachter, *June 2, 1935*

Black, heavy, hung on iron rods, the original
sent to Schwerin for "military economic utilization,"
this casting made from a cast buried

in the bombed and wasted heather, buffed
to a dull shine, she has no wings,
and her eyes are closed. We are in Güstrow,

in the cathedral, taking a tour
of washed and painted brick when the guide
takes us around a corner, points to a rail,

begins talking about Barlach, the Reich,
his radio addresses, letters and petitions,
how his neighbors removed his sculptures,

burned his prints, how one morning his heart
stopped, and war waged on. She hovers
above us weightless, as if she has almost come

into being, as if she is already there
and the idea were what it is to be human,
what it is to be present while still here on earth.

## WHAT GIVES

*Brian Swann*

Old fruit in my garden bobs on the branch,
human, stout. Crows fly in and
take it apart, the way ravens took apart
dead warriors, going first for the eyes.
Over the hill, the tide goes in and out,
a second theme related to the first.
Sun stuns the birds, it does not let them go.
It does not let them through, they're *here.*
It is noon, Roman ghost-time though
this is not Rome where I slept each day
till noon when the wind from Ostia
came through the broken windows and
woke me up. I dreamed in Rome of Rome.
Where you are is never where you are...
Clothes on the roof across from me
billow out and a lovely woman
rearranges them with one hand, the
other holding down her orange skirt.
Later, she and I will meet and at Veii,
by tombs, by ancient rock-cut sacred
bathing places, on the terra cotta earth
that yielded statues of the Vulca School,
among nettles and daisies and buttercups,
to the sounds of frogs and one cuckoo,
make love... Now there's a line of oranges
left at the high-tide mark, blood oranges
from crates dumped or washed overboard
in last night's storm...
One thinks of the human,
meaning the dailyness of things, a family's clothes
on a line, oranges and crates of oranges,
tombs, frogs, cuckoos, the swelling sea,
women, the wonder of women, the importance
of tomorrow which soon comes due, even here
in the mountains where each summer evening
I watch the waxwings find their way home

heading west over my house, cheeping
as they fly, always a straggler or two trying
to catch up and calling louder as the stars
begin to move in, or seem to, as they did
at Veii, Cerveteri, Tarquinia whose augurs
turned them all, birds and stars, everything
back or into the human, prognosticating the
true course and nature of things and on tombs
had painted scenes more vivid than life itself
so what is left behind is not the world
but some version of what it meant
to be alive, not what is given but what gives.

# THE PALERMO ROAD

*Brian Swann*

Outside Trapani, snow on the mountains,
dark red earth,
terraces, orange trees, cars following our
dust-cloud, we following theirs, others
overtaking and
cutting in. A three-wheeler with a black pig
straining in a net, another with three
little girls giggling
waving and choking on our dirt and fumes,
and Walter still fuming insisting on the daily
history lesson
he's memorized: *Between the mouths*
*of the Fiumara Zappulla and Capo D'Orlando*
*was in 1299*
*fought a sea-battle in which...* He slows
slower to think what comes next and a dignified
old man in a
black suit with black armband overtakes us on
a donkey with wood planks strapped to its sides.
In Palermo
a priest frowns when I ask, but points. We
find it after scrambling over iron railings
Judith gets
hung up on and round walls W gets stuck
between: "Teatrino dei Pupi Armati,
Guiseppi Argento
& Figli, Via del Pappagallo, 10."
We enter an empty barn with whitewashed beams,
a few decorations
for Natale, '67, pictures of the palatins
in armor on the walls. A man motions us
to follow him
backstage and up a steep ladder past
grinning cannibals and Moors. At the top
along the walls
puppets almost life-size, rods to hands

heads and legs, the oldest one, he says,
one hundred years,
we can have for eighty thousand lire.
"Ecco Orlando!" A body with three heads,
boy, man,
old man, surrounded by shiny shields that
took a month to make. Back out front
the wooden benches
fill. Six people at five hundred lire each.
Against a painted backdrop and to music
the story of Orlando
unfolds. You recognize him by his cross-eyed squint,
denoting ferocity. He comes to Charlemagne's court
to swipe some soup
and vitals for his mother and sister hiding
in the rocks. He calls the emperor "Magnomagno",
"Eateat", and
runs away pursued by two retainers. When they catch
him he smacks them about until his ma
recognizes them
and they go back to beg pardon of the king
who knocks her down and Orlando knocks him down
and yells:
"I'll kick him in the teeth and knock him out!"
Then Charlemagne forgives his sister,
embracing her
too long for Orlando who yells, "Hey, basta!
Enough of that! Hey, break it up!" More battle scenes.
Swords clash
on swords and shields above the barrel-organ.
Saracens fall in heaps, and twitch,
many with
their heads lopped off. One runs around
like a chicken with no head. And then
the action stops
while the *puparo* runs from behind the scenes
to sort out boys scuffling with the organ-boy
for his job.
The losers settle down to cigarettes and
hacking coughs. After, Walter's miffed.

"Why was there
no Orlando going mad when Angelica
betrays him? I've read the book. He recovers
his lost wits
by sniffing the urn they're in which Adolfo
brought back from the moon, and which..."
"Astolfo," Judith says,
"not Adolfo." Next day we aim for Cefalú,
H mad because J still refuses to share a room,
and still upset
because at a mosaic of a "scena erotica" in
Piazza Armerina of two lovers embracing,
she with her back
towards us, drawing aside her gown to show
her arse, he said he saw J wink at me.
He drives his usual
slow pace, and a donkey-cart with paintings
on its panels of knights and palatins, driven by a woman
who looks like
Orlando's mother careens in front, finocchi bound
like fasces bounce and sway, radishes the size of beets
roll about
as she swerves to avoid potholes and pits.
W curses in German and honks. "Cigarette!"
he calls to J who
pushes in the dashboard lighter. When it pops out
she hands it to him. It's at his lips before
he screams
and drops it in his lap, slamming on the brakes.
"Mistück!" J turns round to look at me,
knowing my thoughts.
A woman walks by in a large black straw hat,
from the top of which the white head of a cockerel
protrudes and,
looking about, crows.

# INTERVIEW WITH MARY KARR

*Stephanie Magdalena White*

*Mary Karr was born in 1955 in Groves, Texas. Her writing career began with two volumes of poetry,* Abacus *(1987) and* The Devil's Tour *(1993), but it was her best-selling memoir* The Liars' Club *(1995) that propelled her career forward. She followed* The Liars' Club *with another book of poems,* Viper Rum *(1998), another memoir,* Cherry *(2005), and her latest volume of poetry,* Sinners Welcome *(2006). Karr's poems, essays, and prose have appeared in* Parnassus, Mother Jones, Poetry, The Atlantic, *and* The New Yorker, *among others. She has a MFA from Goddard College (1979) and has won numerous awards and fellowships for her writing, including a Guggenheim Fellowship, a Pushcart Prize, a PEN/Martha Albrand Award, a Bunting Fellowship, a Whiting Writer's Award, and a grant from the National Endowment for the Arts. She is the Jesse Truesdell Peck Professor of Literature at Syracuse University, and recently she took on the weekly "Poet's Choice" column for the Washington Post's* Book World. *She lives in New York City, where she is at work on a new memoir,* Lit.

*In April, 2008, Karr attended the Festival of Faith and Writing at Calvin College in Grand Rapids, Michigan. There she appeared onstage, along with friend and fellow poet Franz Wright, and talked about her conversion to Catholicism, her writing life, and how the two are connected. Later, she met with Stephanie Magdalena White, who conducted the following interview.*

**NDR:** During your talk yesterday, you said that for a long time after you finished *Cherry*, you didn't want to write another memoir. What made you finally decide to write *Lit*?

**MK:** You know, everywhere I go people say, "You had this terrible childhood, blah, blah, blah, and how did you get out of it?" And I've written two memoirs about sort of living in the house I grew up in, but it's hard to write about yourself when you're older. I think I didn't really have a voice for it or a language for it or an angle on it. I just didn't want to do it. It's like I said, I pray about what I'm supposed to write and even though people were doing sort of a preemptive strike and offering me money to write this book before I wanted to write it, I just didn't want to write it.

And then one day I felt called to. I found myself making notes about stopping drinking, about the end of my drinking and about being a mom and about the difficulties of that, and what that meant, and I felt myself drawn to do it. Again, it's that I try to make those decisions based on what I call "interior movements," that are not exactly feelings. That's what the Jesuits call them, "interior movements."

**NDR:** How do they come about?

**MK:** A lot of it's through prayer. And I just find myself making notes on something and thinking about it, thinking about it and how I would write it. Again, it's a story that I'm often asked about. And I felt called to do it. I feel like it's very hard to write about coming to faith and... And you know what the truth is? I'll tell you the other reason. I've read a lot of books about getting sober, but I haven't read any good ones. I've read, you know, the Caroline Knapp *Drinking: A Love Story*, and it's decent. Or Pete Hamill wrote a book called *A Drinking Life*. They're sort of good pieces of journalism but they don't feel like enduring pieces of literature. Now maybe mine won't be either, but...

**NDR:** But in what way are you trying to make it different from those?

**MK:** I want it to be better written, basically [laughs].

**NDR:** Define that. What does that mean for you?

**MK:** I want the sentences to be more interesting. I want the structure of it to be more surprising. I want it to be psychologically deeper. And mine is more about a spiritual journey. I've taught St. Augustine's *Confessions*—I just taught them again this fall—and about how you enter into a conversation with God. And I was just such a godless little bitch that I didn't know how to write about it. I still don't. I'm sort of just making it up as I go along.

**NDR:** Tell me about your process for this one, then, especially as compared to your processes for *Cherry* and *The Liars' Club*.

**MK:** This was.... I threw away five hundred pages. I wrote, and finished, over a four-year period, five hundred pages. And they would have published it. But I didn't feel like I was writing about what I wanted to write about.

I went over it with my editor. She said, "Oh the writing is really good," etc. She didn't complain about how it was written. It wasn't like she was saying, "Rewrite this, rewrite this." And I got to the end of it and I said, "How about this. Let's just say I throw most of this away. What if the book started like, 'At the end of my drinking, I'd be lying in bed....'" And I remember my kid was sick a lot. And I remember lying in bed and him coughing with the croup, and I would think, "I can*not* believe that little fucker's up. I *can't* get up." I mean, I did get up. My husband was working fulltime and going to school fulltime. He wasn't like some deadbeat dad—I don't want to give that impression. And I was working part time, so it was my job to get up. But I couldn't get up until it occurred to me that if I got up, I could make myself a drink. So I would get up, and I would go in there, and I would have a baby who could not *breathe*, and before I would take him in the shower and turn the steam on, I would go downstairs with him on my hip and fix myself a drink.

**NDR:** So that's how you decided to start the story?

**MK:** That's how I decided to start the story.

**NDR:** What do you think that means, to start with something that is so honest and humbling—such a confession?

**MK:** Well, it's not like I'm throwing him in the oven. It's not like James Frey dramatic. You know, often I tell people when they're having a hard time writing a story, I say, "What is the senior-most thing you're afraid to write, or you feel worst about, or you feel most guilty about. What if you start with that?" And then it occurred to me that that was true for me. That I had this child and, literally, because I was drinking so much, I would throw up in the mornings when I got up, and so I didn't want to drop him off at school because you don't want to throw up in the daycare. You just don't. But that the idea that I couldn't take my kid to daycare in the morning because the sight of children playing made me nauseous, do you know what I mean? And that sense that I was like a vampire. I really loved the dark. I was frightened—I was afraid of the light. That's how I was. It's very savage.... And the only thing that represented hope for me or relief for me was drinking. To really explain that. I wasn't any kind of destitute, grisly, horrible.... But to me, psychologically, I became my mother.

The big fear my whole life was that I'd become my mother. She was the shadow stitched to my feet, you know, that I couldn't outrun. And that I became that. It was hell. It was hell for me. And to have this baby. I loved him, as you are hardwired to do. It wasn't that I didn't love him. I just felt like I couldn't do it. I thought, "This is too hard. This is just too hard." And I'd never really been mothered. I mean, I went to a psychologist because I thought that being a good mother meant doing just whatever he wanted to do. That's the truth. I just didn't know any different.

**NDR:** So do you talk a lot about your son in *Lit*? I mean, is this something that comes up, or is it more based on your relationships, or back to your parents, or...?

**MK:** I don't spend that much time on my parents. Although, my mother got sober right when I started drinking a lot.

**NDR:** Really?

**MK:** Yeah, it was interesting. It's almost like our genetic code owes somebody an alcoholic. It just so happened, I mean. There wasn't a causal link. But the example for me of her sobriety was very radiant. The changes in her were very radiant and obvious. So, it's about that.

It's about being so depressed I checked into a mental institution. It's about checking into a mental institution and thinking that was the low point of my life—a real commencement for me. For me that was a great thing, that was a great surrender. And the truth was, I was sober for nine months when I checked into a mental institution. And I felt *good* enough to check into a mental institution. I mean, that was a step up from how I felt when I was drinking. I actually felt hopeful in some way when I checked into a mental institution in a way I hadn't when I stopped drinking. So it's about that.

And it's about coming to conversion and coming to faith and becoming Catholic. And then, you know, I think we'll end with these spiritual exercises, with me developing a relationship with Christ that feels very real to me, and developing a prayer life that informs a lot of my decision-making and how I live.

**NDR:** It's so interesting, because we're here at this festival where everyone's talking about faith, and you can pray at the beginning of your talk and everyone bows their heads, right? And I can just picture, you know, Zondervan, which is the Christian branch of HarperCollins, picking up *Lit* and wanting to get discussion questions in at the end, and people using it as a Bible study text, and how different that is from *The Liars' Club* and *Cherry*. What do you think about that? And your editor is saying, "Don't put some of that stuff in." Where is this taking you as a writer? And as a Catholic writer?

**MK:** Well, there are these stories I told about meeting my agent and these things that happened to me in terms of my publishing career, and my agent said to me, "You can't write about this stuff." And I said, "But, you don't understand." I met Toby Wolff when I was twenty-two years old and Toby was nobody special, you know, on a white horse. He was a thirty-five-year-old who had published one book with a small press, this guy teaching at a small school in Arizona. And that he became my godfather and actually was my instrument toward baptism. And that he had written a memoir, and that I would write a memoir partly based on my admiration for his work. And the degree to which certain things were standing in line for me to do them and the inevitability of some of the things that I wound up doing and the way that I felt guided by God. I can't not *say* that!

**NDR:** Why?

**MK:** Because that's the *truth* as I experienced it!

**NDR:** And why this…obsession, even, with the truth? When Robert Hass introduced you for the lunch readings at Princeton he said, "She is a person who will say anything true." And, I mean, you wrote *The Liars' Club* and you called it a memoir. It's not like you called it fiction. You said you started trying to write it as a novel, but found you could make yourself look too good. So why this obsession with being honest to other people?

**MK:** I don't know. I don't know. I think if you grow up in a household where there are a lot of lies.… If you grow up with alcoholism, there *are* a lot of lies. There just are. People lie about when they're drunk, when they're sober, what they did, what they plan to do, what they're gonna do, what they have done. People just lie. A lot. It's the common… currency of an alcoholic household. That's just what you trade in, do business in. And I don't know why, at age eleven, I wrote, "When I grow up I'll write half memoir and half poetry." I mean, my sister and I have often tried to think, "What memoirs had I read?" I remember that I read Helen Keller. I read Madame Curie. I read a book when I was in the sixth grade called *Black Like Me* about a guy who became black. I read Sammy Davis Jr.'s *Yes I Can.* I read *The Autobiography of Malcolm X* when I was about thirteen, fourteen. I think I've always been interested in a single person's voice. Which is what interests me about poetry—it's one person's voice, crying in the wilderness. Or it's like when I meet somebody…like talking last night to this priest from Zimbabwe! You know, "What's it like to be a priest in Zimbabwe?" I'm interested in the human story, in one single person's story.

My mother was a portrait artist and, I've said many times, I don't like nature. I'm not very interested in the natural world. But I am interested in humans—very, unusually, interested in just the random human unit that you come across. The human heart, the human psyche, when you hear people's stories, when you become intimate with somebody. And I guess also, I grew up in this household that was so screwed up, and when you get to know people and you hear their stories, you get to hear what other households were like, and other lives are like.

As a young poet, like when I was about twenty-five, twenty-six, when I had just gotten out of grad school, I started reading a lot of biographies and autobiographies of poets. There are these great biographies of Keats and Rilke, and Paul Mariani has done these great books on Lowell and Williams, which are both, really, monuments to the art of biography. They're really great books. And I read the biography of Samuel Johnson. I learned to love history by reading biography. So the idea of that single story. I've since become really interested in history, starting in my thirties, but I was always interested in that one voice, that one person telling their tale.

**NDR:** And you want it to be true.

**MK:** I have limited imaginative powers. I just do. I think God's a better plot-maker than I am. And maybe because I was in therapy so much or because I had such a complicated childhood that I had to be in therapy or something like that... You know, it's the life lived in the scene. My inner life was always so big. I think that's true for most writers, right? We live in our heads a lot. We live inwardly.

And you know, as a graduate student, I was a poetry student, but I remember meeting Toby Wolff, and Frank Conroy had written a really famous book called *Stop-Time*, and they told me about Maxine Hong Kingston's *Woman Warrior* and Mary McCarthy's *Memories of a Catholic Girlhood* and about Nabokov's *Speak, Memory*. And so they told me to read those books in grad school. And people didn't read memoir then, and these guys became these memoir writers.... I sort of can't tell my story and not explain the degree to which—I mean, there were a million places to go to graduate school and I just happened to go to the one where all the people who would write memoir were. And the minute I get sober and start praying, somebody calls me [from the Whiting Foundation] and says, "We're going to give you thirty thousand dollars," and I walk into a room [to accept the Whiting award], and sitting there is Toby Wolff, whom I hadn't seen in, I don't know, six or seven years. It's not like we were close friends—I actually knew his brother better—and then I ran into him at this thing. And so the degree to which I think events conspired to make me do what I did, it just seems like, well, what would you have done, if you had been little Mary Karr and you walked into a room and there were all these guys talking about memoir? Yeah, so I don't know why it has to be true. I don't read novels that way…

**NDR:** I'm going to keep pushing this, though [laughs]. You said of *The Liars' Club*, "I had to write it as a memoir because otherwise I knew I wouldn't write the truth. I want to tell the truth." But why tell people it's memoir? Because, when you went on tour for *The Liars' Club*, you worried, "Surely my family would be held up as grotesques, my beloveds and I. Real moral circus freaks." So why not write it as a memoir in your mind, but then call it fiction, put it out there as fiction?

**MK:** I don't know. I've just always loved memoir. Again, I think it's your psychological proclivity.

A novel has to have a structure. That's the other thing. A novel is a harder artistic form. It just is. A poem's harder than both of them, by the way, in terms of the actual form of it. But a novel has to have a structure and a plot—it's driven—while a memoir is by nature episodic. You know, you're in the fourth grade, then later you're in the fifth grade. Maybe you jump a couple of years, or not, but it's a series of episodes, scenes from a life. And so it's all your interpretation of those events, right? You don't tell the whole damn life. You have to elect some aspect of the life to tell and then you tell that aspect of it.

I mean, when I say it's a corrupt form, what I mean by that is that as soon as you start to write about this instead of that, or your own experience, you've already begun to shape a narrative; you're not walking around with a camera strapped to your head. On the other hand, I know of no better way to describe your psychological state.

**NDR:** You're saying memoir is episodic. You can't put everything in there. How do you decide what to put in and what not to put in? And does that have anything to do with what you want people to know and what you don't want people to know, or is it just a matter of, well, making it a shorter book?

**MK:** Well, it's a matter of what you're talking about. You know, you think you know the truth. You don't know the truth. The chapters that you think are going to be big long chapters, they turn out to be a paragraph. The truth ambushes you. You think you know what the truth is? You don't know the truth. The truth sneaks up on you.

**NDR:** Like what you said in, I think it was the *New York Times*, when you talked about how you always thought that your relationship with your father was that he had left you. But as you wrote about it, you realized that you had left him.

**MK:** I had left him. He never left me. As soon as I looked at the events of my life, that was plain to me. But we remember ourselves in sound bytes. We have ideas about ourselves and our world, and it's very easy to deceive yourself. I mean, that's what I was saying yesterday when I was talking about prayer and making a major decision. I don't think anybody should make a major decision without talking to somebody else. Period. At all, ever, kind of. I think we need each other. I think we need checks and balances, you know?

It's like I said. God is in the truth. I believe God is in the truth. Simone Weil, you know, the famous Jewish mystic, who never was Christian, and never was baptized, and never took communion, but a great Christian writer, I think, I remember her saying, "Spiritual living is accepting reality at any cost." And the thing that I have found, or that I feel, with really good Christians, is there's a sense that they're realistic.

I'm thinking of my friend's mother who is a very very very devout Catholic, very schooled in the Marian tradition, very serious about pro-life, who, you know, spends a lot of time with pregnant women, with little girls who are pregnant, and helping them through their pregnancies, and finding adoptions, and who has made with her life a kind of ministry out of this. And you know that's part of her conviction. It's not like she's beating these girls on the heads with a bludgeon; she's out there, actively participating in helping them. She's like, "Well, you're knocked up. So what are we going to do? Oh, let's see if we can get you a GED. Let's find you a place to live, let's see if we can..." She gets very active in trying to make things better. It's like the lay tradition in the church of people working with the poor, of people being active with the poor. Or, you know, Dorothy Day.

And for me, that's the best part of the Catholic Church—the degree to which people get their hands dirty. In a lot of churches you can just write a check. You don't have to go anywhere or do anything. So there's something about those people that has seemed to me very realistic, sort of like Franz was talking about in that *Image* interview, about people who acknowledge that they're inclined to do evil things, and they don't want to do evil things. They want to do good things instead of evil things. And to some extent it's such a simple statement, isn't it? That they just recognize this is an inclination and a possibility. It comes back to being realistic.

If I was more imaginative or I knew more about the form of the novel, I probably would have written a novel. But it's like I said, it's a much harder form. It's like saying, why don't you just write an epic poem in decasyllabic hexameter. [Laughs.] In Greek. It's like, well? It's like, why don't you write a novel? Because I don't know how to write a novel. Writing memoir is a much cheaper form. What I mean is, it's a much easier form for me to sell to myself.

**NDR:** You tell this amazing story about how you ended up writing *The Liars' Club* and getting published, but you'd written a couple of pages of this memoir before that, right? What made you decide to do that, do you remember? And were you writing it in the hopes of it becoming something publishable, or were you just writing it for yourself?

**MK:** Oh yeah. First I tried to write a novel. I was trying to make some money. I didn't know how to do anything, you know. There are only so many garage sales you can have—you run out of wedding gifts to sell. I tried to write a novel. I was a young poet, I had this baby, I was married. I thought, God, you know, if I could make a little money we could buy another car or something. So I tried to write a novel, and of course I didn't know anything about writing novels. It wasn't a very good thing. And then someone in my writing group said, you know, maybe you should try writing it as a memoir. So I tried writing it as a memoir and then some of those pages I guess someone had given to the Whiting Foundation, and that's how I wound up getting the Whiting.

**NDR:** So did you know, when you started writing those pages, did you know that you were going to be jumping into all this horrible stuff of your past, and that you were going to start remembering things you hadn't remembered, or—

**MK:** [Interrupts] Oh, no. I always knew—there's nothing in that book that I didn't remember. That's what I want to say about both books. There's no event in either book that I dredged up that I did not remember. So it's not like I had recovered memory. It's nothing like that. I always knew I was raped, I always knew my mother had a psychotic episode… I knew those things. But there's a difference in knowing them and kind of entering into that memory and going into that place and feeling how you felt, some of which, as I said before, I had done in therapy. But I was at a place when I started that book—my mother was sober and I was at a place…I guess where I didn't have to worry so much about her killing herself, right? But I'd been talking to her about this stuff for, oh, ten years, since I started therapy. It was something very hard to get her to talk about before she got sober.

But, I guess I thought maybe some small press would publish something, or I could sell a section of it and make a hundred bucks. You know. I didn't think I was gonna write a book and sell it to a real publisher or anything. I was publishing with small presses. I had published a first book with a university press, and New Directions, right around that time, took my second book.

**NDR:** You've written so much about your mother, as you're saying. So, how do you feel about writing about your son in this newest memoir?

**MK:** Well, I talked to him about it before I started. I mean, I did what I would do with anybody. I said, "Look. Here's what I want to write about. Are you bothered by this?"

**NDR:** And what'd he say?

**MK:** "No."

And I wrote one chapter, that I'm still going to use, in the original draft, about him being older. It's kind of a prologue written to him that I think will become an epilogue at the end of the book. It's about him and about thinking, "What is he going to say about this?" I thought about how, everything I've ever said, when I try to tell a story, he's like, "No, Mother. I wasn't twelve, I was ten. No, we weren't in England, no, we were in Venice, and it was my twelfth birthday. Here, if you don't believe me, I have a video." Because he was always walking around with a camera strapped to his face. Starting very little. Like, eight, nine, ten, eleven, twelve, he wanted to make movies.

**NDR:** And that's what he's studying now, right?

**MK:** That's what he's studying now.

**NDR:** That's amazing. I mean, is that hereditary or what, knowing what you want to be when you're ten years old [laughs].

**MK:** Yeah, so I was writing about that, and about saying to him, you know, I can hear your voice in my head as I'm writing this, cause you're gonna say this: "No, no. It wasn't like that. That didn't happen. I wasn't even born when that happened. I wasn't there. You weren't there." And how many times he's looked at me when I'm tearing the sofa cushions apart looking for my glasses, and he'll go, "Mom, they're, like, tipped up on your head. They're on your head. You've torn the house apart looking for them, but they're right there." You know, he's kind of the voice of reason. So I was sort of writing this thing to him and while I was writing it, I had to go out of town. He had a gas leak in his apartment, and they were gonna fix it, and he said, "Can I come stay at your apartment?" And I said, "Yeah, actually, I'm going out of town. You can cat sit for me, take care of the kitten." So, when I come back, he comes downstairs, and he hauls my bags upstairs. And he says, "I was watching some video of you talking to Grandma, while you were gone, for this documentary class." He says, "It was *really* nuts. You were talking about the time she tried to kill you, when you were little." I said, "Well, she didn't exactly *try* to kill me. She sort of threatened to kill me, in a pretty dramatic way." I said, "Yeah, I thought I told you about that." And he said, "Yeah. It's not that I didn't know about it. You have told me about it. But it was watching her talk about it." And I said, "What was weird about it?" And he said, "She acted like it happened to somebody else. Just, her affect was so…. She didn't have any affect about it. She had no feeling about it. I thought, now I understand the way Grandma is crazy. I'd never really understood it until I saw her talking about trying to kill you, *to you*, like it was no big deal. Like, she didn't get it." And I said, "Yeah, well, Grandma's kind of limited, you know, in some ways." And so we're having this conversation.

And I actually wound up going back and looking at this tape of my mother, and she's saying, "Yeah, I just thought, you know, it's just such a terrible world, and I've got these two beautiful little girls, I should kill 'em before they get to do anything bad to it." I had been videotaping her for something else, and I just kept it running, and we're drinking coffee in the house I grew up in, and I say to her, "How much had you been drinking?" And she said, "I hadn't had a drop. I didn't drink at all." She told it to me before she'd been drunk for a week so, you know, who knows what really happened.

So right before Dev leaves, he's packing up all his camera equipment—he's doing this documentary class. He says, "Oh yeah. You know, I remembered somebody telling me that the first chapter of *The Liars' Club* has that scene in it, so I went and read it, to see what it was like."

He said, "It's very well written. It's really well written." And I said "Thank you." He had told me, when he was in the eighth or ninth grade, he said, "I don't think I'm ready to read your books." And I said, "I don't think you are either. And you don't have to. I don't think you have to ever read them, you know. Most of the stories in them, you know from me, so it doesn't really matter." But he said this and, you know, he's packing his stuff up, and he had on, it was so funny, he has this underwear and it has—you know the Dr. Seuss book *One Fish Two Fish Red Fish Blue Fish*? He had on his *One Fish Two Fish* underwear. They're like the cover of the *One Fish Two Fish* book. And he's walking out of my apartment and, you know, his pants are bagging down off his ass and he's got this orange underwear with the *One Fish Two Fish* on it and I just, I had tears in my eyes. I wanted to call him back, you know, and talk to him. And there's something about seeing your kid grow up that's so moving to me, having never kind of been much of a kid, and seeing him grow up, and he's such a great guy. And I wanted to call him back, and I thought, I don't trust this kind of maudlin sentimental feeling I have about when he was little. He's, like, beyond that. He's not interested in that right now. That's none of his business right now. And he's got his girlfriend there and all these cameras.

And I thought, my mother… she had this beautiful, difficult mother. And she painted pictures of her. And I had this mother, and I'm writing books about her. And he's working on this documentary for film class. And I thought, you know, he's writing his own story. And, when he writes it, he's gonna be free. He's gonna be free of me, he's gonna be free of us. He's gonna be his own man, you know, and so I have to just wait and kind of see how he writes that.

And that was something I wrote before I wrote the book. I wrote that almost as a prologue, cause I was thinking, well, how's he gonna read this? And then I asked him to read it, which I've never done. I never have asked him to read anything I write because he knows a little about the books and he's just uncomfortable with it. And I said, "Because I'm writing about you as you are now, I want you to look at this to see if you're uncomfortable with it." It's like, fifteen pages, it's not that long. And he was good with it. So, I'm not done with the book yet, but I think that's gonna become like an epilogue.

**NDR:** Nice. That's beautiful.

**MK:** Oh. Well, we'll see.

**NDR:** Well, do you have some more time?

**MK:** Oh, yeah. Yeah.

**NDR:** Can we talk about, I'd like to talk more about poetry. Do you write poetry regularly?

**MK:** I'm writing poetry all the time.

**NDR:** Do you write memoir all the time?

**MK:** No. I only write memoir when they give me money and make me sit down and make me write it. It's really hard, and I don't much like it. I really do do it for money.

**NDR:** Do you think poetry should be placed in categories like fiction or memoir?

**MK:** I think poetry is it's own category, it really is it's own animal. I don't think it matters.

**NDR:** What is it?

**MK:** Well, it's.... People can write fictionally or they can write from fact, and I don't think it matters. I think the value of the poem is not whether it's true or not. For poetry it's really something else. I mean, it doesn't matter if it's factually true in the world in any kind of journalistic way. Which, by the way, I think is also true for memoir. I mean, I think, it's about how it's written. It's the quality of the writing that makes it great, right? You know, I think Rilke wasn't talking about angels, and I think it's very true poetry. Do you know what I mean? I think there's a lot of great poetry that's not out of lived experience. I think Milton wasn't in Eden, you know [laughs] but I think *Paradise Lost* is still pretty good poems.

**NDR:** Okay. So you wouldn't say it matters if your own poetry is memoir or not?

**MK:** No. I don't think it matters at all. I think it ought to be able to stand on it's own merits as a work of art, as a poem.

**NDR:** Do you usually write from your own—

**MK:** [Interrupts] My poetry's all autobiographical, yeah, for the most part. It's mostly out of my lived experience. But again, that's my psychological proclivity.

**NDR:** So how do you sit down to write a poem, especially as opposed to sitting down to write memoir?

**MK:** Well, someone here was talking about that feeling of inspiration you get when you write, and I don't have much of that. I have inclinations that I get through prayer, and I have tendencies, and I have intellectual decisions that I make, but I don't have a lot of bubbling inspiration. I'm a pretty, you know, bulldog, a hardworking little engine. You know, Franz is very disciplined in some ways. Franz sits down and writes every day, and has done for thirty years. Right now, when I'm writing a memoir, I just keep a notebook. If I'm sitting down to write, I'm either working on this column for the *Washington Post*, or working on the memoir. You know, that's why I finished like twelve of the columns in advance, so it wouldn't interfere with my finishing this book. So I'll just keep a notebook, and then when I'm done with this book, I'll sit down to make poems out of the notebook. But when I'm not writing memoir, I just sit down to write poems on, you know, the days I'm not doing something else. Mostly on Monday, Tuesday, Wednesday. I have those three days to read and write. Those days are sacred. I don't do anything else on those days but read and write.

**NDR:** After you published *Cherry*, you wanted to do a book of poems, and your agent said, "That's crazy."

**MK:** Yeah, she said, "Your next book can*not* be a book of poems."

**NDR:** Why? What was she worried about?

**MK:** She said, you know, there's this tide of interest in memoir right now, and you're at the forefront of it, and you've got this great reputation, and you're losing money, you're leaving change on the table. You need to publish another book right now. And I said, "I'm sorry. I just can't do it right now."

**NDR:** And why couldn't you do it?

**MK:** I just wasn't interested in doing it. I felt like writing poems. I'd been working on all these poems while doing all this memoir stuff, for *Cherry*, and on the road and everything, and it was like "Lemme, lemme" [makes grabbing motions]. You know, I had all these poems I'd been working on for all these years, and putting off working on, and they were standing in line for me to write them. And I was like, "Maybe I'll never write another memoir. Maybe I will, maybe I won't, but I know that these need to be written now. I know that these are my little bastard babies of the week."

**NDR:** So poetry is a constant part of your life. And you told Ron Hogan, you said, "I'm invigorated by language. Poetry saved my life. Really transformed me, really saved me." How did poetry save your life?

**MK:** Well, I've said before, I was a lonely, angry, sad child. I was. I just was. I mean, I was scrappy in some ways. I had some toughness. I had some ability to maneuver into people's lives, is the best way I can say it. And my sister was a good teacher of this. I knew that if I did the dishes at the nice family's house or helped them with the little kids, they'd let me stay for dinner. A lot of people don't have the social skill to figure out how to do that. And my sister was good. She kind of taught me how to get out of the house. And I had some native ability to learn how to do that. But I was very lonely and I wanted connection, and when I read poetry I felt connected. I didn't feel alone anymore. I felt that there were people who were like me, that there were people who would understand me and recognize me for who I was, who would accept me for who I was, and I felt less lonely.

And I think it's Eucharistic. I think you take someone else's suffering into your body and you're changed by their passion, and you take it, like a pill. You take it like bread. And it feeds your humanity, it makes me more human, it makes me think I'm less special, it makes me feel closer to other human beings. I realize our grief and pity join us, as well as our hope.

**NDR:** Has writing all this memoir influenced the poetry you write? I mean, *Sinners Welcome* to me seems very different from the first three.

**MK:** Everybody has said that.

**NDR:** And do you think that?

**MK:** I don't know. They all seem the same to me. The truth is, I don't look at them anymore. I mean, it's not like you write these books and then you go back and study them to see what you're doing. It's sort of like, why? Why would I ever look at them? There's so much else I have to read.

**NDR:** But you read them at readings.

**MK:** Yeah, but not much.

**NDR:** You don't do a lot of readings [laughs].

**MK:** I don't do a lot of readings. I really don't. Unless they pay me a lot of money or there's some real incentive, I don't want to be away from the work.

**NDR:** So you wouldn't be in the camp that says, you know, poetry is meant to be spoken. It must be spoken, so I must go and speak it, as a poet.

**MK:** I write it for the page so that, when I'm dead, it still exists in the right form. I'm a poet who writes for the page. I certainly believe that it has it's roots in the oral tradition, and that that's important to it, but I'm not going to write it so that it's dead when I'm not alive mouthing it.

**NDR:** And what about memoir then?

**MK:** Yeah. Same thing.

**NDR:** But why your life? Why should your life be on the page and stay alive even after your dead?

**MK:** Oh, it's not my life. You have to realize the degree to which I do this for money. I mean, you've got to understand. It's not that I'm not called to do it, but it is so hard, that if somebody didn't pay me for it, I would not do it. Like if somebody said, "Look. Stephanie, I've got a great idea for you. There's a fourteen-foot panel truck out there, and it's got a bunch of equipment in it. Let's move it up these three flights of stairs, this morning, and then we'll do it again tonight, and then we'll do it again the next day, and we're gonna do that every day." You wouldn't say, like, "Oh yeah, I'm gonna get in that big long line to get to do that."

It's very taxing. It's not fun. Fiction writers talk about having fun, but memoir is not fun. And poets, even, to some extent talk about having fun. It's not that it's not hard work, writing poetry, but with memoir it's really—

it's horrible for me. Everyone I know who's ever written a memoir has talked about going a little bit crazy. You have to go a little bit crazy.

**NDR:** You've said *The Liars' Club* was exhausting to write, that you would write and then just fall asleep on the floor.

**MK:** I still have that a lot.

**NDR:** Yeah, I wondered if it was different with these less intense memories. Is it still like that? Is that just the way you write prose?

**MK:** Yeah. It still is like that. I think the psychological work is like... Well, there are two things I can compare it to. And the one is, you know how when you cry, like, really hard, how you sleep? Or when you—you're gonna be teaching, right? Well the first two weeks of any semester are so physically exhausting. Anybody who teaches all the time will tell you, they lose weight, unless they just eat all the time. And I actually had a neurologist tell me once that the amount of energy it takes to isolate and identify faces and figure out who people are—there's a lot of information you get in when you meet somebody. So when you talk to all these people that you're responsible for and that you're supposed to know, through this intense period of time, it's very physically exhausting. And it's sort of like that when I'm doing it in my memory. It's sort of like a mix of what happens when you're doing really hard work in therapy or when you're crying really hard, and when you meet a whole bunch of new people. It's physically very intense and I get very, very tired.

So, yeah, I mean, my writing day is not so long. It's probably like five hours. You know, when I worked in business I worked twelve hours a day. My boyfriend works fourteen-hour days, running a company. But when he sees me do that, he knows I'm not fudging, he knows I can just barely do it. But also, I take more time off now. I'm nicer to myself now. I'm not so desperate. It's a gift of being over fifty.

**NDR:** Back to this last memoir, why is it called *Lit*?

**MK:** Cause it's about being lit up, and it's also about literature being the way that I was first lit up. It's also about being drunk....

**NDR:** So all the things that we're all thinking it's about?

**MK:** Yup, all the things you're thinking, it's about.

**NDR:** That's very clever [laughs].

**MK:** Well, I'm clever that way [laughs].

# SMOTHERED MATE

*Ed Falco*

Stephanie played a king's pawn opening, as usual, and Jay played the Sicilian in response, as usual, and then the game proceeded along predictably careful lines until Jay moved his knight aggressively to g4, in front of Steph's castled king. Stephanie considered the position for a moment before turning away from the board, shifting around in her seat, and looking at the ceiling as if trying to see out to the roof. They were in the spacious kitchen of her apartment, above an art gallery on North Moore, in Tribeca. "I just realized," she said, "I didn't pack Lucian's iPhone."

"Is that your responsibility?" Jay asked. "Packing the iPhone?" Then he added, "What the hell's an iPhone?"

Stephanie said, "What planet do you live on?" She sounded more distracted than interested. Without waiting for an answer, she got up and went to the bedroom. "I can still catch him at the office," she said, mostly to herself.

Jay reviewed the position. Through a tall kitchen window next to the table, the dull light of an overcast day spread over a handsome, rosewood chess board, with inlaid squares and crisp black and white Staunton pieces, hand-carved and triple-weighted. Steph needed only to threaten his knight by moving her pawn to h3 and he'd have to pull it back. He got up from the table, went to the fridge, and poured himself a glass of orange juice. From the bedroom, down a long, high-ceilinged corridor, where Steph was talking to Lucian on the phone, her voice sounded like someone speaking from someplace underground. She was apologizing, asking Lucian to forgive her, and Jay could tell from her tone, her curt, choked pleading, that Lucian was lighting into her for forgetting to pack the phone. From the black surface of the fridge, encased in a magnetically attached plastic frame, Stephanie smiled up at him, looking both more youthful than her 32 years, in the unmarred skin of her face, in the lustrous fall of wispy blond hair, and much, much older, in the world-weary cast of her smile, the longing in her eyes. Beside her, his arm around her, Lucian grinned mischievously.

Lucian was one of those people whose appearance uncannily matches their personality. He was a surly, habitually miserable cynic, blind entirely to any hint of goodness in the world, paranoiac, mean and impossible to like—and that's how he looked. He was average height, five-ten, five-eleven, but he was perpetually hunched over, as if weighted down by the burden of his disposition. His hair was always unkempt, his clothes rumpled, and his face scrunched up as if something were hurting him. In his mid-forties, he was a parody of a curmudgeon. When a computer dating program paired him with Stephanie, and he first met her for dinner, and she didn't immediately run away, he had assumed she was only interested in his money and position—and he told her so. Later, when he found out about the bombing, when she told him about her body, he asked her to spend the night. It was as if, having learned her secret, he for the first time considered the possibility that someone as attractive as Stephanie might genuinely be interested In him. After Steph spent the night, and that went as well as could be hoped for, he proposed marriage and she accepted. They had been together at this point—on this Sunday afternoon of the weekly chess game—for a little more than five years.

Stephanie and Jay had met three years before the marriage, on a Sunday afternoon in Brooklyn. The first time they saw each other, they were both on fire. The flames seemed to be—weirdly, eerily—consuming only specific portions of their bodies. Stephanie was on fire from her feet to her shoulders, yet her neck and arms and face were untouched. The fire clung to her and seemed to be burning hot but without flames. Jay's crotch and thighs and feet were burning, and no other part of him. They were both screaming and running pointlessly through smoke and darkness that had been, an instant earlier, a Brooklyn coffeehouse, where they had come to hear a young, bluesy singer-musician who had died instantly in the explosion, the firebomb intended primarily for him and situated directly under the stage where he was performing, placed there by a fan who believed that his lyrics were commands from the devil ordering her to do exactly what she did: learn how to construct an incendiary device with white phosphorous and use it to burn up the musician and his followers. Most of what happened that afternoon was only figured out much later. That Stephanie and Jay were the two burning figures who ran into each other and, literally, embraced, probably in some partly instinctive, partly hysterical, partly accidental attempt to extinguish the flames, only came out months later, in what was essentially a group therapy session with the eighteen survivors of a firebombing that killed thirty people, not a single one of them yet out of their twenties.

For both Steph and Jay, it was the last thing they remembered of the bombing and they concluded it must have happened within seconds after the explosion. Neither of them talked about it much anymore, but over the years they had worked out the details. The small, cavernous space of the coffee house, dimly lit, a dozen tables and a few rows of chairs. A chord, a few notes picked to begin a song, and then a kind of instantaneous transformation of space during which the stage became a bright light. The order of the room—the carefully arranged tables, the lined-up chairs—did a kaleidoscopic dance of rearrangement, and Stephanie and Jay rose up on fire and embraced.

Stephanie came back from the bedroom, glanced at Jay leaning against the kitchen counter next to the fridge, and then gripped a corner of the table in her hands and leaned over the chess board as if she were about to dive into its engaging geometry of squares and pieces. She wore khaki slacks and a long-sleeved, cotton shirt, green with a button-down collar. She was five-nine, exactly the same height as Jay. What was uncovered of her was youthful and pretty: her face, which was slightly long and made her look serious, as if she should be a professor or a classical musician; her hair, blond and shoulder-length, and obsessively pampered by creams and conditioners and salon appointments; and her hands, long, thin fingers, jewelry-less except for a plain, gold wedding band. She stood in the light from the window, the whole of her, body and mind, absorbed in the arrangement of black and white chess pieces on a board of sixty-four squares. Most of what she kept covered he had never seen, except for her arms; and from that, and from his own body, he could imagine the rest of the disfigurement. She had undergone twelve operations in the years after the bombing. He'd had five. The surgeons had removed what had been left of his genitals, and what was there now even he couldn't bear to see. His burned skin was like the skin of her arms, a doughy swamp of swellings and scars. Like Stephanie, he was blessed in that his face wasn't badly damaged. After some minor surgery he looked pretty much the way he'd always looked, though there were a pair of faint, white parallel lines descending like tear tracks under his left eye—but Jay, mostly, was the only one who even noticed.

Stephanie said, her eyes still fixed on the board, "He can be such an asshole sometimes."

Jay said, "Sometimes?"

Stephanie whispered "stop," and then threatened his knight, as he expected, but with pawn to f3, which opened up the possibility of a diagonal check with the Queen, which in turn made possible a combination of moves that could lead to a checkmate.

"F-3?" he said, across the room, still leaning on the fridge.

"Problem?" Steph looked down at the board again, as if trying to figure out what she did wrong.

Jay returned to his seat at the table and Steph settled in across from him. They were both quiet then, staring at the chess pieces and the board as if there were an absorbing movie playing on a screen only they could see.

Outside, a truck rumbled by, making the window glass rattle slightly.

Jay knew that his next move would be to check with the queen, but he was taking his time playing through Steph's possible responses. She was the better chess player, and he hadn't won a game in months, but he thought he had her now. As far as he could determine, the only way to prevent the mate required exchanging her rook for his knight, which would leave him with a significant advantage. He took his time looking over the position, wanting to be sure he wasn't missing something.

"So?" Steph said. "You put me in check." She made a quick, small gesture with her hands that said "So what?"

Jay moved the queen to b6. "Check," he said, and then added, "Why do you put up with him, Steph? Seriously. Why don't you tell him to come home and get his own fucking iPhone-Whatever and stick it up his ass?"

Stephanie smiled first and then laughed. She was still looking at the board. "I should," she said. "He'd go ballistic."

"So? Why don't you?"

"And then what would we do?" She looked up, pulling herself momentarily out of the game. "If my marriage broke up," she said, "what would we do?"

Jay returned his attention to the board. For the past six months, since he had quit the last in a long series of bullshit jobs, Stephanie had been paying his rent, embezzling the money out of credit cards and household accounts. It wasn't difficult. Lucian made more money than the three of them could spend in multiple lifetimes.

Stephanie said again, "What would we do, Jay?"

Jay felt his eyes beginning to get wet, and he hated himself for it. To make the tears go away, he tapped into his anger, which was always there. "You'd have plenty of money after a divorce," he said. "You'd come out of it rich, and you know it."

"I'm not talking about money," she said, and her voice went up a little and got louder, as if she were insulted that he'd even suggest that money were the issue.

Jay gestured to the board and fixed his eyes on the position. He said, "It's your move, Steph. Just go, okay?"

"Jay," Stephanie said, and in the pleading way she said his name there was a single question, and all he had to do was look up at her to answer it. "Jay," she said again, insisting. When she reached over the chess board to touch him, he pulled away from her. He slid back in his chair and closed his eyes as if that might make him disappear. "No," she said. "Of course not." Then there were several moments of silence in which Jay knew she was watching him, looking across the table at a thirty-five year old man, a man who looked normal as the next guy in his sneakers and jeans and dark knit shirt. She watched him where he sat rigid in his seat with his eyes closed, unable to open them, unable to look back at her. Finally, she said, "Forget it, Jay," and her voice softened to gentle. "Jay," she said, "I'm moving. Look."

At the sound of a piece moving on the chess board, Jay opened his eyes and fell back into the game. She had moved her king to h1, out of check. He moved his knight to f2, putting her in check again, and then she had to take with the rook, exchanging it for the knight—but she didn't. She moved her king to g1, and from there it was a forced mate in three, which he announced, softly.

"Where?," she said. "I don't see it."

Jay showed her the three forced moves, including a sacrifice of the queen, that lead to a smothered mate, a mate delivered by the knight, the king surrounded by his own pieces simply having nowhere to go.

"That's gorgeous," Stephanie said. She smiled, appreciative of the combination's elegance and finality. "I didn't see it coming," she added, and then, as if she were suddenly tired and needed a moment to rest, she folded her hands in front of her on the table and bowed her head. Across for her, Jay did the same. Together, they looked like a family at prayer, two people lost in a quiet moment of reverence. Outside, several car horns screamed angrily at each other. The shrill noise beat against the kitchen window.

# THE ACCORDION PLAYERS

*Peter Marcus*

The poor accordion players of Oaxaca stand on narrow streets
near the plaza, alongside a yellow wall, beside another wall painted
eggshell blue. Stoic in the dry heat, solemn in their scuffed,
black shoes.
Tortillas made fresh upon the griddle only cost a few centavos
and the loveliness of their offered song is free, though the blind
man has already paid dearly with his eyesight and his nine year-old son
with truancy from the local elementary school.
The music hums as vendors pass
with whirly-gig toys, plastic kites and silver bracelets, a rainbow panoply
of helium balloons. The musician's daughter in a frilly white dress,
serenely holds a red plastic donation bowl and waits for every song to finish.
She follows
anxiously behind me, pleading for more pesos. *Señor, señor, por favor,*
*mi madre es muerta.* But I hurry fast away, away from a child's talk of death
over the sun-gold cobblestones.

At the edge of the city I come upon a simple graveyard.
Pastel colored angels shaded by lethargic willows. Is her mother buried here
I wonder. Has anyone left for her a single artificial rose?
I return to the zocala at dusk.
Another boy is playing solo. Accordion on his lap, heavier than his own small torso.
*Donde esta tu padre?* I ask
after dropping a few coins in his dish.
But he doesn't answer, doesn't even lift his gaze to acknowledge
that I've spoken.
He taps the buttons rapidly, fills the old machine
with air. Empties it and fills it, droning on and on with a grave,
ferocious sorrow. *Is your father home asleep? Resting in a nearby bar*
*easing his weariness with friends and a cold cervesa?*
Although I've shut
my hotel window from the midnight sounds of the plaza, their music
seeps inside me. Son and father playing on through the night,
pressing down hard on the white keys of my bones.

# *From* Portions

*Hank Lazer*

### Channel

cryptic & cannot
honor    brief experience
of the great

void    whatever you
are channel to
why make me

beacon or connector
i want simply
to sit breathe

learn empty attention
you make me
traffic tasks exacting

verbal thoroughfare which
is my nature
secret given in

sitting   taking in
holding   letting go
in loving each

### Doorway

word ensues into
light through cracked
doorway hebrew *hay*

archway    *"henry"* he
would say *"lay*
*up    don't hit*

*it in the*
*drink"*  father's esoteric
babble his bible

of physical grace
repetition vision the
game & your

performance in it
what the eyes
imagine done trans

mitted through the
hands no longer
yours or his

**Light**

*(Paris)*

living within variable
durations of emotion
all we wanted

was light bright
clarifying warming blessing
light for the

leaves roses gargoyles
domes the faces
historical markers details

far up exact
structures for the
fruit & vegetable

stalls fountains benches
black hair brown
hair shoes the

gesturing hands light
upon the line
to buy bread

**See**

it was over
thirty years ago
at the time

of my first
marriage i would
go alone many

days to sandbridge
& beyond to
a lotus pond

to a duck
blind to the
inland waterway to

the winter flyway
of the canadian
geese carrying bird

books & poetry
driving writing slowly
learning to see

## Morph

the story you
live within may
well be true

morphine eases the
way i have
seen it twice

once with my
father again with
james odis among

graphs charts monitors
nurses the beeping
lights the hardest

thing a man
must learn is
to relax &

stop breathing so
to cross over
into the next

# Come to a Bird Quicker

*Sarah Bowman*

*And what if I do, and further*
—Hugh MacDiarmid

a blackbird to his silent partner goes
his lazy circling trespassed, arrow-shot
high to a willow

in possession of this sight, a place half-hidden,
a copse from which to watch a pair of birds
and no term to best express this dismissal

if excess could be offered, take the wing snap,
the sheen of dark forms falling, briefly claret,
headlong to the clearing

2.

the currency of a strong heart—
camphor weed holds against the rain, the hill remains
a pock-marked strand

3.

a bucket or two of earth
the edge of the world where trees had grown and none now stand

so slight of color
the cliffs and birds and eggs and shit
the sky already low and dropping
a granite vein run through

4.

slow before a clutch unguarded
marsh grass within a marsh bush
and find the egg is diamond white

# Canvassing For a New City

*—for Mark*

*Sarah Bowman*

*The enamored hunters ride themselves down.*
—Robert Duncan

Hoisted onto the winning horse, all other obstacles cleared,
we had no reason to doubt, alliances were maintained, an avenue of trees circa
1972, Roy spitting at Ethel and the millennium.

As for reasons, love, none's better.
You shrugged mea culpa to make me smile.
It did come back, Master-of-the-House and that pretty girl swaying
as Streisand sang *Guava Jelly*.

When the pain hit, there was Liz in that white dress and the heat
and too much devotion sister-lady. There was whiskey and the guts to stick it out.
And that storm the south got.

2.

It remained to be seen.
Women scattered, showed up later wearing brothel-creeper shoes
and mohair, circled back with round collars, cropped hair, boyish.
But when your lips to her cheek exploded, water in a state of steam
fal-lalled around the room.

On that clear night, Artemis rode through the birthplace of the world,
steep fields, the backbone, the cleve where two lovers slept.
My youth begged one bear, one hound.
I took my loss.

Turned to tragedy, warriors carrying warriors home,
laid my trails and brush-nets in the narrows, cut my markers deep to remember.
Turned then to stony gardens, blood-sweat pared to water, hours.
In some such wood I hoped to find, I found an injured animal.

3.

You stay up late watching TV, I kiss your forehead for goodnight.
Ivanhoe sings 'my heart is all I am' to every castle window.
Then Munich, those faces, a species sees itself and cannot look away.
We draw, we swim in caves, of all the lists to start, why the failing?

There's Zagajewski's mint and cello, our ace-in-the-hole friendship.
But aging has made you nervous.
It's Vivienne Segal and show-tunes from here on out.
Little bird, don't fly yet.

I'm easily distracted by collapse and watch the evening news for implosion.
I've seen Madagascar bleeding its plume of red soil into the ocean.
I wonder what happens after.
That's how it goes.

# *FROM* WALKING WITH ELIHU

*Taylor Graham*

## A Lower Room

*One unbroken, unabated stream it was, of profound and lofty and original eloquence.*
—Nathaniel Peabody Rogers, on hearing Elihu Burritt, 1845

Even in Boston, lighting isn't cheap
in the cause of Peace. Upstairs, the Marlborough Chapel
was brilliant, befitting a New England Convention.
This lower hall so partly-lit,
Mr. N.P. Rogers would have passed right by,

Elihu, but for your voice.
He and his friends had business upstairs.
He knew you only from your writings,
and thought your appearance "original" at best.
He was hurrying forward when your voice

stopped him. Overhead, applause
of the Convention boomed over this silent,
handful audience, this dim space devoted to a speech
against war.
Rogers sat down and could not get up

until you'd finished.
"No beautiful, unmeaning words," he recalled.
"It was all meaning," delivered in a rustic accent
that proved you weren't a college man,
for all your "splendid diction."

You reminded him of Ploughman Burns, with a grace
and dignity that hand-labor
lends book-learning, binding him with a chain
of solid sense that could not
be schooled.

## Boscage

"A mass of growing trees or shrubs, a thicket,
grove, sylvan scenery." From Middle English *boskage*,
Old French *boscage*, late Latin *boscaticum*
from *boscum*; compare Italian *boscaggio,* Spanish
*bosque*. Alternately, from ancient German
(compare *bush*) through Frankish to
Old French *bos* or *bosc*, variants of *bois*—

the origins unclear, but you'd find it one more
proof of the brotherhood of languages, how
*bosc* transformed itself centuries ago,
perhaps on the tongue of a young Frenchman
offering a *bouquet* of lilies to his sweetheart;
and the lisp of his variant made its way
across the Channel into English.

Transplanted Connecticut farmer, your fellow
Yankees wondered if you were still
an American, the way you kept trying to parse
a peace between New and Old Worlds
as you walked the Essex countryside, admiring
in any language that bosky landscape
of field and hedgerow.

## Cadastral

Not by instrument, but surely you surveyed
the world by the light of heaven's stars—
your calculation of their azimuth, influence
and declination.

Trigonometry of the curved surface of Earth,
its land-forms and oceans; its parcels
defined by patterns lined out on-high.

You knew what Homer and the Norsemen said
of heroes roaming under stars, by sea
in search of land—a home.

Perhaps you memorized those lines of the war-
nurse Whitman, *They are alive and well*
*somewhere*—the ones who, by counterbalance,
found what lies beneath

the night sky full of stars, beneath leaves
of grass spreading over a measured earth.
At last, you'd return to *The Seasons*
themselves, and Thomson's musings,

having *sung of Nature with unceasing joy*—
line by plough-line, your own rocky
parcel of Connecticut soil.

# Lost Poem Regarding the Musée d'Orsay, Rescued by Renoir

*Gaylord Brewer*

Somewhere in the dark enticements
of night that wondrous conceit arrived,
some mishap of the past contrasted
to a canvas in the special exhibit.
By morning, of course, this fine wisp
is lost, and not until I am walking in rain
do I recall to even try to remember
and strain toward two or three pairings
so facile, flimsy they're distasteful.
I'm pleased to be out early, returned
to the unexpectant grays of Cherbourg,
wind loosening knots of hot feeling,
unappeased downpour. A woman weighs
butter lettuce, radishes, three fistsful
of *petit pois* in shell. At the boulanger,
where the girl, I believe, recognizes me,
I pretend to study her wooden racks
before choosing Monday's simple baguette.
Back in the flowing streets, my hands
pulse with cold, and as I consider
the arthritis beginning to stiffen knuckles,
glumly consider the future, I get lucky—
a rickety filmstrip begins of an old Renoir,
stick-thin Quixote in sloppy hat
and pointed white beard, the feral eyes,
brush wedged into a deformed root
once a human hand. Frames click past—
handle stabbed into stretched hole
of mouth, some startling atrocity of form
or light lunged at with a gnarled wrist,
brush clamped and parrying again.

## Probably Human

*Gaylord Brewer*

Across the slow cage of hours
I paced, read, dozed, encouraged
clocks to move along, move along.
The martyrdom of stupid fabric,
my cottons, synthetics, delicates
on a drying line in the rain
perform the whole lovely futility.

On a desk, I arrange fragments
from yesterday's cold beach,
pearl contours, the dead polished
in grit and salt. Shards to foretell,
perhaps, some lie or truth we knew
or forgot. I finger each totem
and put it down.
                                        Preparation
for the afternoon's roughly turned
apologies, for night's practiced
and collateral damage—bare feet
bruised on stone, a cantata of glass,
as from the dark something heavy
falling, its single stifled shout.

# A MAN, A BOY, A STICK, A GOOSE WITH GOSLINGS

*Diane Furtney*

*To a long-time friend who asked during a dinner outing (after an afternoon drive and birding), "What about you? Do you want that rescue?"*

A crowd, at blue-checked tablecloths.
A wall of old white windows, one corner lath

showing through. Our table, one of five, juts
toward deal chairs that abut

a plywood bar—earnest about its dozen brands,
tended by eager local boys who try to stand

like sophisticates but look like extremely nice
children. Sugar dispenser, flip-top lid. A brace

of red and yellow squeeze bottles.
Four chairs for us, cushioned, mottled,

on two of which our purses perch
like nesting birds. This was once a church,

the menu says; earlier a mill. Now a rural eatery
prized for weekend fish and chicken dinners, a leafy

five miles east of Sidney—old Erie Canal
quarry town in the Western Reserve, with pastel

courthouse and extravagant Sullivan bank.
Clatter; laughs. A high-school hostess, frank-

faced, blonde, who's sorry about the wait.
Families are in line from the back gravel lot

toward the front veranda, out of sight.
And beyond our wide window, the late

May grass, carrying scattered trees,
slopes down to the Great Miami's

pebbles and water, a hundred feet wide.
Well-behaved trees on the other side

layer themselves up a hill, to rounded clouds.
At left, from a sandbar that fingers down

the river, a great blue heron advances
over the shallows, its neck like a whited branch

whittled to a spear. Now, a dart
of white wing, below our

soundless window glass:
a commotion and flutter on the grass.

Five goslings, water-tumbler-sized,
yellow, wobbly, solemn, fuzzed,

streaked in May with the colors of autumn,
with rubbery charcoal feet, are in a scrum

behind their hooting, nervous father goose,
who doesn't like the surly boy who's

trapped a separated gosling, is about
to pick it up. The parent bird, stretching out

his white neck at the predator, the Breaker of Babies,
has flapped his wings, head down. No doubt he's

hissing like a huge, good teapot.
And the human father shoulders in from the parking lot,

far left. Dark-haired. Late thirties.
Nondescript clothes. Not bad looking. He's

yelled something, scowling at his son;
picked up a six-foot stick; is advancing on

the terrified goose with a shoulder-rolling eagerness
that says everything about his loose,

unloved history. The bird faces this Monster
with wings outstretched. His babies scatter

behind him: he has told them to run.
And for women looking out these windows, even

those who sympathize with or fear
for the man, several things are clear:

that the boy, as you observe, "needs rescue
only from his Dad;" that the Thrasher of Stick came too

tardily for dinner, had to wait in line, resents his son,
and now has a chance to hurt something, someone.

It's clear, too, he's unhappily married,
is unexceptional if not bad in bed,

and it's his own brutalizing father he's turned into,
a man he hated—bibbety-bobbity-boo.

No woman, though, can tap this glass
with authority. No man here wants the mess

of intervention, an end-of-the-week
argument. Ah! but now the stick

is gone: he's tossed it with a wide flail,
a pretense at contempt. (He is not, after all,

entirely sure who owns those birds.
Besides, the goose is big.) He turns toward

the lot and his hand has momentum-swing
as he pushes his offspring,

who now no doubt has learned
something already learned, learned, learned.

What if much of it could be unlearned?
If we could unscar the burned-

in tissue-patterns from our early lives,
those auto-jerk neurons that do us no good? I've

come across, say, a longer-lasting amine
to boost some synapses in the brain—

down in the quick-memory hippocampus
and old amygdala—to revamp us

by allowing for emotional renewal.
Maybe a hormone, Change-a-trol,

for plasticity in the cortex, setting us free,
a little, from our iron-track loyalty

to the inept parenting we endured… This salt shaker
—glass, aluminum-capped—on this blue square:

suppose it offers an option for the human race.
Pick it up and you'll have made a choice

for neuronal newness to be offered to that Son
of Stick (and to everyone) at, say, twenty-one

—by which age that particular boy
may already have married for the first time, O boy,

and be vigorously reproducing his Dad.
"Who will re-teach him?" For now, let's set aside

that good question (recalling that for millions of us,
socialization might have been better done by mollusks).

As he de- and re-learns, could a chemical light
evaporate the damp edges of a bright,

less-hampered self, the categories
of suffering become the categories

of rescue, and hope leap outward to a huge perimeter?
There's no need, of course, is there?,

to wonder about preferences of other
animate matter and what would be their

knowledgeable choice. Every phylum on this planet
would scramble and burst out of its habitat

in a rush for that salt shaker,
the biggest stampede in the history of cell structure.

That dream you once had, remember—of being renewed?
And me, you ask? Do I "want that rescue?"

See me pushing the brass plate on the clinic door.
See my pen pressing the forms ("Your

treatment goal?" *"To be a bit more anserine*
*and much less like a man once seen*

*outside a window."*) And you, who's said that error
is "the hand-me-down from every mother":

if those mistakes could lose their intense
pressure—with your well-raised daughter, for instance:

to see on her face a look of fresh assessment,
see a smile that's rueful or indifferent

in its forgiveness, and know that some deep decibels
of your old call to her are barely audible

and that she's not smaller for her loss, your loved girl. . .
Would you then have a less warm world,

or more? There's a slight chill now across the floor:
today's Fullgrown Misery has come in the front door

—yanking, on an invisible leash,
his hangdog son, then his abashed

and run-down wife, for whom none of this is new.
Given a second chance, what might *she* do?

Meanwhile, the heron has flipped
and gulleted his dinner. Re-dignified, he's stepped,

as you say, "like a new graduate,"
up the sandbar toward the woods. The baked

perch looks excellent. Our good waitress, bonhomous
and bouncy, is penciling nearby. The gorgeous

water that striped past moments ago
has already dropped toward the Ohio

and by Monday will have reached the Gulf.
Are those enough?

Endurance, a pleasant this and that, the pretty glare
of occasional achievement—enough? Or,

to arrive at and keep the decency of a goose.
Here's the salt shaker (a little sticky)... What would you choose?

Note: Serotonin and norepinephrine, two common neurotransmitters, are crucial for recording memories during emotionally significant events. If either chemical is increased at nerve endings in the amygdala and hippocampus areas in the adult brain, it can trigger a greater flexibility to learn new emotional reactions. So far this effect has been limited, but embellishments from genomics, antibiotic chemistry and nano-engineering are being developed.

# THE WEEKEND DAUGHTER

*Jarrett Haley*

Had the accident happened any closer to home, in Barstow or Baker or anywhere inside the state line, he may have had time enough to turn back and enjoy the weekend with his daughter, at home, where he felt he belonged. But the wreck was just outside of Las Vegas—the radio said five cars blocking three lanes—and it was only in this traffic that Bill Corkill checked his voicemail and learned the Energy Outlook conference had since been cancelled. The sun had just set behind him, the desert growing dim and blue. His windshield looked upon an endless string of red brake lights, his rearview mirror a galaxy of white headlamps. Bill sighed, and saw no choice but to merge into the thin procession of cars all edging past the wreck ahead.

He passed the wreck slowly and to himself gave silent thanks for his life and his family; he touched his forehead, his chest and both shoulders, then tugged on his seatbelt where it dug into his paunch belly. And when the traffic finally opened up, Bill eased his Chrysler through the dusk and on towards the murky glow of the city in which he now had no business being in at all.

Outside the Imperial Hotel & Convention Center, Bill with his suitcase stood beside his car awaiting an attendant in the commotion of the driveway. He waited and watched, the bellmen and their brass carts, the valets dodging the lanes, cars pulling up and peeling off, and through all this frenzy he saw for the first time the little girl, on a concrete bench outside the hotel's revolving door—a little girl alone, at night.

The girl sat in shorts, a worn sandal dangling from her toe, her other leg tucked underneath her body like a cushion. The neon glow cast her in anemic fluorescence, and a roof beam from the portico cut a sharp shadow across her bent knee. Bill saw her from such an angle, and this combined with his lingering nausea ever since the accident, he mistook the girl for a young amputee and his heart promptly sank with pity. The sight registered in him deeper than any war-torn image from *Time* magazine or the *Monitor*. Here this girl was blond and fair, and her lanky frame too closely resembled his own thirteen-year-old back in California. And though his Melissa was intact of course, the thought nevertheless resounded in him—that any child, anywhere, could be cut short at the knee and resigned to a life on the sidewalk, full of dust and dependence and the endless handouts of nameless strangers. Right next to the girl the blades of door swung them in and spit them out, gamblers and tourists, conventioneers and lodgers like himself, and there she sat following each with her eyes sunk deep into violet sockets. He couldn't just pass her by, Bill thought. He was different, and he knew he could make a difference, it was small but it was something. Bill tipped two dollars to the valet who served him, and kept an extra dollar in hand. With his suitcase in tow he rolled right up to the girl, and noticing no change-cup at the girl's remaining foot, he instead offered the bill directly to the child.

The money lingered between them for a moment. The girl said nothing, only cocked an eyebrow and looked askance at the dollar, then up at Bill, then back to the dollar, and back to Bill.

"You think I'm *poor*?" she said.

Her eyes, Bill noticed, were not at all sunken like he had thought, but heavy with makeup, a deep, metallic purple. The girl sneered as if she had smelled something awful and scooted further down the bench, uncovering the remainder of her long pale leg.

"I'm...very sorry," Bill said. His forehead flushed under his thinning hair, and he receded back to the hotel door, crumpling the dollar into his shirt pocket, stepping cautiously in-between the moving blades.

‡ ‡ ‡

In his room Bill turned on C-Span for some noise, sat on the bed and kicked off his loafers and found on his phone two messages in his inbox.

The first was a text from his wife, on the cruise:

**B**<br>
**Low battery and**<br>
**left charger at**<br>
**home Tried**<br>
**Sissys but no fit**<br>
**No reception**<br>
**anyway Turning**<br>
**off now S**

The second from his daughter, checking in from the Robinson's:

**D**<br>
**Ok**<br>
**M**

He put down the phone and drew open the curtains. His room did not face the strip but overlooked the hotel's parking garage and out upon the sprawling points of light that made up the rest of Las Vegas. The sky was lit a murky gray over the western mountains that cut a jagged horizon on the landscape, black and massive. He thought of California just beyond them, and the ocean just beyond that.

‡ ‡ ‡

Bill found the hotel's buffet and finer restaurants closed when he went downstairs for dinner. He made do with a bowl of lukewarm soup and cracker packets from the food court, eating it alone among the empty tables as he watched the current of casino guests ebb and flow in front of him. In the gaps between foot traffic he could see now and again the little girl from outside the hotel, standing against the wall now, on the far side of the corridor. She was alone once more but he didn't dare approach her, considering what he must have looked like earlier, offering a dollar to an abandoned girl. But she couldn't be *abandoned*, he thought. She had since changed clothes, now wearing jeans and a loose T-shirt, on her feet a pair of pink cowboy boots. The boots looked glossy and plastic and shone like neon; to Bill, they seemed more like toys than footwear. The girl stood with one heel pressed flat against the wainscoting, her profile suggesting the figure 4. She switched legs every now and then, and from his view at the food court Bill saw how, given a pair of crutches at her sides, he could once again have mistaken her for an invalid. He lost sight of her in a crowd of Japanese tourists, but when she popped up again she was twice as close and darting through the crowd, headed in his direction. Bill feigned a stare into his empty soup bowl. She sidled up next to him and put out her hand.

"Let me see that dollar again," she said.

He took the dollar from his shirt pocket, but held it in his hand a moment before giving it over. The money was now no longer blind charity, and Bill felt it bought him a right to his concern. "Young lady," he asked, "where is your mother?"

The girl looked him up and down.

"Where's your *wife*?" she said.

She snatched the dollar from his hand and marched to a row of slot machines. It took her two seconds to lose.

Bill had his own daughter, of course, and was thereby no stranger to sass. But sass from a stranger was different, he thought, and from a little girl unattended in Las Vegas, roaming the halls in bright pink boots past eleven at night, that was too much. He bussed his tray and wandered in her direction towards the gaming area, hoping to point her out to a security officer, who could perhaps find her parents and hold such negligence accountable.

The ceiling, Bill noticed, was peppered with the round, black housings of security cameras. He thought of how he might look in the camera, in coarse grain and black-and-white silence, and suspected that an active search might seem somewhat predatory. Instead, he sat in a non-smoking section at the far end of the gaming area and slipped five dollars into a video-poker machine. He made sure the machine was just beneath a camera, and figured that if the girl had the gall to sass him again, she would do so caught under the dark eye of casino surveillance.

He sat there like bait for only a few minutes before catching a glimpse of her, just a flash of her bright boots as they strode out of a women's restroom down the hall. From his seat he searched the floor for security, for a waitress, but most of them attended to the smoky excitement of the poker tables, and he could find no one in the short time before the girl had hopped up on the stool beside him.

"You don't know how to play, do you?" she asked.

Bill checked his watch again. He looked past her and down the aisle of the gaming area. "You need to find your mother," he said. "You're not even allowed in this area."

"I *know* where my mother is," the girl said, flashing a wide grin of new permanent teeth, all unbraced and boasting one wayward canine. "I know where security is, too."

Bill pointed to the camera on the ceiling. "Security can see you, too."

The girl huffed. "You know they're only watching their money," she said. "They don't care about me. Maybe they're looking at *you*." She wagged her tongue up at the round black casing. "See? Half of those things are empty anyway. Bet you didn't know that. This isn't *Bellagio*, you know."

The girl wiped her nose with her wrist and looked up and down the aisle. "So where's your wife, anyway?"

Bill waited to answer, wondering if he should simply walk away or stall until some authority happened by. "My wife is on a cruise," he said. "She's with her sister, off the coast of the Baja peninsula. Do you know where that is?"

"But you're here."

"It was a bachelorette cruise," he said.

"Ohhhhh," said the girl, swinging her legs with delight. "I see. Tit for tat, then. You came here to even it up."

"I came for the Energy Outlook conference, for your information."

"*Duh*," she said. "That was cancelled. It was on the stanchion right when you came in. Don't you know how to read?"

"Don't *you* know not to talk to strangers?"

"You talked to me first!" said the girl. "You came up and handed me a dollar like some kind of pervert."

The word. It froze his nerves, it made him suddenly conscious of where he was and what he must look like. He thought of himself again on a security camera; he thought of himself on *Dateline*. He wanted to walk away but thought that might look even worse, like he was trying to get away with something.

"Stranger," the girl scoffed. "There's nothing strange about you at all. You don't know what to do with yourself here. You can't even gamble."

"I…I don't gamble at all," he said.

"Tell me about it. You haven't even started. That's what this is for." She reached a thin arm over his console and punched the blinking button that read PLAY MAX CREDITS. "You see," the girl said through a wicked smile, "this one counts."

Bill stood up and searched desperately over the machines for a waitress, a custodian, anybody in a uniform, and with no other recourse he resorted to flailing his arms up at the security camera.

The girl only leaned further into his machine, passing her index finger over the touch-screen. "You should keep your face cards," she said. "They're the same suit." She punched the button marked DRAW.

When Bill heard the noise he thought it was an alarm of some sort. He assumed he had made contact through the camera, or that the touch-screen had registered the fingerprint of a child, as it now flashed in urgent fluorescent colors. The cards on the screen were vibrant and came alive, their royal faces animated into arched eyebrows and wise grins, as if they had caught her in the act. The alarm rose in pitch and still no guard arrived, only onlookers who began to gather around one by one.

The girl hopped to her feet. "Oh, shit!" she cried, and sprinted down the hall to the elevators. The onlookers parted way for a casino official, an older man with a severe part in his graying hair and a dull black suit and tie.

Bill pointed down the hall. "She went that way, officer."

The man produced a clipboard and requested Bill's name and room number.

"Am I in trouble?" he asked.

"You won," the man shrugged and winked. "That depends on how you look at it."

‡ ‡ ‡

The next morning Bill did exactly that. He awoke, brewed the coffee in his room, sat at the desk and spent fifteen minutes in his pajamas simply looking at the cash. In such large denominations the stack was not even half an inch high, and at just over fifteen hundred the sum was incidental compared to his salary. But it was no less a windfall, a stroke of blind luck, and he regarded the money with a silent, incredulous glee. The bills were new and crisp, sterile and peagreen. He was eager to share the news with his family and called them both, getting the voice-mailbox of each. On his own phone, he found another check-in from his daughter:

**D**
**Ok**
**M**

He sent her a message back, only after he spent ten minutes figuring out how to do so, and his thumbs and patience held out for only two letters: **Ok**.

But in the silence of his hotel room, on a bright Saturday with only the company of his thoughts and a thin stack of money, Bill began to feel that it was not okay—he was sad, the whole matter was sad. His family had cell phones so they could *talk* to each other, he paid that bill for a reason. He was tired of four-letter exchanges from his daughter, tired of being unable to contact his wife, over reception or battery power or vibrate or whatever new excuse she came up with. No, it was not **Ok**. It was pathetic and it was sorry, and he was sorry to see contact between his family reduced to only what could fit on a square-inch of digital screen.

Bill looked to the money on the desk. Maybe it was a sign, he thought, something he could use to bring his family back together. Melissa was too old for Disneyland but they could go somewhere else; there were always teenagers in the audience of America's Funniest Home Videos. They had never seen a redwood either, or San Francisco. Bill considered the options for some time until he noticed, at the foot of his hotel door, a small envelope printed with his name in ornate cursive. Inside he found a card congratulating his win, and two vouchers inviting him to indulge his appetite at the Imperial's sumptuous weekend brunch buffet, compliments of the management.

‡ ‡ ‡

The buffet was a grand and bustling stainless steel affair that snaked along one wall of the dining area in fluid curves, some fifty serpentine feet of sneeze guard and steam tray, and the food, like the white-coated attendants who served it, spanned the spectrum of color and ethnicity. The tumult of the dining area reminded Bill of Sunday mornings at Marie Callender's, especially as he balanced his plate in-between the crowded tables, and found his own table by spying what looked like his daughter's head of blond hair, wet and combed into bold furrows. But as he rounded his table now he saw only a child with plastic earrings in her twice-pierced ear, a blunt stare and a pouty scowl, the face of the little girl who had sassed and harassed him last night.

"So you won," she said.

Bill sat down and ignored her, as he would a bee or a hungry seagull.

"How much, anyway? Hey. Hello?"

She waved her arm between them, and the sequins on her shirtsleeve danced at her shoulder. Her hair was parted and held in place with a cracked barrette, half a steel clip and half a tortoise-shell finish. Bill stayed silent.

"You remember I played that hand for you, right?"

The waitress came to refill his glass. She asked him, "Will your daughter have the buffet, too?"

"Yes," the girl said, "and a glass of orange juice, please." She coolly unrolled her silverware from the napkin, and eyed Bill as she popped off her chair. "You probably don't even know," she said, "but that was the best hand you can ever get." The girl wasted no time at the buffet, returning after a minute with a plateful of bacon strips and two puddles of brown and white pudding. The girl looked at Bill, sighed, then offered a handshake. "My name is Jackie," she said. "Jackie Collins."

"Like the author?" Bill asked.

"What author?"

Bill introduced himself, surprised by the girl's grip and shake. "First of all," she said, smacking on a piece of bacon, "I don't mean to be so rude to you. You seem like a nice guy, but you can't really trust people, especially not here, you know?" She dipped one end of the bacon between the two pools of pudding and swirled the colors into a brindled mixture. "And thanks for brunch too," she added. "You got some vouchers, huh?"

Bill nodded.

"They want to make sure you stick around," she said. "Where are you from, anyway?"

"I'm from Bakersfield," he said. "California. Where are you from?"

Jackie motioned with the bacon. "I'm from here."

"Las Vegas?"

"Uh-huh. Twelfth floor."

"You live in the hotel?"

"Yeah," she said. "It's a suite, two bedrooms and a kitchenette. It's like a regular room, sort of, but housekeeping only comes twice a month."

"Do your parents...*work* for the hotel?"

"My mom used to. She was a cocktail waitress. That's how she met my dad. My dad is good friends with the owner. I met him once, he's real nice."

"Your dad?"

"No, the *owner*. Duh. My dad comes to town every few months. I meet him for breakfast, usually. He's a businessman. My mom doesn't like him, but I do."

"Do you go to school?"

"They teach stuff over at Harrah's, and I could go but don't. That's for tourist kids. It's like daycare only older. I guess you've got kids, huh?"

"I have a daughter," Bill said, "about your age."

"What's her name?"

"Melissa. She just turned thirteen."

"I'm ten, but I'll be eleven at the end of the month." Jackie licked pudding from the stem of her spoon and set it beside her plate. She looked at him thoughtfully. "You seem like a good dad," she said. "You have a nice voice. I bet you don't ever yell, do you?"

Bill felt his face start to flush. "I guess not," he said. He looked to the floor and pretended to check the lock on his luggage.

"Hey, what's with the bag?" asked Jackie. "You're not leaving today, are you? You're just staying one night?"

"My conference was cancelled," he said. "I can't read, remember?"

"Well, wait...hold on," Jackie said. "Look, I already told you I'm sorry for being mean to you. So I'm sorry, okay? Okay?"

"Okay," Bill said.

"So you can't just leave like that." She sat up straight in her chair and leaned over her plate, elbows on the table. "And I know I can't *make* you split that money with me, but if you don't want to be fair, you could at least stick around and do me a favor. So can you do me a favor?"

"What is it?"

"First you have to say yes or no."

Bill considered; he dug in his pocket and checked his phone for any messages. There were none.

"Okay," he said. "One favor."

"Great. I'll let you finish here, and when you're done, meet me at the bellstand. Five minutes, okay? I'll meet you there." And with that, the girl sprung out of her chair and sprinted through the dining room, dodging past the patrons and waitresses, her boot heels clapping loudly on the tile until swallowed by the thrum of the buffet.

‡ ‡ ‡

When he saw her again at the bellstand Jackie was talking with the attendant behind the counter, a man about Bill's age, only thinner and with a thick moustache. She held a long, yellow strip of paper in her hand as she met Bill across the hall. She looped the strip around his luggage handle, then tore off the end printed with his claim number and handed it to him. "And hold on to this, too," she said, handing him a small crescent wrench, the handle warm and sweaty from her palm. From the back pocket of her jeans Jackie tugged out a pink change purse and removed another yellow ticket that she gave to the bellman along with the suitcase. The bellman nodded to Bill, then disappeared through the double doors. "That's Albert," she said. "You should tip him good. They keep our stuff in the back, so it's kind of a hassle for him to get it." Bill sifted through his wallet and took out a five. Jackie waved it off. He took out a ten, and she shrugged in approval.

The bellman emerged from the doors bent over at the waist, wheeling beside him a child's bicycle, a dusty, clumsy thing that seemed to cough and wheeze as the bellman navigated the training wheels around the desk. Across the handlebars a foam tube spelled out the word HUFFY in white lightning bolts, and from one end there hung a tangle of limp pink and purple streamers. Jackie, with one fierce yank, snapped off the wilted ribbons and slapped them into the bellman's open hand. Bill laid the ten atop the strands, then hurried to catch up with her already on her way to the elevator.

"What a piece of junk," she said inside, jamming her thumb at the button to close the doors. "This is so embarrassing. Do you know anything about bikes?" Bill claimed to know a little; it wasn't so bad, he said, it just needed wiping off, maybe some air in the tires. In the back of his mind he wondered how many times and for how many tourists this girl had put on this show, how many new bikes she had been given money for. She had an undeniable charm, of course, and for all this effort Bill figured she deserved one or two hundred dollars, though he couldn't see himself just handing her cash. It would be, somehow, irresponsible. But so would walking away from her in broad daylight, and what a scene that might be, given her capacity for public sass. With his finger Bill cut a streak through the dust on the bicycle seat. "Yeah," the girl said, "it's old and filthy. Probably pretty dangerous, too."

At the seventh floor, Jackie marched out in the direction of the parking garage. In the hallway, she passed a stray housekeeping buggy and, without a break in her stride, Jackie swiped a hand towel and a spray-bottle full of blue fluid. Bill followed and looked over his shoulder to check if anyone had seen.

The top of the parking garage was a wide slab of flat concrete with only two cars parked on it in a far corner. The sun bathed the concrete a blinding white. Jackie took sunglasses from her pocket and started to spray down and wipe off the bike. Bill put a hand to his forehead and looked at the brown mountains in the west. He checked his phone again but found no messages. He called his daughter and left a voicemail; he called his wife and did the same. Jackie addressed the front of the bike with her arms crossed. "Do you still have that wrench?" she asked. "I just need you to take off these stupid training wheels. Then you can go and do whatever, okay?"

Bill knelt down beside the axle and felt the nuts and washers were loose enough to spin in his fingers. "Are you sure this is what you need?" he asked.

Jackie smiled. "I guess you're right," she said. "It could use some air and stuff, too. I know a gas station where they got air. Right by the Flamingo. Have you ever been to the Flamingo?" She straddled the bike and walked it's flat tires between her legs to the exit ramp. "They got flamingos there, Bill! For real! Come on!" Bill followed, slowly as always, as Jackie hopped onto the seat of the bike rolling slowly on its rims down the gray slope of the garage.

Walking down the Las Vegas strip Bill wondered if not just the casinos, but all of Paradise Boulevard was perhaps equipped with security cameras. And if so, what would the surveillors make of this man, a grown man in slacks, stooped over and pushing a pastel pink bicycle, having conceded to the girl who was mortified that she be seen with it—or him for that matter—and so maintained several paces of distance between them, leaving Bill ostensibly alone and somehow mentally unstable with this adolescent relic. "Just stay back some," she had insisted. "I don't want to introduce you if I run into someone. It would be...weird." Bill had agreed, but he now hoped any onlooker would simply assume they were doting father and abashed daughter, and while that thought had struck him dumb this morning at brunch, he now found himself counting on it.

At the service station Bill filled the tires with air while Jackie coaxed a mechanic to tune up the bike in one of the bays. The mechanic was grizzly, fat and thickly bearded, and when finished he stood holding the bike against the bay door, blocking their exit. Only after a nudge from Jackie and her discreet instruction, Bill tipped the man a twenty. She sighed as they walked down the apron of the station. "You need to learn to do that on your own," she said. "It just makes things a lot smoother. Don't people tip in Bakersfield? You tip everyone out here. *Especially* if you win big." At the sidewalk Jackie unraveled a chain wrapped around the seat post. She locked the bike to a streetlamp, then looked to a Bill. "So," she said. "Flamingos?"

‡ ‡ ‡

Atop the entrance to the Flamingo Hotel and Casino a string of pink light bulbs illuminated their slogan in a cursive flourish—"As Vegas as Vegas Gets." And the place did have an ineffable quality of the city, Bill noticed, one that was absent from the Imperial—a sort of plushness, not so much from luxury, but in a spongy, cushioned way. The carpet was thick pile swirling with florid, verdant designs trimmed in signature pink. Jackie, as she strut down the hall in her bright pink boots, seemed to befit the environment precisely, as if she had sprung organically from the décor.

The Wildlife Habitat, as it was called, was a sort of large courtyard flanked by the wings of the hotel and came complete with tropical foliage, wedding gazebo, and water features that wound under footpaths and around bubbling fountains. Jackie dashed to the edge of an artificial pond and took a post opposite a small fiberglass island. "Yeah," she said to Bill, "this is pretty much my favorite place I know." Upon the island, standing regally among brown ducks and terns, a dozen bright pink flamingos each held one leg high into the feathered bulb of their body.

"Look at their necks," Jackie said idly. "They're so long. They look so soft."

Bill had never paid much attention to birds. His daughter had been a fan of things furry or great, the tiger cage or the elephant show, and on trips to the zoo Bill's taste, like his footsteps, simply followed hers. But here, isolated from the more illustrious animals, Bill saw the appeal of the flamingo—its composure among the aggressive swan, its graceful movements compared to the hungry twitch of ducks, its eye like a wise, black marble. The flamingos seemed not to know or care if there was anything outside this manufactured island in a chlorinated pond, in the middle of a casino, in the middle of the desert. It warmed Bill to see Jackie so enthusiastic about the birds; it made the outing wholesome somehow, even educational. He studied the placard at his waist, searching for some fact or piece of information he could share with her, but Jackie had her own.

"Real flamingos are not this pink," she stated. "Do you know why?"

"No," he said, "why?"

"They feed them leftover shrimp. Cocktail shrimp. Cooked ones from the buffet. They just dump the steam trays into the water. I've seen it." She said this with a coy smirk, her words broken up with snickering.

"No they don't," Bill said. "Do they?"

"It's true!" she protested. "They eat all the shrimp, and they're so messy, they get the cocktail sauce all over their feathers!" The girl erupted in bubbly laughter, buckling her knees and swaying by her arms on the rail. "I made that one up, you know."

"Well," Bill said, "I bet you don't know why they stand on one leg."

Jackie stood up straight. "Why!"

"Because if they didn't," he said, "they would fall down."

Bill smiled to himself, but the joke oddly sobered the girl. "Yeah..." she said, "You're right. They must have real strong legs. Look at their knees, they're like knots."

Bill regarded the birds, saw how in the middle of its thin black leg the muscles bulged on top of each other like a bulbous triple-knot. The likeness held Bill's imagination for more than a moment, and for Jackie's cleverness he felt a strange, familiar sort of pride.

"Hey Bill," she said, poking at his elbow. "You got a quarter?" Jackie ran off with the change and returned with a handful of small brown pellets. Bill pinched one and examined it skeptically; for her benefit, he brought it to his nose to sniff and made as if he were to test it with his tongue.

"No!" cried Jackie. "Duh! They're for the birds!"

They tossed the pellets one by one into the water, and improvised a competition out of who could get the most of theirs eaten. Only the ducks responded with any interest; the flamingo only dipped its black beak past the floating pellets and twisted its neck to guzzle upside down, which, Jackie pointed out, was a flamingo's favorite way to eat.

"Does your daughter like flamingos?"

"No," he said. "She likes her friends. She likes her cell phone. She likes the internet and text messages."

"She's got her own cell phone?"

"Unfortunately."

"What kind is it?"

"I don't know. It's pink, though."

Jackie became silent and soon began to throw her pellets with more force, aimed now at the flamingos themselves, especially those that were sleeping with their necks wound up and their heads tucked under their wings. "Wake up!" she shouted. "Get back to work! Can't you see you're on stage?"

Bill caught the glance of a nearby mother with two boys. He put his hand on Jackie's throwing shoulder, and she tossed the rest of her pellets into the water. Bill's hand remained there on her shoulder, rising and falling with each of the girl's heated breaths.

"We should go back," he said finally. "I should probably head home soon."

"It's not *fair*!" Jackie shouted. She ducked from his hand and stepped back to confront him. "You don't even need that money! First *I* won it, and then you just go and give it all to *her*?"

"Jackie—"

"Well I don't care about you, either! So why don't you go ahead, just take all my money and leave!"

Bill felt the stares of several more bystanders now as Jackie stamped away over a footbridge towards the door. He hastened to catch up to her, and he came just within arms length when Jackie spun around on her heels and arrested him with reddened and glassy eyes and a screech from the top of her lungs—"Stay *away* from me, Mister!" Bill stopped in his tracks and watched her walk away, suddenly aware that with any step he took toward her, if she wanted, Jackie Collins could put this stranger in handcuffs.

‡ ‡ ‡

When he claimed his bag at the bellstand Bill couldn't bear the thought of driving home right then. His hands felt dirty from the bike and the city, his keycard was still in his pocket and his room still booked. He figured he would freshen up briefly, wash the episode from his conscience before he hit the road. In his room he lasted five minutes in the silence before he pulled out his phone and called his daughter.

He got her voicemail and left a message.

He called his wife and did the same.

He sat and he waited. For what, exactly, he wasn't sure. He stared at his phone on the table and felt much like a blinking button, over the mountains miles and miles from here, like a pixilated envelope waiting to be opened and heard and deleted. But the phone, these messages, he thought, they didn't much matter anymore. There was never time enough for the whole story, and when he thought about it he probably wouldn't mention Jackie to them either. The whole matter had left him ill at ease, and telling his family would be—as Jackie put it—...weird. And given the fact that he now had a secret of his own, Bill figured his family had plenty of theirs. There was always something unsaid, something left forgotten, an excuse either intentional or not. It could be a little girl in Las Vegas or it could be a phone charger, even one he had unplugged the night before she left, and wound the cord up, and placed in plain sight by her purse.

Bill unlocked his suitcase and took out the leather tote that held his toiletries. Doing so, he disrupted the stack of cash, the bills now strewn about his clothes, as if his suitcase contained its own private party. He washed his face and shaved, then drew the curtains and looked out at the view. The sun was about to set over the mountains and the light entered his room at an angle, in a bright warm column that he let touch his eyelids.

When he opened his eyes there again was Jackie, in miniature now and no larger than a dime, nine stories below wheeling her bicycle across the top of the parking garage. She set herself before a broad, flat space and straddled the bike, then turned and looked up at the hotel, at Bill's room almost exactly it seemed, but it was hardly a moment before she pushed off the concrete with one leg and hopped onto the seat. Her boots found the pedals and she rode down the length of the drive, her hair lifting with the wind behind her and her knees pumping up and down like small pistons in blue jeans. She had just made it to the corner of the garage when the handlebars began to wobble. She leaned into the turn but cut the front wheel too hard, too fast; the bike halted. Jackie was tossed, and Bill watched from the quiet of his room as she hit the ground, tumbling head over heels onto the grit of the concrete.

She lay still for only a moment before she picked herself up and surveyed the scrapes on her elbows and the rips at her knees. She wasn't crying, from what Bill could tell. But as he watched, he found himself secretly wishing she would. He wished he could see her now as fragile as any other girl her age, without the thick skin of a girl who lives in a hotel and plays in a parking garage. But there were no tears from Jackie; she only looked up at the hotel again and walked calmly to where the bicycle lay inverted on the pavement. She righted the bike and with it beside her ran several yards and stopped. The bike sailed from her hands, while Jackie turned and walked back to the hotel, giving not even a glance as it crashed into the concrete wall.

‡ ‡ ‡

As a final effort, Bill made a circuit from the checkout desk through the lobby and back through the casino. When he found her, Jackie was standing in the hallway just outside the Food Court, waiting and watching his approach, as if expecting him. Her jeans were torn, and the scrapes on her elbows were fresh and red. She showed her arms to Bill as he grew closer, wielding them like evidence from an accident he had somehow caused.

"I nearly killed myself on that old bike," she said. "Look."

"I know. I saw you from my room."

"Albert said you hadn't left yet."

"That's right," said Bill. "I've been looking for you. And I have something to give you, something I think you deserve."

He led her to a table in the Food Court. He was relieved to have found her, to be able to clear his conscience, and he felt warm and content with his decision. He slipped his hand into his pocket. "I bought this at the Flamingo," he said. "It's for you."

He gave her an envelope, and inside was a long card with a picture of two flamingos on the cover, taken from nearly the same spot where they had watched them together. A pocket on the inside of the card held three hundred-dollar bills, and on the opposite side was the message—

*A Tip,*
*for Jackie Collins,*
*for being a teacher,*
*a tour guide,*
*and a friend.*
*From Bill*

"You can buy a very nice bicycle with that," he said.

She gazed into the card and fingered the three bills. "Three hundred dollars?" she asked, looking flushed and frustrated, almost about to cry. Bill was unsure of what to do, but he knew what he wanted to say, and he crouched down beside her and put his arm over the back of her chair. "I really wish my daughter could meet you, Jackie. I think you two could be very good friends."

She looked at him sadly. She started to say something, but Bill knelt to the floor and put his arm over her shoulder. "It's okay," he said. "I'll have to come back here at some point. We could meet for breakfast. We could go see the flamingos again."

She leaned into him then, drew her arms around his chest and rested her forehead against his shirt collar. Her voice was calm at his neck.

"My name isn't Jackie, you know."

Against the tile, Bill felt his kneecaps started to ache and his arms felt heavy as he continued to hold them around the girl. Just above them on the ceiling he saw the round glass casing of another security camera. He felt strands of her hair cling to his cheek, and her breath warm against his ear.

"I'll scream again," she said. "I'll scream so loud. And I'll point right at you, and I'll follow you and say whatever I have to."

Bill stared at the ceiling. His image was up there, distorted by the black globe, with the girl's arms stretched around him. He tried to see past the reflection, or deeper into it. Half of the ceiling's camera globes were empty, he knew, but he thought he could see something inside of this one, and he wondered if any camera could tell which one of them had just become the stranger.

## The Day Is

*Kathleen McGookey*

lost and gone. There is palpable happiness between my grandparents in a photo while voices carry across water to me. Each moment isn't precious as its own reward. Not enough space, not enough open day. The dishes still wait. It's unfortunate I don't feel generous when the dog whines at the door, when the sunset turns everything in the front yard to gilt. Possibly none of this is true: words stretch across water, across the light from the lake. The photos are old and not enough is written on the back. The garden's plowed under, no more berries like jewels, small rewards. I won't tell you about night-flowering plants and how I dreamed my hair red: I am tired of human hair used to scare deer from orchards, from hunters. I love deer in their shyness and grace and state of constant flight but can't select the perfect word for them. While the dog barks herself onto the page, some could turn back, but not the princess making love in the garden, not those who seek one true thing. The lake brings light to my face today, a gift. The nearest joy I can imagine is in my own language: light or lake or deer.

## FIELD

*Kathleen McGookey*

The girl in the field picks yellow flowers thoughtfully, as though there were only a few. When she looks down, the creases in her face unwind. When she looks up, she says yes. To the day, to all the yellow flowers in the field. He wants to blow her kisses, but it might look like he was calling her back. The sun is so bright the colors fade but the insect buzz grows louder. A dog barks over and over, three short barks in a row which he tries to shut out. Never mind that people whispered about a grown woman stealing flowers from government property. She is much too complicated for that. She is glad he stands respectfully just at the edge. And see, already the girl has turned into a woman, already things are a bit different than when we began. Because the woman doesn't just love flowers and the man wants his new door to hang properly. This accidental yellow isn't controlled by the clock. She had been listening to advertisements for plumbing and auto repair when he pulled his sleek car to the side of the road, just far enough past the deer carcass he could tell himself she hadn't seen. She tries to make things nice, and so does he, and sometimes they try together. Sometimes they wake from dreams so real it is days before they realize their house has no door the shape and size he talks about replacing.

# On the Water

*Frederick Smock*

> *I never had a patient who spent*
> *part of his day looking over water.*
> —Sigmund Freud

I have sat reading Alain-Fournier's *Le Gran Meaulnes*
in a rented cabin on the beach at Folly Island,
South Carolina, looking up from the page now and then
to see dolphins arcing across the horizon.
I have sat by a rock-pool near an orange grove
in the south of France; the scent of fallen oranges,
scavenged upon by peculiar black-and-white birds,
mingled with chlorine, being the scent of that day—
at the Hôtel de l'Orange, whose proprietress sunbathed
on the roof and dropped pass-keys down to her customers
with always a cry of delight. Sunlight shone silver
on the leaves and shimmered electrically on the ripples
in the pool. I am a Cancer (a water sign) yet even so
it seems to me that we all sit looking over water
as we sit before a hearth, that is, to be returned to life
as it was lived prior to living memory.
With my wife I have gazed out at the Pacific
from Stinson Beach, the two of us just another couple
of boulders (smaller, fleshy) speckling the California coast.
Two reclining figures, eidolons for a Henry Moore,
say, like the one ("Woman at Rest"?)
on the Danish cliffs at Humelbæk, looking out
over the Swedish sound, and, in the far distance,
mists rising from an ancient forest.

## WITTGENSTEIN, IN VIENNA

*Frederick Smock*

*If I were asked to say what is at once the most*
*important production of Art and the thing most*
*to be longed for, I should answer, A beautiful*
*House, and the next thing... A beautiful Book.*
—William Morris

Wittgenstein took three full years off from
philosophy and linguistics—from academia—
to construct a house for his sister, Gretl.
Three years. More time than it took him
to write *Tractatus Logico-Philosophicus*, or
the late work *Philosophical Investigations*.
"If you think being a philosopher is difficult,"
he said later to a colleague, "just try being
a good architect," words to that effect.
He found himself anguishing over doorknobs—
the traditional round tin jobs, or the more
modern levers that were just becoming popular?
How ample the stairs? What plinth the eaves?
How deep and low the window divides?
How about a roof garden, a view to the stars?
Should there be a bedroom on the ground floor—
Gretl will not be young forever, after all—
and should it not face the east? The difficulty,
he said, lay in being practical and beautiful
all at once. Not so different an arithmetic,
where the ideal of the elegant solution still
holds.

# Prognosis: Cataract

*Sean M. Conrey*

Why can't we take this sunlight and cold air,
turn it over like sheet music between beats
and look at what's beneath?

It's the curtain between the room
and the window.
When the cataract's removed, vision returns.

Put a poultice of snow and burnt leaves
on the eyes and wait three days
for clarity. The other night

you asked, Would you make me some tea,
and I answered without saying,
walked to the kitchen slowly.

It was snowing outside for the third time that day,
the trees bent low from the weight.
Today, the snow is blown

round my car in a crescent,
a high and mighty form, a comet
in still frame before I shovel it clear.

It's so bright out, stark and frigid,
the sun's a contradiction,
the houses hold tight to the cold.

Yes, I'll get the mail on my way up, I say,
you at the door in your socks,
and I think, for a second, we're dancing,

the two of us, the first time in months,
the snow and mail just larger hands
at our waists, something bigger

than I alone could make. Everyone clears
the snow from their walk and I think,
Would it all be one white thing

if we could see it all at once?

# THE WORD IN EDGEWISE

*Sean M. Conrey*

Love's rusted edges,
all its dents,
the fundraiser sledgehammer car of all words,
weedy in its dings, sits
till we rend its door open
and look inside. And there

on the passenger side
a drunken stubborn angel
motions us with a mighty hand
to drive. And drive we do

till love burns in the traffic hum,
and each car's passing stereo screams
'the pain doesn't matter much
in the end.' We began

by simply asking this:
What makes us huddle here
naked and clutching love so desperately?
We are not shy on evidence.

The tent revival's matted grass says
widespread love's been had here.

The wind as it spills through the vane,
the ground in the clutches of roots,

the bent tree the cold sky
filters through, so long and empty,

asks, as we idle,
'Can we stand the wind
without love or something like it
in this cold and vast Nebraska,
this unkempt, middling place?'

Just drive, you graceless fool,
before the weather breaks.

## Night of Faults

*Robert Bense*

Those habitual imperfections
the brisk walk
on the model's runway
old designs with new moral edges
gasps at sudden labyrinths
the emerging paths
between waking and sleep
separate ways to the shore, mountains
the plains, ruined cities electrified
splendid former frontiers
still worth detours
the table set for two in the desert
a gritty business
one would imagine
now to begin our talk
angling in a cold stream
of non-companionable air—first litanies
of blame, incomprehension
like the hurtful secret
the slightly forged will
though the sums are large
feuds losing their grip
what is remembered, and especially
what is misremembered
joining a sun at the  teetering edge.

## TAKING FRACTAL DISTRIBUTIONS

*Robert Bense*

A fog of ash this morning.
Raptors have fled their nests.
The mountain crater blows
its magma plug. On the slopes
the distant magma glow. Red
garden cannas in Santa Rosa
feign terror. Always the nod
toward equilibrium.

The yellow bungalow, the house
you grew up in, must go.
How fine the sift of ash
in the end will lie. And you
as well. Though you will not wade
into your biography. Or out.
Neighbors do not rush up and say
we miss your past.

The rise of ash. The fall.
There is no bell curve.
Moon ash. Diesel ash. Fire ash.
Diaspora of ashes. Residue
at the end of the refiner's fire.
You stay indoors. Watch from
the TV. Fall asleep.
Ashes do not have the affinity
of sand for time. The irreducible yet.

# H. G. WELLS INITIATES FICTION WRITING, CIRCA 1895

*Anis Shivani*

**1.**

The boiler, penumbra to rheumatic washerwomen,
reclines in turgid steam, present to its own order,
and the adipose quotidian miracle of the master's house
remaining alive in this same order, day after day,
conjures a comatose fantasy of wellness.

**2.**

The Thames a burglar's whole check.
Passive boaters would not know how to take in a resplendent moon,
should it occur out of time.
Hearts beat like thick sludge.
Who takes measure? Who keeps time?

**3.**

At the smaller lending libraries in Putney
volumes of girl's romances are dog-eared in what must surely be
acts constituting the antithesis of romance.
Reading has to acquire its passionate following of would-be grotesques and silent rogues,
or else wither of overuse, of course.

**4.**

Thomas Henry Huxley, Darwin's bulldog, retools young scholars
in his own laborious image, scholars to a new age
of dog-eat-dog, and youth at any cost—
oh, I am Faust, I am Faust!—who love to tell the tale,
and I one of those scholars at South Kensington,
before T.H. got ill, and I too in his image,
became a buried flower, before my time—
no churchyard stone to sing of how I came to be.

**5.**

It can't be literature.
I am no Verne. I am no James. I am no Conrad, even.
The *Pall Mall Gazette* is a gasbag of the golden age.
Man reads man to swallow him whole.
A new question about Victorian England:
Who will bury the cosmic corpse,
and at whose expense?
Serial rights set the bar to profligacy,
though I thrill in this new proficiency.

**6.**

England, behind the city's scenes, smokehouse and workhouse,
bread and butter on the cheap, machine work never easier,
the hedges trimmed by knives sharpened through instinct,
mothers embosoming workhorse sons by night,
bewitched swallows sorting industrial rust,
new plagues infesting factory floors,
alleys dark hours after noon—
and myself no social observer.

**7.**

No, Mr. Ford, in the kingdom of letters
only boilerplate counts, only how you boil the common man's
astute sensibility.

**8.**

The discovery of the future is a prophet's melodrama.
It serves the earth-based ants right.
On the edge of Bloomsbury there are witnesses
to Carlyle being a sort of Quaker who preceded his time
by many millennia. Such strong will
in the face of menace and worry.
God's creatures are nothing if not aged.

**9.**

It is a time of fantasy and fable.
The century has proven elastic beyond measure.
Do we not behold democracy's final barricades
falling before our eyes? It is a time of fantasy, indeed.
Then there will be a future to reckon with.
Iron wills and iron skills,
for an age of prophets thrilling with palsy,
and weapons that dignify death
by its sheer quantity.

**10.**

The grotesque is a paradigm of beauty.
See how the failed chemist from the Potteries coughs blood
but keeps it secret from the housekeeper?
We travel through time to meet ourselves
in an earlier state of disguise.
And it is wondrous how often our disguises are intact after piercing.
Wondrous is the state of brotherhood,
as England travels through time, salvaging workmen's finest crooning hours.

## TO EDWARD UPWARD*

*Anis Shivani*

How slick the tuxedo-outfitters' dishonesty!
How astute the winners in investment banks' lunch rooms!
Old colonial memories, shared by colonels long out of distress,
evoke a vague collective miasma of nervous fritter,
which we are one and all glad to have stylized.
Everyone dresses now as integral widows at too-cold northern
seaside resorts, where gulls swoop down with loss of wings,
and magicians and clowns stop to admire painterly
stillness. Every man has been trained to think
mathematically. My fragile mother deserves better.
These days bones, teeth, hair, skin, membranes are first to go.
What is left is the filament-trace of the body that used to wander
night-time hells, persist in advocating for the twilight idols
to take their place in the stately front of the audition room.
Chance, and its betters, have been victorious,
have pushed aside the programs of our youth,
and isn't it right that we are present at these denials of our friends?
Isn't it appropriate that not a one will admit to having fallen for
Stalin or his ilk? A purity without puritan hurt haunts
the new legends, as they dedicate their works to future generations,
asking only that they be read with a measure of forbearance,
and please to shell the pound or two for the glossy journal than circulate worn copies
checked out of public libraries. I admire their need-bruised wit.
There used to be women one presumed to be nurses.
Somewhere beneath white sheaths cold medicine lurked.
Could we have escaped the wavelike transitions from drunken decade to drunken decade?
The shops, as I said before, want to equip us in knightly armor
for our small domestic battles, and we mock Tolstoy's mockery
of Shakespeare, ascribe it to old age's crankiness.

* Edward Upward (born 1903), is a member of the English "Auden Group" of the 1930's, having influenced Auden, Spender, Isherwood and others with his early Mortmere Stories, above all *The Railway Accident* (written in 1928). Leonard and Virginia Woolf published his influential novel *Journey to the Border* in 1938. Unlike other members of his literary circle, he never moderated his socialistic views.

# THE MARRIAGE BED

*John Estes*

*If the bee disappeared off the surface of the earth, man would have no more than four years to live.* Albert Einstein

First, there's the guilt—at least
for those who grew up
hooked on *Little House on the Prairie*,
watching Pa tenderly
cobble Ma a hickory-log frame
for her hand-sewn mattress
stuffed with tall grass;
or those who cannot undiscover
the climactic *anagnorisis*
of Homer's *Odyssey*,
where Odysseus passes
crafty Penelope's identity test
by describing, with meticulous detail,
how he built their bedroom
around the four-poster,
hand-hewn around a rooted olive tree—
the guilt of buying one's marriage
bed off a showroom floor.

In the *Georgics* Virgil describes
how if one's honeybee hive—
Latin *cubile*, the same word used
for the bridal chamber
couch Tithonos and Aurora share
each night before she,
replenished, arises
at dawn to don her saffron robes—
goes dead and silent
one calls it back to existence.
Whether killed off cursed
by nymphs or mutant fungus
or just bad luck, despite the alert
protections of Priapus,

one must sacrifice a young bullock:
stuff its orifices with marjoram
and thyme, beat its bones
and innards soft then let it rot
in a closed-up hut
with four small windows.
Then, after a hot and windy
season, *mirabile dictu*: this fermenting
viscera will burst forth
a buzzing, nectar-sucking swarm.

Second, there's the rift—
though we agree that any debt
is better than sleeping
ensconced in the cheap veneer
of Mexican-made consumer goods—
between what we say,
what we are
and what we recognize as so.
Am I a giant-eyed drone?
Are you an egg-rich queen?
Are we no more than common
workers, bees
of an easily blighted invisible?

## NOTHING...

*Sandra Kohler*

helps. Not the day: pristine, autumnal, clear
as glass. Not being in the garden, where there
are yellow German iris and violet Siberian iris
blooming, where the buds on the peonies are fat
and sticky with ants, where the clematis climbs
in huge purple flowers, and the bleeding hearts
are a jungle, each of them a square yard high and
wide. For grief there is no garden. Where pinks
are opening, crimson, white, fuchsia, acid pink,
and dahlias thrust up tight bursts of crisp leaves.
For fear. Where the coneflower are studded with
the green skeletons of what will be blossoms when
they put on the flesh of colored petals. For disquiet.
Where stiff stalks of loosestrife and liatris bloom,
the opening throats of lilies. Anxiety. Panic at
the profound indifference of the real to our fears,
gestures, our superstitious attempts to temper,
propitiate, control, foresee: the cold corridors
of time that memory opens and walks down,
the high clerestory windows of rooms where no
exit is possible into the light, the long shafts
of absence gaping beneath your feet.

# TURNING

*Sandra Kohler*

Apricot-tinted open sky beneath clotted gray
cloud. Spider's glinting strands, telephone wires,
asters, the first chrysanthemums. The sun's
a colder bloom. This is my hour. I am trembling
like the broken-off rags of cumulus. The wind
is hard-edged. A woodpecker in the old dogwood
is stolid, repetitive; a jay's shrill announcements fly
out of the turning leaves. Daybreak surrenders
to our longing to be made selves by our separations,
each from each. By the light falling and the light
rising, the contradictions of weather, the hands of
a fate we recognize when it has finished with us.

A brother suffers, a sister revives, a child walks
away and finds a world to stand in. The new shape
of a life is written, black foliage against whitening
sky. All the people of two decades of memory
gather in one dream and conspire to forget me.
I am in love with their beautifully turned backs,
the glowing cigarette ends which dismiss me.
Smoke, fog, steam, cloud: who can distinguish
these white masks, their different sources: fire, river,
machinery, air? The days build structures before
we perceive them that will bear names—brother,
sister, child—yet have nothing to do with our blood,
our bones, genes. All this seems the turning of
a cheek, the faint breeze of autumn upon it.

# VENEZIA NOTTURNO

*Leslie Ullman*

Liquid streets. Their shimmer—
the space between Petrarch's first line
and the sonnets he left in his wake—

pathways between houses where I
feel my way out of my neon century
to a bridge barely visible in the damp

arrival of dusk. I would borrow a sliver
of lamplight edging from high shutters—
I would borrow a whole slice of

someone's evening after he's closed
his shop full of yellow ceramics
and poured red wine into a tumbler,

spreading the day's news by his plate
and leaving his shutters open
as the mist he's used to

settles like a hush, a caesura
in the metrics of history which only seem
to pause at the present—a trick offered

to visitors from my country, where no one
has ever carried groceries over
cobblestones softened by hooves and blood

or lived in a city where houses rise
right from the water, their foundations
part salt, part tidal drift.

In Venezia, a single gondola glides
now and then through the sleep of those
who were born to the sound of sealed wood

parting water, the near-silence from which
the gilt and filigree of the Renaissance rose
like hothouse vegetation to become cathedral

and palace, each piazza a fugue
of torso and limb, gilt wings of cherubs,
marble carved to a froth, busy frescoes

climbing the Doge's walls one frame at a time—
thus the metropolis of ceilings
came to be, a painter secured by ropes

suspended beneath each one, his palette full of gold
and a blue that was even harder to come by
while the lagoon continued its slow art

below, even at night, stroking stone to silt.

# CENTERS OF ORDER

Leslie Ullman

> *"If we give objects the friendship they should have,*
> *we do not open a wardrobe without a slight start."*
> —Gaston Bachelard

Wood that once was the cool interior
of tree. Inlay of insect passings
and leaves that never made it out of solitude—
its grain is an old conversation with water
and damp nights. Was once
tree hugging itself in rings.
Now, in part, is clothes
salted with lavender, harvest of linen
gathered from fields grown golden
with sun and sparse rain
far from home, where our brief
knowledge of them has nearly faded—
oh Tuscany, we hated to leave you behind, your
fine bread and narrow streets we could have
shaken hands across from fifth-story windows—
and the Alps, where we drove into Austria
by mistake and paid handsomely
for the privilege, pooling our Euros
into white military gloves while geraniums,
corralled in identical boxes, waved
gaily from chalet balconies—and the red-
tiled towns heaped along the Adriatic
wherever Rome had left remnants of aqueduct
and turret.... At first we spoke
in whispers, erased by vaulted ceilings
and catacombs built from blood and rude tools,
or spoke not at all, for hours at a time,
before paintings that had glowed for centuries
in their tarnished frames without
any help from us. Then we folded ourselves
back into our bodies, slurping gelato
among the ruins, aiming our cameras
at baroque instruments of torture

and swigging bottled water the avid way
our countrymen do. Flying home
on a Swiss plane, tucked in our seats
like socks in a drawer, we had our last
good cup of coffee.

## DRIFT—

*Jared Harel*

This is how it starts: my family
slouched before a digital camera, feigning
a smile, not even a smile, just the lifting
of cheeks, tightening of muscles.

This is how it starts: a cosmic white light,
everyone blinded, father stunned
to find his face in the camera, how quick
it all happened, how old he's become.

Then later, a couple Mexicans
move through the house, changing
light-bulbs, fixing the grill. Their soft eyes
assess the damage, smile as I pass.

This is how it starts: my parents passed
out by nine at night, separate couches
shielded in plastic; the glow of some program
waltzes on the walls.

This is how it starts: a shot of my mother
in short purple shorts, an easy smile
as though she's been sailing.
A shot of my father. His arms around her.

Now faces rotate on the family computer.
Smiles hedge and break
down screen. This is how it starts.
I feel it drifting. The slightest touch

and we will all disappear.

# THE NAMES OF BIRDS

*Megan Gannon*

Somehow stark
  and mysterious—as the names
    *lark,*
*starling,*
  *linnet,*
    *swift*
limn so little
  of the wheel,
    dip and tilted
drift, but twine
  bright skeins
    of air between
the plumped and heated,
  beating breast and their
    idea. Days
you savor this
  newness, walking around quiet
    as an egg, small
trapped tide rocking
  against the chitin;
    now tangible
as an emptied
  dish, now unknown,
    airy—so far
inside you it seems to sever
  galaxies
    with its beam.
Is it being up inside
  so much spent breath
    that thrums each one
like a wet reed,
  or the trilling
    that brings a bursting
only a hollow-boned
  body can answer?
    All I know is, it wasn't

the faint music
    of a curlew or any air
        I have a name for
that cast me
    outside this evening
        to stand by the hedge—
as if somewhere
    there is a song and senselessness
        is the only way into it.

## Etymology of Evening

*Megan Gannon*

Not darkening, but balancing, some thing
weighed against its absence and dissolving
from a source that can't be seen. The cool
of the sheltered beds, the shortening
of corridors. And the words we circle in this
leveling—*wisteria, lilac*—resting in eddies.
This is where what you can't horizon
increases incrementally. The gift is, in this world
no hole is dense enough to swallow
semblance, the field of wildflowers blurring
around a rumor of hues. *Evening*, as dependable
as circumstance, as the assurance that
all sorrows, all joys are exactly divisible
in pairs. Any number of atoms seeping
toward a moment of precision when nothing
can pierce the drowsing houses. So everywhere
and even-handed—the restlessness, the centerless
days. In the hour when grips loosen

their hold and breath has a presence no suddenness

can disperse, bathwater's drawn, a hand

rends a hem, and *when* is not a question

you care to counter.

## The Mask

*Lisa Ampleman*

When we helped Tony move, some odd objects
did not fit into boxes and, so, sat separate on the lawn,

awaiting the truck: a rack for drying dishes, a set of weights,
a heavy ficus, and a wire mesh mask with the imprint of his face.

I thought first of a death mask, the angles of the nose
and cheekbones sculpted, but nearly animate, the eyes

as detailed as if they could open any minute. Perhaps
it was an art project, some grad-student friend casting his face

for a class on bust-making. But, because the thin wires
crossed themselves to make a mesh, I thought it a fencer's mask

and pictured him en garde, foil at the ready,
the mesh able to stop a swordpoint within an inch of his face.

But it had no strap to hold it to the back of his head,
and the holes at top and bottom, he said, held screws

to attach him to a table and keep him still
while radiation fired on the lymph nodes he had left.

A picture in a box of frames showed him bald and grinning.
His hair had grown back curly in remission.

The mask had traveled here with him and would go along
to a third city. He tried to explain to us, the untouched,

why he kept it, but could not.

## MY ONLY DEFTNESS

*Lisa Ampleman*

You say that if you field-dress the turkey, steam rises
from the viscera because just minutes ago, this body

was alive. When you open up the crop and gizzard,
you can tell where the bird's been: pine needles

or duckweed. I wonder if there are feathers everywhere
but forget to ask, picturing you as deft,

as you tell me about removing the head, the wings,
the feet and spurs. But first, you say, you must

make sure it's dead, so I imagine with you:
you stand on its neck. The bird is calm

until right before death, when it "goes nuts," you say;
it flaps and writhes and then is still. I can't feel

the triumph of arriving home with dinner
which you describe, and I haven't seen the fields

that sprawl below your family's home. "If I
were a poet," you say, "I'd be able to say

something about how they look in the morning."
I cannot, either, but here, in the limit of words,

is an exchange: yourself in a sort of portrait.

# Accident

*Helena Fitzgerald*

## 1

Last week I got into a motorcycle accident. Tried. I tried to get into a motorcycle accident. Last week I tried to get into a motorcycle accident.

It's these times I'm glad I don't have a wife. Or a girlfriend. Or a best friend. If I had anyone in my life with whom I shared a degree of that scratchy and uncomfortable cultural obsession *intimacy*, then I'd be listening to their protests right now:

"Gabriel, don't do this. Gabriel, really, stop, are you sure you should do this—This is ridiculous—I'm worried about you—stop it—take care of yourself—at least wear a helmet—don't do this—you're such an idiot, Gabriel."

But the great thing is, I don't have a wife. Or a girlfriend. Or a best friend. I don't even have a band or a manager anymore. I exist only to credit card companies and ConEdison.

Actually, that's a lie. I also exist to a tattooed hipster kid in a broken-fenced empty lot under the Williamsburg Bridge who is selling me his Triumph 650 Bonneville, a very specific and hard to find British-made motorcycle. Anyone who owns a Triumph must be quite serious about motorcycles. I don't know what it is that makes a Triumph special because I don't know shit about motorcycles, but I know there is something that does, and this kid knows what it is. While he talks, he keeps one hand on the bike, like a teenage boy holding onto his very first girlfriend at a college party. I cross my arms and wait for him to be done.

"I just…I gotta pay for grad school, man. You know? And I love this bike, I love this bike more than my girlfriend, more than my mom, even, but I got into grad school, and I have bad credit and I can't get any loans, but I gotta go, man." He looks up from his litany of sorrows, and something dawns on him.

"Hey!" He jabs a finger at me as though he were an archaic detective assembling the last piece of a mystery. "You're that guy! With the band…my friends and I saw that one concert…with the car. That was pretty fuckin' cool. We all though the album pretty much sucked, but you guys were fuckin' rad in concert, man."

I hand him an enormous wad of small bills before he can say anything else.

"Cool, man," he says. "Cool." He looks down. I get the distinct impression that he's trying not to cry. At last he says in an unsteady voice,

"So…um…what're you gonna do with it, man?"

"Crash it," I tell him confidently, and leave his breaking face in the sound of wheels and engine.

On July 29, 1966, Bob Dylan split his career into two analysis-inviting halves when he crashed a motorcycle on the side of a twisty back-road in upstate New York and nearly killed himself. The accident, making mercy and gift for critics, has been called everything from luck to attempted suicide. It happened a few months after he returned from the European tour partially documented in D.A. Pennebaker's brilliant *Don't Look Back* and Dylan's seminal "Royal Albert Hall" live album. Although this tour established him as a prolific figure, and is the temporal site of a number of central Dylan myths, including that of him smoking out the Beatles for the first time (a negligible but undeniably seductive little legend), it also saw his visible personal breakdown, the usual rock star's combination of quick fame and hard drugs. After Dylan's time in London, John Lennon declared that he "didn't think Dylan had very long." In his essential 1991 biography *Bob Dylan: Behind the Shades Revisited*, Clinton Heylin calls the pre-accident Dylan "death-ridden." Then there was the accident. It seemed to shake mortality into him. He moved upstate with his wife and family, swore off both drugs and entourage. One might have quoted Rilke: "You must change your life." The accident seems to have been such an edict. He changed his life. He also changed the face of rock 'n' roll forever with the album that hit the charts the very next day while he recovered in a hospital in upstate New York. When asked what he had to look forward to after *Blonde on Blonde*, he replied, "salvation," and quite seriously told reporters that the album was about "the second coming." Dylan described himself as "saved" more than once, of course, most famously in his born-again Christian days, but the first time he invoked the concept was in reference to *Blonde on Blonde*. Although the album was written and recorded before the accident, the accident symbolically sums up the self-destruction out of which his most brilliant album was born. The motorcycle accident and *Blonde on Blonde* are inextricably linked. The accident is the central myth. The accident is the key.

I ride the motorcycle down Kent Avenue, where the East River hangs onto the last moments of the old neighborhood. Along the water a soon-to-be-gone Brooklyn asserts itself in dirt and barbed wire and broken-car refuse, even as the foundations of multimillion-dollar condos arrive, laying concrete and putting up skeletal towers. Picasso said that all his life he learned how to do that which he could not do by doing it. That's how I learn to ride the motorcycle. I learn where the brakes are and how to use them when I nearly crash into a coffee shop on Bedford Avenue, at the last minute discover which thing to grab and squeeze the life out of, and reel back into the correct lane to continue toward Manhattan. I nearly die exactly twenty-eight times from the Lower East Side up to where Inwood abandons the city and gives into the postcard scenery along the Hudson, and in those twenty-eight scrapes with death I learn to use, one by one, the accelerator, the brakes, the side mirror, my knees, my feet, my hands, my arms, the handlebars, the speedometer, the clock and the gas gauge. And then I'm on an open road and, no longer a half-dressed virgin at a frat party among the cabs of Manhattan, I can live all the songs about motorcycles.

I tear down the open road. I ride free under the big sky. I fly on my bike. I am the king of the highway. It is beautiful. It is awesome. I am awesome. I am a rock star with a motorcycle and I am awesome.

Seriously, I am so scared. I think I'm going to piss myself.

There are cars. There are cars everywhere. And trucks. There are trucks the size of houses, the size of towns, there are all these cars and all these trucks all going really, really, really fast and I am riding, in the open, without a helmet, on a glorified bicycle in the middle of the highway and I am going to die.

"Please don't kill me," I implore a fifty-foot truck.

"Please, please don't kill me," I beg the murderous sports cars.

"Please don't kill me. Please don't kill me. Please don't kill me, I'm a rock star, I matter, I am essential, you care, don't kill me."

At last (oh blessed, blessed, sweet, sweet mercy) I turn off the main road, when an exit promises the mythic land of "Woodstock, NY."

This is where it all happens.

"Come on," says Bob Dylan's voice in my head. "Hit the gas, man. Hit the fucking gas. You gotta go faster! You can't be self-destructive at twenty-five miles an hour!"

I press on the gas, increase my speed to nearly forty miles per hour, and wobble down the two-lane road toward Woodstock. A minivan speeds by, swerves into the opposite lane to get around me, and leaves me in its dust.

"God, you're such a fuckin' pussy!" I imagine Bob Dylan throwing back his head to laugh at me. "I can't believe anyone ever thought you were a rock star!"

"Shut up!"

"Why don't you just get a real job? Go home and get a real job." He rolls his eyes. Bored with me, he examines his sunglasses.

Half of my brain wonders along with Dylan why I haven't yet gone home and gotten a normal job with a suit and a steady paycheck and no obligation to flirt madly with death, but I ignore that half. Instead I turn the dial up on the part of my brain that knows I am a glorified hero figure, the hard-bitten wanderer of America. Determinedly, I picture flames and guitars and naked women and my photo on the cover of *Rolling Stone*. I am self-destructive. I am. You'll see. I press the gas, fingers curled white like I'm choking something. I bite my bottom lip hard enough that my mouth is full of blood when the bike lands.

Adrenaline pumps its addictive wings through my body between muscle and bone, and the bike reels, tilting, unsteady, from one side to the other. I come toward a curve in the road, one of those with no discernable midpoint that seem to slide sideways forever in an interminable half-moon.

Oh shit.

I've seen pictures of where old friends and groupie-historians surmise that Dylan's crash might have occurred, a bend in the road, overgrown with summer-lush new England weedy grass, hung with sleepy shading trees, a metal guard-rail curvaceous and slightly dented, the grass tufting its way onto the road, negotiating to gravel the border between pavement and woodland. I can't just crash anywhere. I have to crash at an overgrown, shaded, guard-railed obscure bend in the road on my way to Woodstock. The closer I get to where the curve becomes explicit in the road, the clearer it is that if this is not where Dylan's legendary crash occurred, it is certainly the uncanny twin of every photograph I've ever seen of the event's location. One part of my brain, the one resolutely thinking of guitars and flames and naked women and the cover of *Rolling Stone* triumphantly yells, "You found it you found it you found it!" But my body and my logical, educated self have never been less happy about anything. Because I found it, and that means now I have to crash the motorcycle.

2

I come up on the edge of the curve and start leaning sideways. The guardrail stares me down. "Come on, asshole," it taunts. I know that's what I have to do. Drive straight into it. This is how one crashes a motorcycle. Unless you want to do it the way Dylan did. Do you want to do that? No, I didn't think so. Drive into the railing. Drive into the railing. Drive into the railing.

When Dylan famously crashed his bike, he flew right over the handlebars. In an interview with Sam Shepherd in *Esquire* many years later, he said that he stared into the sun and was blinded by it and, while remembering how he'd been told as a little kid never to look directly at the sun, he panicked, lost control, slammed the brakes too fast which caused the rear wheel to lock, and went flying over the handlebars. The impact when he hit the ground left him with cracked vertebrae and a mild concussion; he was incredibly lucky to have broken neither his neck nor his spine.

Before I got on the bike this morning, I had fully intended to do exactly that. I would ride right into the sun, stare at the sun, go blind, lose control, slam the brakes, fly over the handlebars, crack my vertebrae, and be the next Bob Dylan.

But history, I began to reason as I unsteadily cheated death all morning, never rewrites itself in perfect imitation. Something's always off. Changes in the details denote progress, the mutation of trends from era to era. When Christ comes again, he isn't going to be another skinny, longhaired thirty-three year old.

So I don't *really* have to fly over the handlebars.

And anyway, I can't write the next *Blonde on Blonde* if I'm dead.

Crashing the motorcycle, however, is still imperative. I can do it in a less dangerous way, but I must do it, or slink off into eternal anonymity. I will not be anonymous. I will not move to suburbia and wear a tie and send my children to boarding school. I am going to be the next Bob Dylan, and I am going to crash this motorcycle into this railing, and I am going to do it right now. I put my head down and aim at the railing.

"Salvation, salvation, salvation." I talk to myself as though I were a high school sports coach. "Think of salvation. Self-destruction leads to salvation leads to writing *Blonde on Blonde*. Crash the bike! Drive into the guardrail! Salvation, salvation, salvation!"

I close my eyes, clench my hands around the handlebars, and start to drive toward the guardrail. The high-school coach keeps up the pep talk.

"Speed up! Fast! Crashes happen fast! Rock stars do not drive slowly!"

I slam on the accelerator, but drive right past the long curve in the road. The overhanging trees fall away and a sunlight-soaked field takes over.

Shit.

No one saw. I can do it again. I pull the bike over to the side of the road, but I don't actually stop. I'm pretty sure that if I stop this bike, I will never get back on again. I turn the bike around. I prepare to drive into the guardrail. This time I will do it. It's ok. It's just like bullfighting. It just takes a couple times. It takes a bullfighter a couple times too. Think of bullfighting.

Why bullfighting? I have absolutely no experience with bullfighting!

How the hell is that supposed to make this easier?

I hate my brain. I like my body, and I hate my brain.

It is problematic to like one's body when one is trying to convince oneself to slam it into a metal guardrail going seventy miles per hour on a glorified bicycle. My body has been very good to me over the years. I have little desire to destroy it.

But all I want, all I want in the whole world, is to write *Blonde on Blonde* and more importantly, you see, Bob Dylan dared me to do this. Bob Dylan told me I couldn't write *Blonde on Blonde* and I am going to prove him wrong.

The bike jumps back onto the road and we're racing toward the guard rail, around the curve and here, here's the moment to lose control, fly out spinning beyond my own hands and grabbing knees, turn terrifyingly weightless, let go, let go, let go, come on, let go, it's all you have to do, just let go and it will happen, let go, think of salvation, oh shit.

I pull off the road, having driven past the guardrail again.

Ok. We're just going to keep trying until it works. You could stay here for days, you know, I reprimand myself. It's not like you have anything to do. It's not like you have a band anymore. This is it, Gabriel. Drive into the railing. Drive into the railing. Come on. Think of bullfighting.

Shut up about bullfighting! You are not Ernest Hemingway! You have never even seen a bullfight! Why bullfighting? Why?

From the opposite direction now, I attack the curve with my bike, testing the limits of the road. I bunch my chest and forehead over the handlebars, driving into the reckless wind of the world, and here comes the critical moment and I think *Blonde on Blonde, Blonde on Blonde, Blonde on Blonde, Blonde on Blonde,* salvation, salvation, salvation, salvation, salvation…

Dammit.

The sun-streaked gravel beside the field catches in my tires and flies up like churning water. Don't stop the bike, I remind myself through gritted teeth, don't stop the bike. If you stop the bike you will never start it again. Turn around, try again, and do it right this time. Don't think about bullfighting.

Speeding, again in the other direction, bike humming discarded rubber against the road, disdaining yellow lines, disdaining roadside speed limits, disdaining all of everyone ever and myself first of all, full of massive and powerful disdain for the road and the bike and myself and everyone who's never been brave or careless enough to crash a motorcycle, yes, yes, this is good the disdain is good, this is going to work, ok here's the railing, drive, drive, drive, drive…

It was the closest one yet. Maybe it's going by degrees. Maybe I just have to build up to it (Like bullfighting.) (Shut up!). I got near enough that I could see the dents in the metal, it rose up toward my face, and then at the last moment I decided that I like my face better than I like rock 'n' roll immortality. I wrenched the bike away so quickly that I almost did crash, reeling like a drunk trying to walk a straight line across both lanes until I settled at last in the shade-wet gravel here, the bike twitching because if I stop the bike I will never start it again. So I'm driving in ever yet smaller circles, like a nervous hand gesture, getting ready to go again. This time. This time it will work. I clench my teeth. I feel sick to my stomach. I'm getting a headache. And a sunburn. This is all getting profoundly uncomfortable. Sweat sticks the back of my shirt to my shoulders. I need to crash this motorcycle now. I need this part to be done.

*Blonde on Blonde* is such a good album that I can't even listen to it anymore. Whenever I put it on and "Rainy Day Woman No.s 12 & 35" starts, I feel sick with aching nausea because I didn't write it. Dylan already wrote it. I can't ever have written it because Dylan got there first. I haven't listened to *Blonde on Blonde* once since my band started to get successful. I take it everywhere with me, but I haven't played it in a year. I try and it hurts too much. I clench my teeth and my eyes water. I pick at my skin. So I leave the album on the floor of my car, on night tables in hotel rooms, on shelves and on top of speakers, and it taunts me. It sits there like a vulture, huge and silent and threatening. "Do something about me, motherfucker," it whispers. "Do something."

I think of Dylan's blurry photo in brown and blue on the album cover, looking like a delinquent Jewish school child, wearing that stupid scarf, and I start the bike again. Something has to be done. And anyway, I probably won't break my face. Or my neck. Or crack my vertebrae. I bet I can actually aim at the guardrail, if I really concentrate, so that I avoid my face completely. My arms, too, my arms are important. Maybe I can just break an ankle or something. I'll try to hit the railing with an ankle; an ankle wouldn't be so bad. In fact, I bet I can do this without getting seriously injured at all. I don't actually have to break anything in order to have a revelation. Often people get in crashes and have to go to the hospital but don't sustain any injuries. Ok, here it goes.

Except I never speed up because the bike's rearview mirror turns all red and blue and white and sure enough, there's a police car slowing down behind me. I putter right by the guardrail, which had been so ready to oblige me and my legend, and pull off to the side of the road.

This is perfect. This fixes everything. The policeman pulls up alongside me. I wait for him to get out of the car. He'll slam his door and he'll level all sorts of charges at me, he'll be puffed up on his false adulthood, and in my broken-down leather jacket, my chaotic hair, my smudged, hard-lined face, I will squint up at him with all the half-stoned (I put a hand in my pocket to check. Yes, I am in fact carrying marijuana right now) disdain of American youth deluded of its own immortality and I will not agree to anything he says. I will be difficult and taciturn and incoherent and he will grow flustered and angry and arrest me for many things and, yes, this will be an even better legend. This is much better than the motorcycle crash. The motorcycle crash has been done. I'll be arrested, and someone will have to come and break me out of jail. The story will circulate, and I'll tell people, "Salvation. When I broke out of that jail up near Woodstock after being arrested for false charges, that's what it was, it was salvation, and that's how I wrote this album." No, wait! I won't have my friends break me out of jail. I will go to jail, and stay in jail and write my album in jail. This is brilliant. This is ultimately bohemian and ultimately American. People won't just compare me to Dylan; they'll compare me to Thoreau and to the Beat Poets. I will become canonical, obnoxious graduate students will write their dissertations about me, kids everywhere will wear "FREE GABRIEL SHAW" T-Shirts, and—

The policeman rolls down his window and leans out, friendly and unconcerned.

"Hey kid," he says, "Put your helmet on, ok?"

And he drives away down the road before I can protest.

My mouth opens and closes like an aquarium-bound fish. "WAIT!" I yell, "POT! I had marijuana in my pocket! Look, it's illegal, look!" I take out the small plastic bag and wave it at the back of his car. He doesn't notice, or at least he doesn't care. The car goes around a bend and I can't see it anymore.

It begins to get dark while I stand, caught motionless between the bike and the guardrail. I become aware that I've stopped the bike. "You knew what would happen if you stopped the bike." I stare at the guardrail, but it wants nothing to do with me. I've failed at this legend. Dylan: 1. Gabriel: 0. And now I have to ride this ridiculous thing all the way back to the city. I unhook my helmet and put it on. The cop was right, after all. Helmets are important.

Salvation is a great word, and a better concept. It sounds like exactly the kind of thing about which you'd write a rock 'n' roll record. It'd be a nice thing to have if you could buy it with a credit card and store it on a shelf near a desk, take it to the studio with you in your backpack or tape it to your guitar case. But it's what comes before salvation that's the bitch of it. The problem is that you have to be saved from something. And with all the time I've spent being a rock star, I've still never quite gotten the hang of self-destruction.

I miss my car. It's the only thing I can really think: I miss my car. God I miss my car. I think none of this would be happening if my car were still alive. I think everything that's happened since my car died is only because I don't have that car anymore.

Bob Dylan never had a car. He had a motorcycle. I settle into self-loathing as the highway follows the day's failing light back into the city.

3

I should tell you that this is all Amsterdam's fault.

The day the band broke up, I got very drunk and ended up at the international terminal of John F. Kennedy airport. I stood in the airport, wearing a huge pair of sunglasses I couldn't remember having put on, and stared at the "Departures" board.

London, Geneva, Prague, Dublin, Paris, Budapest, Vienna, Cairo, Sydney.

No, no, no, no, no, no, no. No. Uh-uh. No.

Then the word "Amsterdam" appeared in little green letters. That's a good idea, I thought.

I had absolutely no reason to be in Amsterdam, but I had a credit card in my backpack. My band had broken up. Our tour was cancelled. Our album was cancelled. Everything that I had planned to do for the rest of my life was cancelled. So I got on a plane for Amsterdam, a place where rock stars are supposed to go.

I checked into a very expensive hotel and got directly to doing absolutely nothing. I turned off my phone. I stopped wearing socks. I stopped brushing my hair. Sounds became faint. I wondered, idly, if the tour had left me partly deaf. I didn't talk to anyone. I wore the same pants for ten days. I stopped wearing underwear. It was great. Maybe I'll just stay in Amsterdam forever, I thought.

After a couple weeks, bills began to accumulate under my hotel room door. But it's not like they were real. I shrugged at them. I made collages and sloppy origami creatures out of them. My hotel phone started to accumulate messages. I regarded the red, blinking light on the phone as a night-light. The light was there to keep away the monsters. It helped me sleep.

From a corner of the hotel room, my guitar looked at me as though it were a demanding old girlfriend. I decided I had never seen it before and had no idea what it was.

"Who are you?" I asked it. "What do you want? Go home!" I shooed it with my hand, convincing myself as I did so of the instrument's autonomous nature: It had brought itself here, and therefore must be capable of leaving on its own if encouraged correctly. "Go home! Leave my hotel room! Go!" It glared at me. I glared right back.

I wandered around the city. I got drunk in the street. I got high in cafes. I never smiled. I listened to Lou Reed all the time, and knew that I was the only other person in the world who had ever really known what Lou Reed was talking about.

Basically, now that I no longer had a band and was no longer playing music, I felt more like a rock star than I had in my entire life.

The TV in my room got American cable, and although one bill had promised (before I'd cut it with toenail scissors into a paper-chain of Christmas elves), that it would soon be turned off if I continued not to pay for it, as yet no one had made good on that promise.

So it was about three in the morning, I guess. I'll call it three in the morning. So it's three in the morning and I'm in my hotel room in Amsterdam. And at three in the morning in Amsterdam, a VH-1 special on Bob Dylan comes on TV.

Bob Dylan just doesn't like people. He's always been unconcerned with consistency or truth in interviews. If he's in a good mood, he uses them to fuck with people. If he's in a bad mood, he insults the interviewer. But he's more famous than just about anybody, so magazines and TV stations and determined, terrified journalists keep on interviewing him. I imagine that to the person on the other end, a Bob Dylan interview is kind of like a bullfight. You go in knowing that you're probably going to get gored by the bull, and at least you're going to get very injured. But if you survive, you can tell people for the rest of your life, "I was in a bullfight."

I really have no idea when this thing with bullfights started.

So some stuttering brat, who can't possibly be out of college yet, is trying to ask Dylan about his career and his latest album.

"So...um...ok, so like...are you..." I think the kid's going to pee. I keep watching because I want to see this kid pee in fear all over Bob Dylan. Then I start coughing and when I stop, the kid is still trying to ask Dylan a coherent question. He hasn't peed yet, but that's just luck "...your, um... tour, um...what, um, you know, um, did you...did you, you know, have a reason..." he grabs the question and hangs on for dear life. "For-the-tour-did-you-have-a-reason-for-it-what-was-it?"

"No." The kid looks terrified. He stares blankly until Dylan elaborates, "No, there's never a reason for a tour, you know, you just go on tour."

Dylan's disdain is pure genius.

"I wanna be disdainful," I mumble in a sloppy voice. I ash my cigarette on the carpet. "Fuck, it got on the carpet," I observe out loud and don't clean it up.

The kid tries again. "Well, um, your, um, new, um, album, um, is it, um…"

"The album's just an album. I don't have to justify it. Not to you."

Now I think the kid might throw up. That'd be even better. He manages to get words, rather than vomit out of his mouth. I'm intensely disappointed.

"Well…uh…ah…are there any…ah…new…ah…rock artists who you, um, you know, um, like?"

Dylan looks straight out of the screen and right at me. My brain thumps like a heart.

"I hate Gabriel Shaw," he says.

"I'm sorry, who?" The interviewer asks.

"Gabriel fuckin' Shaw. Gabriel motherfuckin' Shaw, what a total pussy, right?"

"I am NOT!" I yell.

"You are TOO!" The kid turns his head to reprimand me, and then turns back to Dylan.

"Yeah," Dylan continues, "First of all, his band has such a stupid name. Who would actually call themselves "The Unholy Hipsters?" The whole point of being a hipster is to pretend not to be one. Real hipsters hate hipsters."

"It's a reference!" I yell at him desperately. "Don't you get the reference?!?"

But he just goes on.

"If Gabriel Shaw were a real rock star, which he's not—"

"AM TOO!!" I yell.

"You are NOT!" Dylan and the kid answer in unison this time. I hate the stupid kid so much. I hate him. I hate him and I bet he has never ever had sex once, not once, not ever, never.

"But Gabriel Shaw—" Bob Dylan just keeps on talking about me. I get up and hide behind the couch, but that doesn't stop him either. "Gabriel Shaw is just a preppy suburban kid who doesn't know the first thing about music. His whole act is so stupid, and that's why his songs are so hollow and so fucking forgettable. He's completely useless! He's a spoiled brat! He's boring! He's never lived! He has nothing to write about, he has never fucking lived. You know what I mean?"

"Of course I do," says the stupid kid with great rabbit-eyed earnestness.

"You know, man," Dylan's getting friendly with the kid now. He seems to be enjoying himself. He reaches out and puts his arm around the kid's shoulders. "You know, it's different with me. I've lived life, right? I never had it easy. I grew up in Duluth, right, and I had to find music on my own and no one helped me and when I came to New York you know I lived on the subway for a week? Yeah, and I've been fucked up and I've loved and lost and gotten my heart broken and I crashed that fucking motorcycle in Woodstock in 1966 and I lived and I mattered. Everything I've done has mattered, man! But Gabriel Shaw has no right to even call himself a musician—"

"Oh, and you do?" I jump up from behind the couch, gather words like a messy pile of dirty clothes and fling them at him. "You can't even sing! You can't sing! You can't sing you can't sing you can't sing! Your voice is terrible! It's awful! Everyone knows it! Everyone knows that you can't sing! Can't sing, can't sing, can't sing!"

Dylan very slowly turns away from the kid and stares at me. Through his enormous out-of-style sunglasses, his three-sizes-too-big suit jacket, and his terrible white-man's-afro hair, he drips disdain.

Literally.

It drips out of the screen in big sticky amber drops; it forms a river down from the television, over the mini bar, and spreads across the carpet toward me. "And who's going to clean that up now?" My mother's righteously indignant voice asks.

"Mo-o-o-om..." I whine, batting at her voice with my hands, "Mo-o-o-om, go awa-a-a-a-a-ay..."

"My terrible voice is the very essence of rock and roll..." Dylan tells me. The word "essence" splatters and starts coming toward me out of the TV in another gelatinous river.

"When the fuck did you talk like that?" It's all I can think to say.

"Oh, I'm sorry, let me try again—Yeah, man, it's like, the very fuckin' stuff of, like, rock and roll, man, yeah. Does it make you more comfortable if I talk like this, Gabriel Shaw? I could talk in eighteenth century spondaic metered verse, I could talk in heroic couplets, I could imitate Homer's dactylic hexameter too, you know. Maybe that would make you more comfortable, you studied all that at Yale..."

"Fuck you, I did not go to Yale."

"You did too," says the interviewer brat.

"I did NOT!" I try to pull myself off the floor and stand up to him. But now the TV is very high up above me. I don't know when it got there, but the ceiling has risen to heaven-reaching arches like the ceiling of a Gothic Cathedral and Dylan is on the ceiling, calling down to me in unassailable authority like Michelangelo's God and oh *fuck*.

"You're just such a bad liar, Gabriel. I mean, sure, lie, great. It's all I ever did, but the thing is, I did it well. I knew why I was doing it. I was a goddamn genius at lying. You're just a whiny little amateur, and by the way where's the next album, Gabriel? Yeah, that's right. Where's the next album? And where'd your band go? Why won't your band play with you anymore? Huh? What are you doing with your stupid little life, huh? You drove your band away because you're such a bad musician and such a bad liar. Look at you. When was the last time you picked up that guitar over there?"

Bob Dylan and I look at the guitar in the corner of the room.

"I have no idea what that is or how it got here!" I yell.

"Oh man, you're a fuckin' mess, you stupid little kid. Let me ask you one more time Gabriel: Where. Is. The. Next. Album?"

He stares down at me from the ceiling and waits for an answer but I don't have one.

"Where'd you put it, huh, did'ya lose it, misplace it, some airline lost your luggage, you asshole?" He laughs an enormous big belly laugh, and while he laughs the room spins faster and faster and faster and then rights itself when he stops.

"You want to know why I'm so famous, Gabriel? You want to know why I'm a genius and a rock star and a legend and will never, ever, ever die? I always had another album. You've had one. One! One album hardly counts, that's hardly a scratch, right, dude? Hell, people barely even remember my first album! Where's your *Bringing it all Back Home?* Where's your *Blood on the Tracks*, Gabriel Shaw? When are you gonna revolutionize the form of modern rock music? When are your concerts gonna cause riots? Where's your *Highway 61 Revisited*? Where's your fuckin' *Blonde on Blonde*?"

"I'm—" I try to answer him but he just starts laughing, and the room picks up speed again. It's lifelike and inhabited, the walls crawl and squirm. There are things living in the walls! There are lizards in the walls! The lizards have faces, their faces turn into colors, then into all these reaching, grabbing hands and then it all stops when Dylan stops laughing. The room is just a room, the walls are blank, my stomach is very angry with me and I can't find my cigarette. Bob Dylan is still on the ceiling. He walks, slow and ominous, down the wall as he talks to me.

"What were you gonna say, Gabriel? Were you gonna tell me that you're working on it?"

In fact, that's exactly what I was going to tell him.

"Yeah, *working on it*," he continues as he slides off of the wall, "How long you gonna work on it, huh? You gonna work on it until your money's gone, you gonna work on it until you get a nine to five job and no one remembers that you ever touched a guitar? How long are you gonna be *working on it*? You're not a rock star. You're not a musician. You'll never be immortal. Talk to me when you write "Just Like a Woman." Talk to me when you write "Sad Eyed Lady of the Lowlands." Yeah, how 'bout "Sad Eyed Lady of the Lowlands?" Write that, Gabriel. You go, and you write that, and then maybe we can talk. In fact, I dare you. I dare you, Gabriel Shaw, to write the next *Blonde on Blonde*. You write that, and then you come back and talk to me, why don't you?"

"I'm going to! I am! I'm writing it right now! It's almost finished! Maybe I just don't want to show it to you, Bob Dylan!"

The TV is at once very small, and I am very large, sitting cross-legged in front of it like a kid at sleepover camp. The room's silent and I'm yelling at the television, which is currently playing a rerun of "Friends." I try to turn it off and discover it has no off button. Oh shit.

Bathroom, I decide. Bathroom is the answer.

I get up to walk to the bathroom but the room shifts, spins and evades me. I know the bathroom was closer than this. I'm walking down a very long hallway. The hallway has a low ceiling, is made of stone and lined with blazing torches in wall sconces. I am going to call management. This is definitely not the room I'm paying for.

"Well, maybe you should have paid all those bills..." My mother's voice drifts down the hallway. She floats along right next to my ear. I slap at her like a mosquito.

There's a door at the end of the hallway. I recognize the door. It's the door to my hotel bathroom. Bathroom. I found the bathroom. I found the bathroom and now everything will be OK.

I reach for the handle but the door is barred by two large men.

"I'd like to ask you to elaborate on a certain paper you wrote during your senior year at Yale." The man who spoke is very short and very beautiful. He has curly brown hair and a Caesar hairline and looks very familiar and oh shit, is that—

"Gabriel," says the other man, "What did we tell you about doing drugs?"

"Dad?" The other man is my dad. He's wearing a tuxedo.

"Dad, is that—"

"Answer the question, young man!" says the first man. He walks toward me. Actually, he limps toward me. He has a limp and yes, ok, now I'm sure that—

"Dad, is that Lord Byron?"

"Oh yes," my dad says. He pushes his glasses up his nose "That's Lord Byron. We're lovers."

"MOM!!!!" I yell. Lord Byron is also wearing a tuxedo. My dad and Lord Byron start making out. My Mom does not appear.

"Bathroom," I say very slowly, in a determined voice. "Bathroom." I jab my finger at the door in sticky slow motion.

"Oh, all right then," says my dad. He and Lord Byron stand back and allow me to open the door. Inside, the hotel bathroom is unchanged. It might be the most reassuring thing I've ever seen. Then, with a sound like an enormous gust of wind, the door swings shut as I hear Lord Byron yell,

"Gabriel Shaw, I LOVE YOU! I LOVE YOU! I LOVE YOU!"

The door slams behind me. The room is empty and still. I throw myself at the toilet. Everything I've eaten for the past month pours out my mouth into the toilet in a wrenching, streaming flood. I cling to the porcelain edges of the toilet bowl, as though my face had fallen off and were swimming like a goldfish below me, free of the tyranny of my body. This seems to go on for hours. At some point, cool hands reach down and pull my hair back from my face. The hands rub over my back in gentle, hypnotic circles. When I stop vomiting, they rest, comforting, and then slide slowly away. Panting, I look up for the owner of the hands.

There's a red-haired woman sitting on the counter above the toilet, wearing tight jeans, playboy bunny ears, and a "FREE GABRIEL SHAW" t-shirt. She straddles the toilet's back as though it were a motorcycle, and looks down at me lovingly.

"God, you were bad in bed," she says, and then she throws her head back and laughs and laughs and laughs.

‡ ‡ ‡

The next morning the hotel informs me that my TV service, along with all other amenities, was cut off three days ago after my failure to pay any of my bills. They also explain that my behavior was becoming an embarrassment to their establishment, and could I please pay my bills and get the fuck out of their hotel?

The hotel manager is so well groomed and dressed that it hurts to look at him. It's some disgusting, bright hour of the morning. My head throbs.

My skin aches. I wrap myself around the edge of the door. He looks down his nose at me.

"Anyway, I've been sent to ask you to pay these bills promptly and then vacate our establishment. We request that you do both these things as quickly as possible." I squint at him. I really want a cigarette. What time is it? "Now, Mr. Shaw. Right now, please."

"But I'm a rock star—" I mutter, voice edging into a whine.

"Who and what you are is immaterial, Mr. Shaw, except that at the moment you are a disruptive individual who owes our establishment a great deal of money. And anyway," he says, and I could swear he smiles, "Didn't I read that your band broke up last month?"

I glare at him, and go to find my credit card.

That very day, after repeating "rock star, rock star, rock star, rock star, rock star," under my breath in order not to panic as I signed away an amount of money which would be impolite to enumerate, I took a plane to New York, determined that the first thing I'd do when I got back would be to crash a motorcycle.

# Interview with Anita Nair

*William Wolak*

*Anita Nair was born on January 26, 1966, in Mundakottakurissi, near Shornur in the Indian state of Kerala. She grew up in Chennai (Madras). After studying English language and literature in college, she worked as a copywriter and journalist. In 1989, she moved to Bangalore and worked as an advertising agency's creative director. At that time, she began writing short stories which were later to be published as her first book entitled* Satyr of the Subway. *Her early writing earned her a fellowship at the Virginia Center for Creative Arts. Over the next several years, she turned her attention to writing novels. Her first one,* The Better Man, *appeared in 1999, and it was followed by* Ladies Coupé *in 2001 and* Mistress *in 2005. She published her first selection of poetry entitled* Malabar Mind *in 2002. In addition, she has written several children's books and edited a book of travel writing about Kerala. Currently, she lives in Bangalore with her husband and son.*

*William Wolak conducted the following interview in Anita Nair's home on July 19, 2006, while he was in India on a Fulbright-Hays fellowship.*

**NDR**: How many languages do you speak?

**AN**: Five. I speak Hindi, Tamil, Malayalam, Kannada, and English.

**NDR**: Which language do you consider your "mother tongue"? By that I mean which language did you speak with your family when you were growing up?

**AN**: My family was bilingual. I speak English and Malayalam about the same.

**NDR**: Why have you chosen to write in English?

**AN**: Primarily, because that was the language that I grew up with, the language I studied, the language that I heard. Secondly, I love the language; I mean I just love English.

**NDR**: What percentage of the Indian population read English for pleasure?
**AN**: A really small percentage. I mean I could be horribly wrong, but say

maybe ten percent.

**NDR**: Are you considered "unauthentic" or "un-Indian" because you've chosen to write in English?

**AN**: Now this is a question I would need to elaborate on. What causes this aspect of being "un-Indian?" The thing is, in India, you do have an image of what an Indian ought to be like, or an Indian poet, or an Indian writer. And it could be just physical traits; it could be the way you look, the way you are, and so forth. And the moment you break away from that, immediately you are suspect. So because of that, I am suspect to a certain extent. Now to the question of "unauthentic;" I think, initially, when my books first arrived, there was that question. I mean, "What does she know about India?" I didn't have to say too much because my books spoke for themselves. And the literary establishment could see that. I write about rural India; I write about suburban India. Whereas, most Indians writing in English write about urban India. So, it can't get more authentic. The acid test, of course, has been that my books are usually published in India first. So the critics here and the readers here will not allow anything that is remotely unauthentic to get past them. So in that sense, that test has taken care of the question of authenticity; that's no problem. But I did have that problem when I began writing.

**NDR**: Have your works been translated from English into any of the other Indian languages?

**AN**: Yes, my works have been translated into two or three other Indian languages: Malayalam, Marathi, and Hindi. Mostly the novels, not poetry. Some poetry has been translated into Malayalam.

**NDR**: How do you conceive of the poet's role in India today?

**AN**: There isn't a role at all.

**NDR**: As a poet, do you feel like an insider or an outsider in India?

**AN**: I feel like an outsider.

**NDR**: Are poets respected in India?
**AN**: Poets are respected, but seldom read.

**NDR**: The title poem of the book "Malabar Mind" establishes the tone of the book. It has as its setting the spice laden, rain soaked, emerald green shores of Kerala in southern India. How would you describe this poem?

**AN**: That's actually like a historical document of Malabar because it brings in various bits of history as well as contemporary life there.

**NDR**: There's a brief footnote to the poem; could you speak a little bit about what you mean by "Malabar Mind" and the historical context of what was once known as the Malabar coast or district?

**AN**: You see, Malabar actually referred to a section of the western coast of India. And when the British came, they had what they called the principality of Madras which included Malabar. So Malabar was a geographical place; it was a geographical destination. It had a map; it had boundaries. But after Independence, they divided the country into states on a linguistic basis, and so Malabar was assimilated into what is Kerala now. With that assimilation, Malabar as a place ceased to exist. So now it's really something that's alive only in the oral tradition. People say, oh, you're from Malabar, aren't you, because that's the way you speak. Also, what it means is that Malabar was a place that was traditionally open to the sea but closed by land. So it had a lot of influences from the rest of the world, but no influences from the rest of the country of India. Which is why Kerala is a kind of very strange place for most people who come from outside of India. People ask why is this place so different from the rest of the country? And it's simply because it was inaccessible by land till about a hundred and fifty years ago. And the other thing, of course, is that in Malabar probably because of the weather and because of the abundance of natural wealth, there is a certain attitude that people have. It's a very laid-back attitude in which you live and let live. They're not a very proactive sort of people. Whereas, in comparison the people of the southern part of Kerala were very different. That was a land where people had to work to cultivate; they had to persevere and fight with the land to make it yield. So they tend to be hard working; they tend to be aggressive; they tend to be go-getters. Whereas, traditionally Malabar is a kind of laid-back principality more than anything else. And that mind set exists to this day in people from there. You tend to be a little easy; you tend to allow people to come and make themselves at home. So it's a kind of mind set which allots things inwards and doesn't expect too much, you know, in terms of giving in return. Which is what I wanted to play upon in

*Malabar Mind* because in some sense many of these poems are about invasions and acceptance. And it's about letting things go. For instance, even in a poem like "You Said, I Agreed" or if you take a poem like "The Face Mask," there are so many examples where it's not a question of someone who stands up and fights; it's about someone who allows things to happen.

**NDR**: The title poem "Malabar Mind" also juxtaposes a lush sensuality in lines like "She licks his eyes and wills him/ To take her in rhythmic ecstasy..." with a lurking undercurrent of madness in lines like "In his eyes, the lunatic gleam."; "Look at this girl, the lunatic stares..."; "Madness threatens to erupt at any time."; and "Courage and the soft breeze/ Will cure madness, they say." Is that the feeling that you are trying to convey; that people are always on the brink?

**AN**: I think so, all the time. And these are some factual details: Kerala has the highest number of suicides, and its madhouses are absolutely overflowing. You have the highest literacy in Kerala, but you have the highest unemployment rate as well. It probably has to do with the high level of awareness, which is what I've said. How can you be content once you know your rights? The moment you know your rights, then you are demanding that they be met.

**NDR**: Do you feel a "weight of tradition" when you're writing as an Indian poet? Let me tell you where this question comes from; here, in *Malabar Mind* there is a poem entitled "The Cosmopolitan Crow;" in section two of that poem, one persona says the following: "She didn't understand/ How can she? Of what it is/ to be anchored by a thousand year old tradition." Do you feel this weight when you write like an "anchor of tradition?"

**AN**: No, I don't. It's just the persona speaking. That person speaking is the Mother Crow, and she feels that way.

**NDR**: Are you a materialist? This question is derived from the same poem as above where is says: "How can they live like this?/ Content to be thought of/ as transmigrated souls of human ancestors." Is that a persona speaking or are you commenting on Indian tradition?

**AN**: No, that's partially me speaking. One thing that I constantly find myself having to fight against is this Indian cultural tradition which allows karma to rule. It's a very fatalistic attitude. And I've always tried very hard to go against that. You can't dictate to destiny, but perhaps you can persuade it to slow a bit.

**NDR**: So how do you conceive of the self then if you don't believe in atman, karma, or dharma?

**AN**: No, I believe in all of that, but I also believe in the human spirit. And, I think, for me the balance is to find that point where both merge harmoniously rather then letting one preside over the other.

**NDR**: So you believe that individuals determine their own freedom?

**AN**: Oh, absolutely. In fact, I believe in freedom to such an extent that in all my works of fiction that theme keeps resonating again and again. If there is a choice between society and the individual, it is always the individual.

**NDR**: Are there any obstacles to being published related to gender today?

**AN**: No.

**NDR**: Are there any obstacles to being published related to caste today?

**AN**: No.

**NDR**: Is globalization making life easier for women in India?

**AN**: I'm not so sure if it's making it easier because what happens is that with globalization you know what the available avenues are; you know what the things are that you can do, you know what are the things that women all over the world are doing. And it does take a little bit out of the person living here when you realize that in some ways society in India still expects a woman to fulfill all her traditional roles, which means that she has to put some of her desires on the back burner.

**NDR**: Could you explain a little more about an Indian woman's traditional role?

**AN**: Well, we do have the religious texts and the oral traditions which are probably more powerful than any sermon or any kind of religious dictate written now. Because from the time a woman is born, the women in her family go on about how you have to do this, otherwise when you grow up your husband's not going to approve, and your in laws are not going to be happy. So somewhere in you, you're very slowly and meticulously being brainwashed about the kind of roles that you have to fulfill as an adult woman. And these roles have to do with being a good wife, being a good mother, a good daughter-in-law, a good daughter, a good aunt, and all the family roles that you are expected to play. Nowhere is there any kind of space allocated for being a good woman. A woman per se. A woman is always perceived from a paternal or masculine viewpoint. So, in that sense, a woman has desires of her own; she has dreams of her own. Usually, she's told that either she can try and marry her desires for the common good around her, or if it's not possible to marry her desires, then she puts them on the back burner. I constantly hear women saying, oh, I was waiting for my children to grow up in order to start doing this, or I was waiting for my family to settle down, so that I could do this. So there is a kind of censorship that is self inflicted rather than inflicted by the society.

**NDR**: The society gives you a certain role, and it's difficult to find a way out of it?

**AN**: One of the things is that the society in India has a very crucial role to play. The society and family. One thing is that we don't have is a social service scheme. The family actually works like a social service scheme in the sense that if you are in trouble, it's the family that comes in to support you. If there is trouble in the marriage, the family becomes the mediators. All kinds of things are covered this way. If there is a death in the family, they provide a home for you. So there are very few people who would stand up against the family because that would mean being ostracized. Not many people have that kind of courage to say, okay, I don't care; I'll just live my life the way I want.

**NDR**: How did you go about finding a space for your creativity? I mean, how did you establish a zone and the time required to do your creative work?

**AN**: Well, one thing, of course, is that I am fortunate in having a family that is not so didactic and nor do they impose themselves on me. But, also, it involved a great deal of compartmentalization where I had to carve out bits of the day for myself and keep them sacrosanct; so that they were completely inviolable in that sense. It isn't easy, it wasn't easy, it still isn't easy.

**NDR**: Do you work? Do you have a job?

**AN**: Not any more.

**NDR**: Let me ask you a question concerning relationships prompted by a passage in your poem entitled "Lullaby." The passage reads, "Neglect is a habit you need to learn young; Or, like me, in the downy confines of your bed/ You'll have to let yourself be held, caressed and even subjugated; A kind of whore, I trade my body/ So that at night, I don't have to dream alone." What does this passage say about Indian relationships?

**AN**: Well, you see mostly these are arranged marriages. In some sense, these are marriages where you trade one set of things for another. For instance, you give your time, your body, and pretty much your energies into running a man's home, keeping him happy, and stuff like that. And, in turn, you know that you are going to be taken care of for the rest of your life because usually marriage in India is forever. Divorce is really not common. So it's very much like barter, and it resembles very much a business relationship. In that sense, there is no room for feelings. I mean that is a very cynical way of looking at it perhaps. I must have been in a very cynical frame of mind when I wrote it. So it is about saying don't expect more than you're going to get anyway; because if you do, then you're going to be unhappy. But you learn this as a woman in India. Concerning children, for example, females are always neglected when compared to the males. It's something you have to learn; otherwise, you're constantly going to be saying, why am I being treated like this? Then you end up feeling like a victim or a martyr.

**NDR**: May I ask, related to the quotation above, whether your marriage was a love marriage or an arranged marriage?

**AN**: It was a love marriage.

**NDR**: Can you elaborate a little bit about how India has changed?

**AN**: In the last ten years, I think the change that has taken place in the country has been amazing. Everything has changed, you know, the way people live, the kind of access we have to various things. The food patterns, the consumption patterns, everything has changed. For instance, I've had family living in the United States ever since the mid 50's. So when they came back, they came back with gifts for us, and these were things that you could never for a moment imagine that you could buy in India. They brought back bottles of whiskey and bourbon, and they brought chewing gum, and they brought toys, and they brought polyester stuff, and things like that. And in India, we still didn't have any of that or it was not available unless you paid a lot of money for it. But now when they come back, they discover that what they bring could be bought here for half the price. Right. So that's just talking of the material changes. But, also, there are changes in the minds. Because one thing that we have is cable television and it is really cheap in India. I mean for a hundred and fifty rupees, which is the equivalent of three dollars, you get one hundred or one hundred and twenty channels into your house. And most homes have television, or at least there is a community television. So you see how the rest of the world lives. You might not adapt it into your life or even adopt some practices. So it's not as if we are the people who listened to someone who came back from the West and who first told us about ATMs, and told us about a hole in the wall into which you put your card, and you got money out of it. That was like a miracle. Not any more. Because we have ATMs here, all these things are here now. Things have changed so much, and particularly in the past ten years because the government has adopted a very liberal policy about import, and things are sold here. People are going abroad and studying. Earlier, perhaps about ten or fifteen years ago, you never heard about people traveling abroad on work or for pleasure. Now if you go to the airport, everybody is zipping into the United States, zipping into Europe, into Australia.

**NDR**: That's one thing I've noticed this time in India; almost every Indian I've spoken to knows some one in America; he or she might have an uncle in New York, or something like that. And so there's this connection between India and America that I'm finding more and more.

**AN**: Absolutely, you find that all the time. Like for instance, if you were to take a flight out of Bangalore, the flights are packed; you have to book months in advance. Everyone is traveling to either the U.S. or the U.K. or they're going into Europe. It's so difficult to enter a plane and find an empty flight. And these are daily flights.

**NDR**: Do you think the people are benefiting from the kinds of jobs being created by the influx of the multinational corporations?

**AN**: Well, I think typically what happens in countries like this is that the rich get richer and the poor get poorer because the distinctions between rich and poor are becoming so much wider. What is happening is that the upper middle class, for instance, have a lot more money to spend. They have the money to indulge in fineries and luxuries, but these are things that are not so easily affordable. The poor find it impossible to reach those levels. So the distinctions between rich and poor are growing.

**NDR**: Do you have any faith in the ability of the state to ameliorate the conditions of the poor?

**AN**: I think that will happen when we have politicians who are not into politics to make money for themselves. What I've been noticing, not so often, but I see stray cases here and there, is that people with very sound educational backgrounds from good monied families—it's not the rags to riches story—are entering politics. They bring with them the wealth of their education and their experience. And perhaps what they don't bring is greed. In which case, there is a chance that the state will be able to formulate policies which will help the poor rather than formulating policies that benefit themselves and their cronies.

# Pectus Excavatum

*—In Memory of Sara Glosik*

*Derek Mong*

1.

My listening leads
to nothing, his wingbeats so
faint that should I hold

a glass to the glass

I'd catch only brief
rainfall drumming the porch boards.
And so I watch him

twitch between the screen

and the glass pane, moth-
wings written against the flash
of a bug lamp as

it lights up a kill.

2.

When I was twelve the doctor named
my chest and said I would be healthy.

He called it genetic and, smiling
like we had shared a sick joke

blamed my father
for the sternum missing to the right

of my heart. He told me the pallor
meant nothing, cleaned his stethoscope,

left the room. In the evenings
when I can't sleep, I twist bedsheets

into knots and press them against
the groove, muffling the rhythm within.

This chest could double as a sundial.
The shadows pool on my heart.

3.

How quick it must have been:
the windshield blown outward
like confetti, then sprinkling itself,
moonlit and minute
over a neighbor's front lawn—
followed a blink later by her body,
gymnastic, tossing

its weight past the dash
and over the spasm of hood,
the seizured fender, still tumbling
till the headlights like crossed eyes
hone in on her stillness, the slivers
of oak bark and blood. God—
how quick it must have been

4.

before the suburb settled, and the trees
breathed once more. She left only
a turn signal clicking
its cup of fire and a street's length
of porches waking to yellow,
the sound of storm doors
swinging at the hinge. Later the voices—
crawling on their little wounded feet.

5.

When I press my palm
to the window the moth stills
and moonlight goes pale

to my skin. His wings

are veined transparent—
I unbolt the lock and let
the moth flutter in.

Outside another

mosquito sizzles.
The current cracks an angry
note, my room goes blue,

the moth hurls himself

at my chest. My hands
make a loose skin over him—
I count each beat on

the palm of my hand.

The rain pours. The air's
warm. His little wings tremble
like leaves before storm.

# Water Garden Triptych

*Marjorie Stelmach*

**i.**

In the shallows among the water-grasses
where you buried a score of bulbs years back,
fragile roots
have silked out and held,
and lilies have risen again this June,
bobbing in tough, deep-green
encasements
like snake heads convened among the weeds

*—the first dream asks:*
*does a shell-garden dropped in a water glass*
*envision seagulls?*

—among the weeds,
just as you planned when you brought them here,
so far to the north, wrapped carefully,
and everything in doubt;
where at summer's end you left them to the lake – no escape
from the waiting.

Responsive to remote urgings, under water, under ice,
a fertile dark something took hold and longed upward,
dreaming a future,
dreaming:

*a whole-cloth summer, rolled and ready for*
*the cut of costuming:*
*latent dragonflies, water-striders,*
*a cast of virtual minnows, the passing*
*shadows of gulls,*
*a blue stir of lacy photon curtains*

**ii.**

Far to the south,
three aunts planted their dutiful selves
that winter,
descending in planes, bearing resolve,
arranging for school shoes, haircuts, and,
one of them
thinking to lift the sorrow, bringing the gift
of a single clamshell, carefully placed in a water glass
on a bedside table.
We watched it rock to the bottom as slowly
as treasure in a ghost-ship's hold,
and in an equivalent silence.
Obedient children,
we said our prayers and sank
into mothering dreams

*—the second dream plays on a physics of strings:*
*translucent equations, cats' cradles of the ten*
*dimensions, a vision*
*of absences, tucked*
*and guarded*

—sank into dreams
and woke
to vertical gardens of silk and paper, a lurid spread
of petaled dyes—deep reds and purples,
trellised on tap water visibly rife with a chemical glint.
And nothing to do but wait
for the weight and fade, for the bleed.
By mid-day, sodden on its thread, the garden
had shed its colors
into a tube of corrupted sun,
its silks a pool of filthy brown,
burdened by gravity,
bowed.

*—the third dream, too,*
*evades understanding, posits*
*a landscape of lack, vast*
*and so close*
*as to open within us*

**iii.**

They rise this summer among the rushes; a June sun labors
over the Christening:
*Fire Crest, Chromatella, Yuh Ling.*
By noon,
they're a table laid for tea: twenty petal-cups arrayed for twenty
luminous guests;
place-settings of silver, aglint on a cloth
of shimmered tapestry.
Some of them pink on their saucers
as the secret blush of daughters; others
shading to the pearls and mauves
of eyes worn old
from watching the absences widen
through years.
Come dusk,
they're tucked for the night, dreaming
of deepening roots, rich silts, the passing
shadows of wings.

*—a final dream surfaces now, risen*
*from among the dimensions:*
*a three-fold vision containing*
*encasements, a silk of unfoldings, the fertile soils*
*of a lifetime's shadows,*
*a dream of a lasting truth,*
*one*
*to question all visions, decry*
*all poverty of vision.*

# POME

*Gretchen E. Henderson*

*Hit with Cupid's archery,*
*Sink in apple of his eye.*
—William Shakespeare

Here we are, king
in a garden
and I can give you this: flesh
of legend in my hand, an apple. Still
you cannot look me in the eye.
For once, take
this, and listen—not to me, a vagrant
but to seeds in my hand. I will not
bid (like couples did in Attica
sharing a *pome* each nuptial night)
but clasp this fruit to ask:
Did the serpent tempt with a *pome-*
granate? Did Mohammed inhale
eternity by this flushed scent?
What of Daphnis
and Atalanta?
Knowing what's forbidden: I want to
see through the adage, hark-
ening back to Deuteronomy, King
Alfred, *et cetera,* since what matters
is the ability to grasp
history as palpable, as malleable
as us—
prompting you to notice
a detail so intimate (in this vagrant's
flushed eyes)
peering into *pupils* (derived from
*child* and *little corpse,* morphing) to see
a globe spin round this glob.
I see you now, king,

face to face—here we are
in a garden
and all I have is this:
(do you see?)
my own reflection
in your eye.

## Welcome to My Cabaret

*Angie Hogan*

I am that pillow in the couch-corner,
red-faced and ready to lose its tassels.
Those filmy letters from the newspaper
still haunting your green-veined hands—that's me.
Twenty-four colors of countertop, three-inch squares
strung together on a link chain.

I am in your unconscious
pretty little head. Buy a few
drinks; put a buck or two in the band
of my rabbitless fedora.

A mouse with a Butterfinger
wrapper rustling through the dark,
I am the tricks
up my own unbuttoned sleeve:
a voice,
a one-man show.

*Stay awhile, one more cup of coffee,*
welcome, I'm your host.

# English with Subtitles

—After *The Lovers on the Bridge*

*Angie Hogan*

And sometimes I just want a postcard,
him to air mail a sad Renoir—
*I miss buttering your thighs,*
something eventful—*Le Mistral*
*doesn't pipe without you.*

There is nothing like the night
we didn't speak—couldn't—
but let the flick of our fingers, Paris
lights illuminating the river, the room.

A two-way *tu es:* his because
I didn't understand what came after,
mine because *you are, you are* is all
I could think to.

Sometimes I want to begin in the middle.

And wouldn't he say *you have something,*
letting the thing be mine? And
wouldn't my words be more to him, more
*croissant crumbs in the pubes*?

Loic,
Say *I want to paint the shutters*
*blue with you. The grapes are big as plums*
*this year.* Say *I don't love you anymore.*

I want it plainly.
I want it unsigned.
Sometimes I want to start
in the middle, a sad Renoir, *je ne...*
eyes slurring, flutter, lash.

# *FROM* THE ALMANAC

*Chi Elliott*

## December

Mark the dwindling year (1941)
by rationing rubber.
Or building an A-frame shrub castle
of old 2x4s and ties
to protect the plants from frost.
A rose, maybe. A yew.

Blame it on the full moon
on the $25^{th}$ minute
of the $19^{th}$ hour
of the $4^{th}$ day.
Or on the meteorite that fell
in Weston, Connecticut in 1807.
Everything starts with brass tacks
and ends with ice.

December's cold air
stopping Big Ben.
December's Ember Day
twice in a row.
It's thirteen words
for snow, you know
one of them.

**January**

It helps to restrict the gaze,
to have a method for looking and averting.
So focus: on Elara, one of Jupiter's moons,
discovered in 1905. On a saying:
*Love, cough, and smoke can't be well hid.*

Too many things on this page:
the first successful caesarian
in America in 1794, waves ranging
from 8.6 to 10.1 feet
on Plough Monday.
Dates, feasts, fasts,
aspects, and tide heights.
And because you suspect
your brother of intemperance,
and your boss of whimsy,
turn to the handwriting section;
ponder the letter O.
It looks more certain
with a fully closed top
and no extra loops.

Believe me when I tell you
about the rain coming in April.
When to plant the peas,
and how deep.
Believe me when I tell you
that it was the 12$^{th}$
when William Tell
hit the apple.
Because his son stood there,
stock still.

## February

*ask me the name of the moon in the man.*
—e. e. cummings "27"

To keep him, it's good luck
to wear blue, new things.
And money—to hide it near the foot.
Good luck to wear something
you'd like to steal.

Saturday the 4th is auspicious for weddings.
And on the 27th the moon
will be as close as it gets,
a mere 217,000 miles,
an extreme perigee.

My friend says to avoid green towels
so my husband (if I had him)
won't cheat.
She also says not to touch
the straws of a broom.

Moon: to behave in an idle,
dreamy, abstracted way,
as when in love.
Moonshine: smuggled whiskey;
foolish, idle talk.

There's a snow moon on the 12th,
when Abe Lincoln was born,
a full moon on the 23rd hour,
44 minutes into
the 43rd day of the year.

# A Brief Biography of Pieter Claesen

*Elizabeth Klise von Zerneck*

In the painting, the snow descends
on the house of Pieter Claesen
of Breuckelen, while outside the snow descends
on my Brooklyn house too. Pieter Claesen
was born during the last days of the Holy Roman Empire,
and moved to New Amersfoort after leasing
land for years from the Rensselaer patroonship.
That's about as much as we know about
the crisscross of his life, and I won't bore
you with the crisscross of mine. Suffice it
to say that neither Pieter Claesen
nor I lives in those houses anymore.
What I want to note here is how—once—both
of us wore our houses like bodies.
How astonishing that there exists a painting to recall it all:
the splendid, shouldered roof, the bright army of windows,
the broad ribcage of façade,
and how heartening to see that when the snow fell,
for a short while,
the house stood
and took it.

# ATHENS

*Elizabeth Klise von Zerneck*

The fact that the ancient Greeks
and Romans used buttons,
but that buttonholes were not
invented until the thirteenth century—
that is what I'm thinking about tonight.

I have pondered this notion
far longer than I'm willing to admit,
trying to find the metaphor.
I have sat here, considering what a name
derived from both rosehip and thrust
might imply. And how it would feel
to be traded as currency, one
among many in a cotton sack.

Or something about how a piece of horn
sewn onto wool is like simplicity.
And how—like propriety—a brass button
might be lashed to a blazer cuff.
And how the march of pearl buttons
down a dress could exemplify comfort.
Or conformity.

I have toyed with the idea of a person
coming undone over time,
come loose somehow, or lost—
like beauty coupled with age, perhaps—
threads fraying and long, unraveling.

I've thought about how to relate all this
to the notion of heaven,
or the onset of autumn,
or that complicated thing between us.

Tonight, whatever comparisons I make,
nothing seems to catch. And maybe it
won't for years. Not
without a buttonhole.

# "Writing Poetry After Auschwitz is Barbaric"

—Theodor Adorno

*Steve Rood*

At Montpellier, in 1552, the Inquisitor of the Faith
burned students of theology at the stake.
Felix studied shapes of leaves and flowers there,
(keeping his religion to himself) and pressed
herbs into books for drying. Searched out natural
affinities and uses, accidents and essences.
Outside the walls, people were hung on gibbets
and wheels. Or trussed with straw for the fire.
Felix gathered pomegranate blossoms.
Sustained himself on his memory of the beauty
of horehound and woundwort, purple-crested
cow wheat, henbane and agrimony. Even as a student,
he joined the great plantsmen—Theophrastus,
Ghini, Cesalpino, Turner, Gesner, Johnson, Ray—
forward and back across the centuries,
and the lovely gardens of exotics from the Levant.
All the men delighting together in tulips,
while the world collapsed on them, again and again.
In 1696, John Ray, isolated in his Essex cottage,
legs covered in sores, which he bathed
in a mixture of dock root and chalk,
invented the word at last, growing
from its Greek root, the word to describe
2000 years of labor, and to supplant
*planta, stirpium, res herbaria.* Botany.

# THE QUALITY OF THE AFFECTION

*Steve Rood*

I don't hear the Scarlatti I'm playing.
Slow it down, I tell myself. Otherwise
it's no better than TV in the next room.
Which keeps me from loneliness a little,
but why waste the music that way?
Why bother to hold this fragrant guitar—
mine since I opened the case in my grandmother's
knotty pine den when I was thirteen—
trembling and warm against my stomach?
Why, if not to watch the music in the dark
while it sleeps, breathing quietly?
Why, if not to stare at it like my son's face
when I'm taking an eyelash out of his eye?
Why, if not to have breakfast with it,
and talk for hours, until we say "Basta,"
and then stroll by the river
where kids are swimming with dogs,
and a young woman asks if we are father and son?
Why, if not to use it to call the owl down from the wires?
Why if not to sit in it, a small boat, loose,
without oars or sails, rocking on the swells of a clear sea?

# Interview with A.M. Homes

*Jaclyn Dwyer*

*A.M. Homes was born in Washington D.C. in 1961. She graduated from Sarah Lawrence College and earned her MFA from the Iowa Writers' Workshop. She is the author of the novels,* This Book Will Save Your Life *(2006),* Music for Torching *(1999),* The End of Alice *(1996),* In a Country of Mothers *(1993), and* Jack *(1989). Homes has published two short story collections,* The Safety of Objects *(1990), which was developed into a feature film in 2001, and* Things You Should Know *(2002). She recently published a memoir,* The Mistress's Daughter *(2007), about her experiences as an adopted child. Homes has received a number of awards, including a Guggenheim Fellowship and a National Endowment for the Arts Fellowship; she has also written for television, the Showtime production,* The L Word.

*Jaclyn Dwyer conducted this interview over e-mail from January - August 2008.*

**NDR**: As a writer, you achieved success at a fairly young age. How do you think this affected the trajectory and expectations of your writing career?

**AMH**: I think I've had the good fortune to be published and reviewed since I was a very young writer, but was never either graced or damned with enormous success that could perhaps cloud my or my publishers expectations of what might come next. I've had books like *The End of Alice* that many publishers were told they couldn't buy and others that I would have thought would do well in the US but have actually done better in Europe. *This Book Will Save Your Life,* is what I think of as a deeply American story. It got a lot of reviews in the US, two very bad ones just as it was coming out, and it kind of tanked here, but did very well in England, Germany, Italy, etc. My hope for my writing career has always been the same, to have the energy and passion to keep writing and the good fortune to be published, and it's very nice to be able to earn a living doing the thing you most enjoy.

**NDR**: You've mentioned frustration at people who think your fiction is true? Do you think it's a problem that so many writers, particularly young writers are using their lives to churn out first novels, so that we've reached a point where fiction is expected to be factual?

**AMH**: I think we've lost track of what the differences are between fact and fiction and on a more depressing note, I think we've lost the idea that people can IMAGINE something, that a person can extend beyond his or her personal experience and into a realm where they understand the experience of others.

**NDR**: I see your work as thematically similar to Joyce Carol Oates, who has also been labeled controversial. You're both women who write stories that explore the psychology of your characters through violence and sexuality. Did she influence you at all as a young writer?

**AMH**: I admire her work, both the range and prodigiousness. She's really a major force, but when I was younger I wasn't so aware of her. I grew up reading Albee, Pinter, Kerouac.

**NDR**: Which emerging writers do you think are important now?

**AMH**: There are many, many interesting younger writers, I just judged the *Granta Best American Novelists Under 35* and was so impressed at the range of voices and seriousness of the work

**NDR**: What are your intentions and expectations when you're writing a story or novel? Do you want the reader to think and to feel something in particular, or do you just want to write a good story?

**AMH**: My intentions and expectations change from story to story, novel to novel, but always the goal is to do the best job I can representing the characters and telling the story. With everything I write I think about why I am asking the reader to interrupt living their own life to come into my world and what I want the reader to come away with. That said, it's never a specific message, it's really more about provoking thought—getting the reader to think about his/her own life and how they view and deal with their own experiences.

**NDR**: Because your work is often labeled controversial or unsettling, the reader's perception or response to your work becomes very important to the work itself. How conscious of you are your reader when you are writing?

**AMH**: My responsibility is to my characters and I can't begin to allow what others might think about the work influence my work habits. Opinions of literature shift over time as does the impact of any particular critic, I just try to keep my head down and do a good job.

**NDR**: Your work is controversial because it is so incredibly real, and this, I think, is what makes it unsettling to some readers. At the same time, much of your work is also very surreal. Throughout *Music for Torching*, I kept saying to myself "This can't be happening," but at the same time, I kept believing. How do you achieve this balance between the surreal and the very real?

**AMH**: It's funny you ask about this, and in such a wonderful way. I'd say that the balance between the real and the surreal is getting more difficult to achieve as our world becomes increasingly surrealistic. I think of a writer like John Cheever as a great American surrealist and yet his work is very "realistic." In my work I go for a kind of psychological reality, which brings a kind of heightened realism, realer than real or Kodacolor quality that's also about the heightened intensity of fiction vs. reality.

**NDR**: In nonfiction, because it's supposed to be true in a factual way, do you feel like your more at risk of "getting it wrong" since, compared to fiction writing, there's a higher expectation of "getting it right," because the story is about your own life?

**AMH**: I think both fiction and non-fiction have the ability to really "get it right." What disturbs me is how these days, so many people have lost track of the difference between fiction and non fiction. I am very aware that there is a fact base and a chronology that comes with non-fiction that can't be violated. As someone who has written fiction and non-fiction I believe that writers know when they are making it up, and I am deeply bothered by memoirs that are in fact novels…though as we know for centuries there have been novels that were actually memoir, i.e. when in doubt claim it is fiction. But if you're really writing non-fiction then you'd better be sure you've got the story straight.

**NDR**: You've said that you don't particularly like memoirs and that you're not comfortable with non-fiction. Had you thought of writing *The Mistress' Daughter* without publishing it?

**AMH**: When I started writing the book, I just wanted to get the story down, and create a document for myself. I wasn't thinking so much about publishing it, but as people heard the story it seemed like everyone wanted it to be a book, and I realized that it might have value and meaning for others, and so then I felt compelled to finish it. There are lots of memoirs written every year, but not too many are written by people who are already writers, my point, I think my experience as a writer gave me a very good skill set for writing about a very difficult experience, i.e. finding language for the difficult and primitive emotions that are shared by many adopted people.

**NDR**: You've said that you're fascinated by the boundary between public life and private life. Are you mostly interested in your characters revealing parts of their private lives within the story or in exposing private lives in the work itself? It seems the very nature of writing about private experiences—I'm thinking of sexual acts in *The End of Alice*, "A Live Doll" and "Georgica"—thrusts them into the public sphere.

**AMH**: I'm interested in the splits between who we tell ourselves we are in our public lives and how we behave privately, and also how we can sometimes convince (or not) ourselves that we're something other than what we are. Long story short, I am fascinated by human behavior.

**NDR**: When you're writing a novel or short story, do you know the end, or do you just wait and see where the story wants to go?

**AMH**: Sometimes I do know the end, even before I begin. Other times the end emerges or shifts as I'm writing—with *Music For Torching* I knew the last line for a very long time. Mostly I try to tolerate the not knowing because as wonderful as it is to begin a book knowing where you will finish, I think the process, the discovery of the story is also a wonderful journey, and it's in part about tolerating all the unknowns.

**NDR**: You've said, when referring to your students' work, that content is important. Where do your ideas for content come from? Is it all just inventive and imaginative, or do you also pull things from the media and people around you?

**AMH**: Content comes from everywhere, the imagination and the world surrounding us. There has to be a reason for a reader to suspend her own life and start reading your story or novel...i.e. there's got to be something in it for them.

**NDR**: Several of your characters with children are either overwhelmed with parenthood or are just inept and incapable of parenting. How has motherhood affected your writing, in both finding time to write and if parenthood itself has changed the way you would write about it now?

**AMH**: It's hard to know how life in general affects how one would write differently over time. All I can say on the subject is that parenting makes writing novels look easy, it's hard work, and takes enormous amounts of time, but it is real life and forces someone (ME) who is not so inclined to live in the real world to stay there for hours and days at a time.

**NDR**: In the past you've written for *The L Word* and now you're developing a new show for HBO. Can you talk about the show and writing for TV? How is it different from novel/short story writing and how much creative freedom are you allowed?

**AMH**: It's entirely different, one is a labor or love, novels and short stories belong to the individual author, and quite literally a TV show belongs to the network. It's written/rewritten to suit their desires and specifications. That said, I find it a lot of fun, to write for someone else, to essentially be dropped down into a story and asked to turn out dialogue etc. I started as a playwright and do enjoy this kind of thing, and you get to work with other people—something I hadn't done in 20 years.

**NDR**: Your last novel (*This Book Will Save Your Life*) was unexpectedly optimistic. Is this the direction you see your fiction moving?

**AMH**: If you look carefully you'll see that *This Book* (my most recent) and *JACK*, (my first) have a lot in common. The ideas and themes that run though all the books are similar, but you're right, I did want to write something more optimistic; we're living through a very difficult period of history (post 9/11) and I was thinking about how does one live optimistically during such a dark period. As for where I'm going next, well, I recently published a piece of something new called, "May We Be Forgiven" in *Granta*'s 100th issue; it's a deeply dark story of two brothers, and there will be more to come of that as soon as I buy brighter bulbs for the house.

# A Fastidious Brewer of Tea

Michael Longley. *Collected Poems*. Winston-Salem, North Carolina: Wake Forest University Press. 2007.

*Lars-Håkan Svensson*

1.

"Sea Shanty," the opening poem of Michael Longley's fifth collection, *Gorse Fires* (1991), is a modern version of the kind of introductory poem with which ancient poets liked to preface their collections. The speaker has entertained grandiose plans which have, however, been modified or even been made to seem redundant by the Muse or some other powerful agent of good taste. In Longley's case, the motif of the poet's artistic re-education is expressed as adjustment to new and less glamorous circumstances. Thus, the speaker, who "would have waited under the statue of Eros / While the wind whistled in my bell-bottoms," now finds himself wearing long johns on "the high ground of Carrigskeewaun" in Co. Mayo, Ireland. His "repertoire of sea shanties and love songs" seems very much a thing of the past, though he watches "Lesbos rising among the islands." The value of this vision may be illusory, though, for as the poem ends with an echo of a well-known Sapphic fragment about being stood up by one's lover ("At midnight the moon goes, then the Pleiades"), the light of the distant stars is replaced by—or perhaps reflected as—"A spark of sand grains on my wellingtons."

What we can expect from this collection, then, is not the sophisticated love poetry that the poet might have produced had he lingered under the statue of Eros. Still, this does not mean that love as a theme is absent. "Aubade," a poem placed at the centre of *Gorse Fires*, is a clear indication of this. Despite its title, "Aubade," a free translation of an Irish poem by Nuala Ní Dhomhnaill, is an affectionate if low-key love poem spoken from the perspective of lovers who are also parents. Like "Sea Shanty," which programmatically states "I must make do with what is left me," it reinforces the poet's concern with workaday realities by emphasising that "we must make do with today's / Happenings." *Gorse Fires*, then, is a volume concerned with articulating a new sense of sobriety, of accepting that the plenitude earlier taken for granted or aimed for is no longer on hand. The sense of loss is introduced even in the italicized quatrain commemorating the poet's parents prefacing the volume, and a wealth of intratextual echoes makes sure that the lesson isn't lost on us. For example, a phrase intimating the parents' closeness in death ("her ashes settling on to his collarbone") is recalled in "Sea Shanty" where the speaker claims to have "dozed on her breastbone" (a passage in its turn recalled by a later poem where someone, presumably the poet's wife, "crouched over me / And protected me with your shoulders and hair" when he tells her, on the day his mother died, " 'I am an orphan now' ").

*Gorse Fires*, in other words, is a collection concerned with reorientation in an artistic as well as a general sense. It is the work of a poet who has been forced to make a virtue of necessity, who has had to turn paucity into wealth, and who in fixing his eye on himself and his immediate surroundings has also been able to tap his own past in new ways. This is noticeable in a variety of respects: through his remarkable poetic *Kleinkunst* (many of the poems in this collection are diary-like improvisations not longer than five or six lines); his fine-tuned renditions of the barren landscape near Carrigskeewaun, which serves as a "home from home," the poet's first home being Belfast where he was born in 1939, grew up and still lives; his ability to transform the subject-matter of classical poetry (Longley studied classics at University College, Dublin) into pertinent if indirect comments on the tragic situation in his home country.

The need for a home—and the complications involved in trying to invest permanent energy in a new one—is a motif revisited time and again by Longley. The alternating roles of Belfast and Carrigskeewaun in his life found a memorable expression in an early poem, "The West," exploiting one of his favourite formats, a poem consisting of two five-line stanzas:

> Beneath a gas-mantle that the moths bombard,
> Light that powders at a touch, dusty wings,
> I listen for news through the atmospherics,
> A crackle of sea-wrack, spinning driftwood,
> Waves like distant traffic, news from home.
>
> Or watch myself, as through a sandy lens,
> Materialising out of the heat-shimmers
> And finding my way for ever along
> The path to this cottage, its windows,
> Walls, sun and moon dials, home from home.

A new, powerful example of Longley's ability to orchestrate such notions is found in "Homecoming," one of an introductory series of poems exploring Carrigskeewaun as an idea of home. Following closely (in the original 1991 edition of *Gorse Fires* directly) upon a poem in which the wind in the chimney of his Belfast home is described as a "voice-box" impersonating the animals of Carrigskeewaun, this poem—which is a free version of an episode in the *Odyssey*—provides another version of home by describing how the sleeping Ulysses, returning to his native island, is "lifted out of his hollow / Just as he was [...] And put [...] to bed on the sand, still lost in sleep." The Ithaca to which Ulysses is coming is both hibernicized, being full of *bullauns* ('a square or cylindrical stone block') and modernized, Ulysses's ship being described as a "complicated vessel;" the Greek original (*Od.* xiii.117) refers to it as 'hollow' (*glaphyrés*), a standard adjective in this context, but as the Phaeacian ship which carries the sleeping Odysseus is magical, Longley's phrase has a felicitously ambiguous resonance.

The collection as a whole is full of such *nóstoi*, or home-comings; moments in which the poet plants fragments of the past in the present, endowing it with a miraculous and closely observed elasticity. In one poem he undertakes a transatlantic journey, visiting cousins (and "the ghosts of the aunts and uncles I never knew") in Mississauga. In another, an ingeniously appropriated version of another famous Homeric episode—Penelope's realisation that the stranger she has just met is really her long-absent husband because he is able to describe in detail how he designed their bedroom—the poet and his family travel to Italy by couchette in a "room on wheels [which] has become the family vault;" the other travellers include a mummy-like "lady / We met four thousand years ago in Fiesole." The Holocaust and the Odyssey are unexpectedly, but very movingly, brought together in a poem adding to commemoration of Argos, Odysseus' old dog, mourning for pets taken away from Czechoslovakian Jews waiting for transportation to Auschwitz:

> We weep for Argos, the dog, and for all those other dogs,
> For the rounding-up of hamsters, the panic of white mice
> And the deportation of one canary called Pepicek.

The *Odyssey* is again called upon in the very last poem, "The Butchers," which recounts Odysseus' terrifying revenge on "the disloyal housemaids." Technically perhaps best described as a free translation, the poem glances at the Northern Irish situation through a number of references which have a particular significance in Irish English: "Until they came to a bog-meadow full of bog-asphodels / Where the residents are ghosts or images of the dead." As an indictment of the mentality resulting in sectarian violence, this poem can hardly be bettered. In addition, it shows the range of Longley's ability to appropriate and domesticate his Greek models: having earlier been the recipient of the reader's benevolence as he arrives home and is united with his family, Odysseus now becomes a symbol for the worst instincts of man.

2.

I have dwelt at some length on *Gorse Fires* because it seems to me that it represents a crucial moment in Longley's poetic career. At the time of its publication, twelve years had elapsed since the appearance of his previous collection, *The Echo Gate* (1979). It is true that fifteen new poems, written after *The Echo Gate,* were appended in a section called "New Poems" when the first four volumes were reprinted in *Collected Poems 1963-1985* (1985). (In the new *Collected Poems* under review here a sixteenth poem has been added, and the title of the section is simply "Poems.") Nevertheless, as one peruses the new *Collected,* the overwhelming impression is that Longley's oeuvre to date is made up of eight collections which can be subdivided into two large sections comprising four collections each. While each full-length volume certainly represents a new development and emphasizes different concerns and themes, the sixteen poems, as I see them, do not quite amount to a collection that can claim to be treated on a par with the other ones but are better seen as a bridge linking the two larger sections. This is not to diminish their artistic value. In terms of quality, the sixteen poems deserve the reader's full attention, but as a collection they cannot measure up to Longley's other volumes, all of which constitute full-length and carefully realized sequences.

It is undeniable, I think, that Longley's silence during these years—by his own admission, partly caused by writer's block—affected his career in important ways. The 1980s were of course—as were the 1970s—a highly politicized decade in Northern Ireland. The Troubles left their imprint on the work of Longley's friends and colleagues from Belfast—notably Seamus Heaney, Derek Mahon and Paul Muldoon—who published important collections during these years and began to become well-known outside Northern Ireland and the UK. Heaney, who had moved to Dublin in 1976, took up a post as visiting professor at Harvard in 1979, and Muldoon moved to the US in 1987, eventually joining—and heading—the Writing Program at Princeton. Mahon, whom Longley got to know well while they were both students at Trinity College, had left Ireland even in 1970. Like Medbh McGuckian and Ciaran Carson, Longley remained in Northern Ireland and Belfast throughout the Troubles. After a brief spell as a schoolmaster, he worked for the Arts Council in Belfast until 1991, when *Gorse Fires* was published. This job took up much of Longley's time and energy, and is likely to have been one reason why he wrote comparatively little during the

1980s. Another circumstance which—ironically and paradoxically—may have delayed Longley's recognition as a major poet was the fact that while Edna Longley, to whom he is married, did much to promote Northern Irish poetry during this important period, she almost invariably, for obvious reasons, said nothing about Longley's work in her highly influential articles and books on Northern Irish poetry.

The upshot of all this was that Longley's reputation in Ireland and abroad was fuelled neither by new books nor by critical attention during the 1980s. When *Gorse Fires* appeared, to enthusiastic reviews, in 1991, this situation began to change. By now, Longley is recognized as a major poet, and is the author of one of the best-known political poems to have come out of Ireland in recent decades. His work is the subject of a perspicacious and sensitive monograph by Fran Brearton (*Reading Michael Longley*, 2006) as well as a growing number of articles, some of them collected in a volume edited by Alan J. Peacock and Kathleen Devine (*The Poetry of Michael Longley*, 2000).

3.

The title of Longley's first volume, published in 1969, *No Continuing City*, might easily be construed as referring to the Belfast of the Troubles which were then entering a violent phase. However, the political overtones are far and few between in this collection. The title-poem deals with love, not politics; in fact, it forms part of a group of poems, many of them on Homeric themes, which deal with the speaker's transformation from Odysseus-like rover to responsible husband. Almost without exception, these are rhymed poems, based on intricate stanzaic patterns borrowed from Renaissance poets or of Longley's own devising, and often adapting, as "Epithalamion" does, lessons learnt from John Donne's poetry to a modern situation.

One reason why Longley's first collection does not relate to the current political situation is that nearly all of its poems were written much earlier when Longley was still studying classics at Trinity. Moreover, these are poems written by someone who is still to a large extent in search of his own voice and who, given his background—Longley's parents were Londoners who had settled down in Belfast some ten years before the poet was born in 1939—may not have found it altogether easy to decide exactly what 'home' (a pervasive motif in these early poems as well) might mean. In a 2003 interview, he commented: "From an early age, I drifted between Englishness and Irishness, between town and country, between the Lisburn Road with its shops and cinemas and the River Lagan with its beech woods and meadows."

A poem that looks forward to Longley's mature manner is his elegy for his father, "In Memoriam." Composed in unevenly rhymed iambic pentameter (many of Longley's early poems stick doggedly to rhyme and metre), it introduces a more personal, almost colloquial register, and turns the father-son theme explored in some of the Homeric poems into something much more intimate. In Longley's second volume, *No Exploded View* (1973), this lament for his father is followed up by another similar poem ("Wounds") which also draws on his father's memories of WWI, connecting them now with the sectarian killings that were taking place in Northern Ireland at the time. In this poem Longley has found his unmistakable idiom. He buries his father and

> Now, with military honours of a kind,
> With his badges, his medals like rainbows,
> His spinning compass, I bury beside him
> Three teenage soldiers, bellies full of
> Bullets and Irish beer, their flies undone.
> A packet of Woodbines I throw in,
> A Lucifer, the Sacred Heart of Jesus
> Paralysed as heavy guns put out
> The night-light in a nursery for ever;
> Also a bus-conductor's uniform –
> He collapsed beside his carpet-slippers
> Without a murmur, shot through the head
> By a shivering boy who wandered in
> Before they could turn the television down
> Or tidy away the supper dishes.
> To the children, to a bewildered wife,
> I think 'Sorry Missus' was what he said.

The Longley manner which emerges here is not only characterized by its quiet mastery of a certain neutral, almost colloquial register occasionally shot through by striking or terrifying images such as the nursery night-light which is put out forever, but by a striking ability to take in everyday sights and endow them with emblematic significance—or, as in another poem, "Ghost Town," to depict visions of seemingly real places with painstaking exactitude: "I have located it, my ghost town—/ A place of interminable afternoons, / Sad cottages, scythes rusting in the thatch; / Of so many hesitant surrenders to / Enfolding bog, the scuts of bog cotton." (Incidentally, it is this concern with perception that has given the collection its title: as "Skara Brae" makes clear, 'exploded view' is an architectural term for being able to see both depth and surface.)

*No Exploded View* is permeated with poems mentioning or alluding to the group of poets responsible for the upsurge of vitality associated with Northern Irish poetry during the 1960s and onwards. Several poems address Seamus Heaney, James Simmons, and Paul Muldoon, who together with Longley formed a small group of friends in Belfast who, initially under the tutelage of Philip Hobsbaum, read and commented on each other's work—and Derek Mahon, who was never part of the Hobsbaum circle but with whom Longley continued to stay in close touch. These poems naturally touch on artistic issues, and sometimes amount to miniature metapoetic treatises; but Longley finds room for meditations on the art of poetry in many other poems as well. And many of the poems in his third collection, *Man Lying on a Wall* (1976)—the title is a homage to the painter L. S. Lowry—deal with or embody the slippery area between life and fiction. "Ars Poetica" rehearses, in fantastic fashion, some of the seemingly autobiographical themes Longley's readers are accustomed to by now: one is not surprised to learn that "I go disguised as myself" or that the speaker expects that "The judge will at once award the first prize / To me and to all of my characters." The next poem, "Company," which revisits the same issue in a more sober and down-to-earth tone (the critic Michael Allen has pointed out that Longley often places two poems dealing with similar material in different ways next to each other), is made up of a single sentence extending over 44 lines. Divided into two equally long stanzas, the poem envisages two possible futures for the speaker and his companion, one located in a big city such as Belfast, the other in Co. Mayo. The tone of both sections is slightly diffident as the speaker, who envisages himself as still at work on his poetry, does not appear to believe fully in the success of his art—or perhaps of art in general—and also appears to have grave doubts about the political climate: there are references to vigilantes in the city and suspicious impoverished households in the countryside; only the intimacy between the speaker and his companion is not doubted.

By the time Longley's fourth volume, *The Echo Gate* (1979), appeared, the most recent, violent phase of the Troubles was in its tenth year. Of all Longley's books this is the one that deals most directly with the Troubles, and it is no wonder that *The Echo Gate* is full of poems that describe and allude to terrorism and acts of political violence, but in characteristic fashion Longley blends the violence of the Troubles with his father's WWI experiences. In a way that is going to be even more typical of his later volumes, Longley collects poems on similar themes in groups while also inserting subtle intertextual links between poems at some physical distance from one another in the sequence. In this volume there are, for example, poems about the Troubles and its victims; poems about the Irish countryside (notably a diptych called "Home Ground" dedicated to Heaney and Muldoon respectively); poems about WWI, its combatants and poets; poems about remarkable and heroic women ("Florence Nightingale" and "Grace Darling"); and poems celebrating love and peace. The effect is to put the Troubles in a wider perspective, which makes the impact of the poems which address the Troubles directly and in matter-of-fact tone, such as "The Civil Servant," "The Greengrocer," and "The Linen Workers," even more powerful because they occur in a context where alternatives to the atrocities taking place in contemporary Northern Ireland are also given memorable expression.

4.

One of the poems in *The Echo Gate*, "Peace," deserves special attention. It plays a significant role as the longest in a series of war poems, and as the subtitle "after Tibullus" indicates, it is a free version of the Roman elegist Tibullus's anti-war poem, "Quis fuit horrendos primus qui protulit enses?" ('Who was he that first discovered the horrid sword?'). As such it points forwards towards an important strand in Longley's work (and in contemporary Northern Irish poetry in general). In Longley's next four volumes translations, imitations, and adaptations of various kinds play an increasingly important role, and are sometimes difficult to distinguish from poems which merely make the thematic content of foreign originals their subject matter. Poems exploring episodes in the *Odyssey* loom large in *Gorse Fires*, as I have indicated, but Longley's next volume, *The Ghost Orchid* (1995), contains an even larger number of poems of this admittedly elastic description. The source languages vary more than in any other of his collections: one poem is "after the Dutch," another is a rendition of one of Cavafy's poems (without its status as translation being acknowledged), yet another is called "Sorescu's Circles." A considerable portion of the book is taken up by poems ultimately deriving their inspiration from Ovid's *Metamorphoses*, thus bearing testimony to Longley's obvious enthusiasm for Michael Hofmann's and James Lasdun's *After Ovid* where they were first printed. Some of these pieces such as "According to Pythagoras" display Longley's mischievous sense of humour while his version of "Baucis & Philemon" combines an Ovidian lightness of touch with an unsentimental ability to write movingly about marital love. The best-known example of Longley's involvement with imitation and adaptation—perhaps one of his best-known poems—is a sonnet he wrote when the first ceasefire was about to be announced in 1994. This poem is a condensation (and a reorganisation of the events) of the famous episode in the *Iliad* where Priam comes to fetch his son Hector's corpse from Achilles who has defeated and killed Hector:

I
Put in mind of his own father and moved to tears
Achilles took him by the hand and pushed the old king
Gently away, but Priam curled up at his feet and
Wept with him until their sadness filled the building.

II
Taking Hector's corpse into his own hands Achilles
Made sure it was washed and, for the old king's sake,
Laid out in uniform, ready for Priam to carry
Wrapped like a present home to Troy at daybreak.

III
When they had eaten together, it pleased them both
To stare at each other's beauty as lovers might,
Achilles built like a god, Priam good-looking still
And full of conversation, who earlier had sighed:

IV
'I get down on my knees and do what must be done
And kiss Achilles' hand, the killer of my son.'

Written just before (and in anticipation of) the ceasefire in August 1994 and published just after it in *The Irish Times*, this poem justly has become one of Longley's best-known poems. It is a moving plea for forgiveness which aligns itself with Seamus Heaney's "Funeral Rites" towards the end of which a noble heathen, the Icelander Gunnar of Hlidarende, is used for similar purposes; though dead by violence, Gunnar was left unavenged. Longley's poem is not uncomplicated, though; as he himself has pointed out, the Trojan war did not end with this episode, and Achilles himself was killed. But by disrupting the chronological order and ending with what should have been the beginning, Longley's sonnet emphasizes and celebrates the moment of forgiveness in full awareness of its fleeting nature.

Longley's preoccupation with changeability and metamorphosis, to which his imitations and translations testify, pervades *The Ghost Orchid*. The idea is introduced in the very first poem, "Form," in which the hare's body is contrasted with "the grassy form" it occupies in its "makeshift shelter" on the ground, thus subtly mixing Longley's interest in metamorphosis with the equally important notion of home. Given this interest in adaptability, it is no wonder that Ovid's *Metamorphoses* supplies the material for a number of poems in this collection. In some cases (in "Perdix" for example) metamorphosis is something good, because it involves an ability to create something new out of seemingly disparate elements. In "After Horace," however, postmodernism's desire to marry totally incongruous materials just for the hell of it is castigated in a humorous tone though one suspects that Longley is not out only to amuse us:

> If a retired sailor
> Commissions a picture of the shipwreck he survived,
> We give him a cypress-tree because we can draw that.

However, despite his numerous references to other poets Longley is not a bookish poet. Many of the short poems that predominate in this collection seem to be born effortlessly out of the poet's alertness to quotidian human experience. At any rate there is almost never a tonal difference in his translations and adaptations and such poems as seem to be jotted down on the spur of the moment as a result of something that he witnessed or happened to think about.

Many of Longley's poems in the two late collections *The Weather in Japan* (2000) and *Snow Water* (2004) are reminiscent of classical Japanese or Chinese poetry. The exquisite title-poem of the former collection, which is more rhetorical than most of Longley's later poems in that it makes use of the ancient figure of chiasmus, is a case in point:

> The Weather in Japan
>
> Makes bead curtains of the rain,
> Of the mist a paper screen.

The poems in these two collections are written by a master in full command of his powers who can seemingly transform any experience, thought or event into memorable verse and express himself with an ease that makes the lines give the impression of having written themselves. Many poems address relatives and friends or are elegies for friends and relatives; some are based on his father's experiences of WWI or occasioned by the writings or lives of English poets of who took part in it; others still are improvised reflections on sights chanced upon at Carrigskeewaun or experienced during trips to foreign countries. As this is the stuff that Longley's mature poetry is made of, it is remarkable that he is able to evolve new aspects of his subjects. Through the particular method of organising his collections that I have described earlier he makes his poems enter into conversation with each other and the reading of his collections a multifaceted experience.

Not the least of the many pleasures afforded by Michael Longley's poetry consists in the way in which he manages to rejuvenate seemingly well-worn topoi. I began by discussing an introductory poem in which he poses as a sophisticated love poet turned sailor. His latest collection to date, *Snow Water*, begins with a poem, also called "Snow Water," which recycles the ancient idea of water as the source of poetic inspiration in a manner which is as elegant and ironic as it is ambiguous:

> A fastidious brewer of tea, a tea
> Connoisseur as well as a poet,
> I modestly request on my sixtieth
> Birthday a gift of snow water.
>
> Tea steam and ink stains. Single-
> Mindedly I scald my teapot and
> Measure out some Silver Needles Tea,
> Enough for a second steeping.
>
> Other favourites include Clear
> Distance and Eyebrows of Longevity
> Or, from precarious mountain peaks,
> Cloud Mist Tea (quite delectable)
>
> Which competent monkeys harvest
> Filling their baskets with choice leaves
> And bringing them down to where I wait
> With my crock of snow water.

# "As Close as Possible to the Site of the Outrage": The Poetry of Thomas Kinsella

Thomas Kinsella. *Collected Poems 1956-2001*. Winston-Salem, North Carolina: Wake Forest University Press. 2006.

*James Matthew Wilson*

Thomas Kinsella began his career as a poet more than five decades ago with brief lyrics whose tense, cryptic energy proclaimed his debt to the early W.H. Auden. His "Midsummer" and "A Lady of Quality," for instance, adopted that favorite stanza of Auden's, the romance-six, but sometimes hobbled along because of a blood-bitter austerity present in Kinsella's style reluctant (though not absolutely) to imitate the fleet, ironic balladeering typical of such early Auden as "A Summer Night." Whereas early Auden routinely deployed stanzas as discrete units of syntax, Kinsella frequently enjambed stanza after stanza, driven not by a spirit of excess but of furtive inquiry. "Midsummer" concludes,

> We have, dear reason, of this glade
> An endless tabernacle made,
>         An origin.
> Well for whatever lonely one
> Will find this right place to lay down
>         His desert in.

No doubt, one hears Auden's "Out on the lawn I lie in bed, / Vega conspicuous overhead" percolating through these lines of the apprentice Kinsella. But, Auden's poems throughout his career delighted in balancing endless tabernacles and interior deserts within the dualistic play of his larger debates on human ethics in the age of anxiety—and they display a restless experimentation in poetic voice that ranges from the bathic to the telegraphic. Kinsella's more sober sensibility inclined him toward thorough scrutiny of the "desert"—eventually at the expense of his impressive, but narrow, talent for the well-wrought late-modernist lyric. After Auden's emigration to the United States and conversion to Christianity, his style grew unbuttoned and chatty while his poetry as a whole became more explicitly concerned with ethical questions. In the nineteen-sixties, Kinsella's style also underwent a sort of declension, with his incomplete elimination of formal in favor of free verse. Only rarely would his mature work echo the chiseled tableaux that compose the early *Moralities* (1960). "Sons of the Brave," a poem from that small volume, serves as a typical specimen of the marmoreal early work:

That great shocked art, the gross great enmity,
That roamed here once, and swept indoors, embalmed
Their lesson with themselves. We shade the eye;
Our mouths have never filled with blood; the shot,
The sung, entwine their ghosts and fade. The sty
They rooted in retains its savour but
Their farrow doze against a Nightmare slammed
Shut in their faces by the prating damned.

The subsequent change in form did not lead to a looser voice but to one more fragmented and evidently disturbed by the outrages of cultural and natural history, of ancient myth and contemporary Irish politics. Through their uneven and broken structures, the poems also came to wear outwardly the processes of their composition. "Down Survey (1655-1657)" from *Littlebody* (2000) shows Kinsella handling a theme similar to "Sons" in the later style:

The young men chanted beside the public way:

*Is there any sorrow like ours*
*who have forfeited our possessions*
*and all respect?*

And the virgins of the Parrish of Killmainham
hung down their heads.

Such lines read like a ragged sheeve torn from the archive of Irish oral history, and properly interpretable only in the context of *Littlebody* as a whole. Indeed, this and other later Kinsella poems open out by allusion and incompletion to his entire body of work to the point of rendering any one poem dependent on that ever-growing corpus for its meaning.

The poems on either side of this stylistic change in the sixties are less varied and less beautiful to the ear than Auden's, but demonstrate a persistent and sophisticated search for the nature and meaning of human culture at its points of origin—an authorial ambition unmatched by any of Kinsella's Anglophone contemporaries. Like Auden and other modernist poets, in other words, Kinsella has built his poetry into a coherent structure for the interrogation of how human beings can live in a world superficially overwhelmed by disorder or evil. We can now see how systematically Auden's work probes the distinctions between[,] and origins of[,] lust and love to discover how ethics might steer the appetite; how Eliot's poems trace a quest to escape the prisons of selfhood by at last relativizing the human creature through the recovery of his humble origin in the love of the divine Creator; how Pound's *Cantos* map out the exemplary heroism of poets, rulers, and other men of action to explain the political achievements and failures of history in terms of aboriginal or archetypal myths. Kinsella's poetry as a whole touches on all three of these quests for origins but finds its formal principle at that particular originary locus where biological life melds with cultural life. The prose introduction to the poem sequence *Wormwood* (1968) sets forth as explicit a mission statement for his work as we are likely to get:

> It is certain that maturity and peace are to be sought through ordeal after ordeal, and it seems that the search continues until we fail. We reach out after each new beginning, penetrating our context to know ourselves, and our knowledge increases until we recognize again (more profoundly each time) our pain, indignity, and triviality...Sensing a wider scope, a more penetrating harmony, we begin again in a higher innocence to grow toward the next ordeal.

Observe how this brief outline of the quest for the properly lived human life insists upon a teleology—we must indeed move in a particular, progressive, direction. But, in an anti-Romantic reformulation of Goethe, each step forward toward knowledge entails a falling back as well; we are advancing, but the *telos* toward which we aim changes and, as it changes, recedes, until our own intellectual and emotional growth comes to substitute for some objective and definable finality at which we had hoped to arrive. The embodiment of thought becomes tentative, immanent heir to the soul's hope of taking wing. Kinsella frequently captures the tragic implications of this endless quest to arrive at ourselves; the grub in his "Leaf-Eater" "gropes / Back on itself and begins / To eat its own leaf." And "Phoenix Park" develops this connection between the reason's desire for knowledge and the purely animal appetite with a confession that there may be no final cause that sets the reason in motion and that alone can, therefore, bring it to rest:

> Laws of order I find I have discovered
> Mainly at your hands. Of failure and increase.
> The stagger and recovery of spirit:
> That life is hunger, hunger is for order,
> And hunger satisfied brings on new hunger
>
> Till there's nothing left to come;

Such passages do not express the conclusions Kinsella reaches in his poems. Rather, they describe the methodology ordering them. Within the earlier collections, the different poem sequences offer a succession of approaches to different points of origin, different starting points for human knowledge. *Downstream* (1962) and *Nightwalker and Other Poems* (1968) primarily explore Irish colonial history, modern "types" of Irish character, and above all the recent history that made possible the "modern" Ireland of Seán Lemass. Particularly in "Nightwalker," Kinsella explores the disparity between the drama of Ireland's national origin in an inspired revolution and its present as a minor modern state pathetically seeking foreign investment in the European Common Market (Recent Irish poets have proven adept and obsessed with alternately mythicizing and interpolating their national identity, but only in Kinsella's poetry and a few late poems of Denis Devlin do we find serious scrutiny of the Irish State as it came to exist after the Anglo-Irish war). In *Wormwood*, Kinsella follows Auden in turning from public history to the intimate relations of "Love the limiter."

With *New Poems* (1973), Kinsella's archeology of origins takes on greater breadth and a consequently greater obscurity attributable to his increased reliance on intertextual reference. In this volume, Kinsella focuses on images of his grandmother as "ancestor," that is, as the frightening and elusive biological source of himself. The image of the egg—a chicken egg and the embryonic self—governs the mode of inquiry in these poems, returning always from the cultural terrain of memory to the pre-cognitive conditions of birth. These empirical considerations of Kinsella's immanent origins prepare for the fragmentary scenes from creation myths in *From the Land of the Dead*. The dark images of his grandmother and a repeated scene of a chicken egg dropping and smashing similarly anticipate the originary violence Kinsella explores through these myths. If "The Route of *The Táin*" is primarily concerned with the local violence found in Ireland's ur-historical prose epic, "The Dispossessed" paraphrases Ernest Renan's *Vie de Jésus*—"One morning, in a slow paroxysm of rage, / we found His corpse stretched on the threshold"—to underscore that the whole history of the Christian West, in its most divine aspirations, begins with the murdered body of Christ.

Shortly before publishing *New Poems*, Kinsella began experimenting with the brief chapbook as the medium of his works' publication, and these Peppercanister Poems have become the standard units in his serialized quest for origins ever since. The early *Butcher's Dozen* (1972) is an occasional poem protesting British military and judicial abuses in the North. It and the more recent *Open Court* (1991) and *The Pen Shop* (1997) are largely written in tetrameter doggerel couplets intended to echo the public ballads of the Gaelic poetry Kinsella has translated. In general, however, the Peppercanister Poems continue to explore a wider range of historical experience, with a heavy reliance for their meaning on intertextual references to an intriguing but eccentric archive. They also persist in a fragmentary, prosaic free verse that does not usually impress in quotation, but which provokes and intrigues (much as does Pound's *Cantos*) when read as a single, ever-expanding work.

*One* (1974) returns to specifically Irish origins through elliptical tableaux taken from the late medieval pseudo-historical *Book of Invasions*. A *Technical Supplement* (1976) explores that most obvious yet mysterious origin of human life—the body itself—through a commentary on the anatomical drawings of Diderot's *Encyclopédie*. And *Songs of the Psyche* (1985) makes explicit the Jungian exploration of cultural archetypes that has subtended much of Kinsella's work by facilitating the movement from the merely biological to the cultural through the modern gateway of the psychological. The most successful of the twenty-two Peppercanister chapbooks that constitute almost three-quarters of the *Collected* volume, however, is *Out of Ireland* (1987). The poems in this sequence are set near the grave of the modern Irish traditional musician, Seán Ó Riada, whose vocation partly stirs Kinsella's meditations on the writing and fate of the medieval Irish theologian, John Scotus Eriugena. The subtle theory woven in the poems suggests that the complex counter-point of Irish music, with its apparent chaos of parts ultimately reconciled in a harmonious totality, provided Eriugena with his vision of creation itself as a swarming numerical mess that shall form a beautiful ordered whole in the divine eye of providence. Eriugena's "harmonious certainty" promises

> that the world's parts,
> ill-fitted in their stresses and their pains,
> will combine at last in polyphonic sweet-breathing union
> and all created Nature ascend like joined angels,
>
> limbs and bodies departing the touch of Earth
> static in a dance of return, all Mankind
> gathering stunned at the world's edge
> silent in a choir of understanding.

In like fashion, the unpredictable turning-over of diverse originary moments synthesize compellingly in Kinsella's poetry. Although he is quick to remind us that Eirugena died "at his students' hands // They stabbed him with their pens," Kinsella's poems tirelessly search out the redemptive and reconciling powers of love—human and divine—that are founded on and struggle to rise above aboriginal violence. No contemporary Irish poet has taken up the epic ambitions and fragmented, spatial practices of the modernists with the sophistication of Kinsella. Indeed, Kinsella is almost alone among living poets in his use of his art as a means of discovery, critique, and transcendence of the primordial conditions of human life. This uniqueness becomes even more apparent in *Godhead* (1999), where the biological, psychological, and cultural meditations of so many of his poems are deepened through theological reflections on the pattern of human origins and experience. The poems contemplate the Trinity and the hypostatic union—the Incarnation of God as man—as glosses on the compound condition of human beings as flesh and spirit in union.

And yet, for all Kinsella's architectonic brilliance (a gift that preserves coherence amid eccentric choices of reference and a typically modernist obscurity that only the books of his several superb exegetes can help us overcome), the deliberate laconic plainness of the writing limits his achievement. A Kinsella poem can be counted on to provide a grim naturalistic image of physical appetite, such as that of the predatory owl:

> the drop with deadened wing-beats; some creature
> torn and swallowed; her brain, afterward,
> staring among the rafters in the dark
> until hunger returns.

But, such stunning compounds of gorgeousness and terror, suitable though they are to a poet especially concerned with charting the material foundations of art, history, and the psyche, become redundant and are seldom relieved by other voices, tones, or visions. When Kinsella returns to formal verse, he seems deliberately writing at less than full power, insisting that rhyme read as doggerel and satire. For all the immense variety of his subject-matter, in other words, the stiff, austere voice of the poetry does too good a job reconciling all to one bleak vision. Taken together, the poems illuminate but sound redundant—and they lose much of their significance read independently[.] Perhaps an Irish reader—especially a Dubliner—would detect more nuances in Kinsella's language than can an American ear. Unless this is the case, one must conclude Kinsella is a poet of almost unequalled brilliance who has failed to develop the material of his art—language—into the varied palette one would normally expect to find in such a long career.

# THE AMERICAN TRACT

Susan Howe. *Souls of the Labadie Tract*. New York: New Directions Publishing Corp. 2007.

*John Wilkinson*

Some of the greatest poetry in the English language has been written in the United States in the past fifty years. A salient feature of this extremely various poetry is a density of presence that cannot be satisfied with any existing assumption about individual or collective consciousness, or the way in which consciousness receives the world or the world is composed. Such a phenomenology is highly sceptical, but regards the poem, as painters contemporary with the New York School regarded the canvas, as an exemplary site for securing the plenitude of presence, even if its securing will always demand further acts of revision, further critique, further wagers. Such art is constitutive presence, a thick here and now alert to conditions on its borders. This achievement makes it all the sadder that new American poetry can exhibit a relatively uncritical relationship with a past it retrieves continuously, so as to refresh a mystic connection with a land belonging to others (that is, native Americans) until the recent past. It is sad that an admittedly ever-deferred transfiguring can be held to overcome and by implication to justify such appropriations, redeeming history and catching up the indigenous and colonising, the oppressor and oppressed in a utopian or heavenly community. This American project can be articulated openly as the basis for ambitious poetry, even now, for example in the work of Susan Howe.

Susan Howe is a poet whose writing is revered for its spareness, its scholarship, its implicit feminist politics, and its exploration of what it is to be American. It draws for its prime example on Charles Olson's *Maximus Poems*, an epic of migration and American colonisation making much use of documentary materials, a debt which Susan Howe generously affirms. Her book-length projects of reading and recovery, starting with *My Emily Dickinson*, substitute for Olson's vitalism an attachment to the tradition of American transcendentalism. She writes in the 'Personal Narrative' introducing her recent book *Souls of the Labadie Tract*:

> If I were to read aloud a passage from a poem of your choice, to an audience of judges in sympathy with surrounding library nature, and they were to experience its lexical inscape as an offshoot of Anglo-American modernism in typographical format, it might be possible to release our great great grandparents, beginning at the greatest distance from a common mouth, eternally belated,

> some coming home through dark ages, others nearer to early modern, multitudes of them meeting first to constitute certain main branches of etymologies, so all along there are new sources, some running directly contrary to others, and yet all meet at last, clothed in robes of glory, offering maps of languages, some with shining tones.

Nothing like this could have been written by a European. The carefully contrived term 'library nature' is designed to evoke Thoreau, and advertises the library, an English-language library, as a wild place, a place of thickets where the attentive citizen can hear the calls of destiny. Using theological language, Howe envisages a text where "all meet at last." True she acknowledges the millennial "common mouth" will be "eternally belated," but she stacks the odds in favour of a "common mouth" coming to pass, by positing "an audience of judges" as the present occasion for then slipping into a use of "our" which can anticipate the "all" of "all meet at last."

This 'Personal Narrative' was originally a talk to the MLA Conference, the professional body for American teachers of literature; how did they react to being cast as saints, elected to lead an English-speaking procession to the Promised Land, or at least, the Promised Text?

Imminent transcendence and aching postponement, erasure and reframing characterise Susan Howe's poetry, and have been accommodated by her readers to theories of the lyric horizon, and to the belatedness and postponement of meaning in lyric poetry. Her poems have been lent to discussion of authorship and origination, with the status of found texts as poems animated by their position within a sequence and on the page. These matters are of course central to contemporary poetic theory. But the neat little poems of the titular sequence 'Souls of the Labadie Tract', six to eight lines each, two to five syllables, remind us that 'Tract' begins as a literary term, becomes a scriptural term, then becomes confused with 'trace' and 'track', the words being used interchangeably, before meaning an extent of territory; all these meanings are at play in Howe's title and poetic sequence. So this one word traces a movement from the library to the "shining tones" of the scriptural tract, to the almost vanished traces of the Labadist Christian sect, to the territory they occupied—a name and space on the map released by this poetry from an antiquarian interest, and transformed into pure potential.

Although the Labadist sect was more exclusive than the MLA, its tract leads to the same destination, as the last three poems in Howe's sequence disclose:

Longing and envying rest
after a little—garden under
trees but better still likely

to be still more anxious to
get to just daylight all I've
always pushed backward

---

That's the "Labadie Poplar"
Labadists—New Bohemia
little is otherwise known
Our secret and resolute woe
Carolled to our last adieu
Our message was electric

Will you forget when I forget
that we are come to that

---

"America in a skin coat
the color of the juice of
mulberries" her fantastic

cap full of eyes will lead
our way as mind or ears
Goodnight goodnight

As published these poems are surrounded by an enormous quantity of white space holding at bay the library from which their words are extracted so as to enter the space of revived meaning. And 'space is God', Howe asserts in the book's concluding text, 'Fragment of the Wedding Dress of Sarah Pierpont Edwards'—a very nineteenth century sentiment. Extracting words releases them from the textual ground where they have been buried, so they become those ghostly but sainted ancestors whose muttered intimations "get to just daylight." The ancestral words of the Labadists are aligned with the ancestral words of Emerson and Thoreau, the ancestral forms of Emily Dickinson, summoned at once by the appearance of these tiny poems on the page with their dashes, the diction of Walt Whitman in the odd use of the word "electric," and the textual authority of Anglo-American modernism, especially Louis Zukofsky and at the end T.S. Eliot. With all that historical text at work, the 'Souls of the Labadie Tract' themselves occupy the surrounding white space as myth, as invention. The souls are ghostly footfalls. Howe has solicited their myth early in the sequence: "Authorize me and I act | what I am I must remain | only suffer me to tell it." This formula, poised against the white of pure potential, conforms exactly to the formula for American ethnic, gender, or victimised identity. It is also the formula for God's work, whereby the community or the conference is transfigured into the band of saints, and anyone is already a part, so long as God will "only suffer me to tell it," to tell "all I've | always pushed backward."

The "fantastic | | cap" in the last poem of 'Souls of the Labadie Tract' combines "Greenest green your holy cope" from an earlier poem, with a forest, a library and a priest's dress, "a skin coate of grasse greene," from a later poem, and belongs to a weft of short 'a' sounds running through the sequence—the mulberries cited in the last poem converted into the silk threads of text or textile. This all leads to America's "cap full of eyes," like a cap full of a magic draft or drug, and like millions of Americans under their baseball caps, their logos asserting their identity, their "I." The goodnight into which these poems fade is the white page, the transcendent text.

This particular poetic practice, then, is nothing like so theoretical as it's often held to be. Although it parades its linguistic construction, the language doesn't do much heavy lifting; it falls into line with American literary, social, religious and political life—at its most high-minded, at its most admirable. But isn't there something strangely immaterial about all this, despite its obsession with materials? There's a strong feeling for a formative past, but a past consisting of ghosts wandering about a wilderness. Howe's poems do include the traces of native Americans, but lightly registered in the language of settlers. The text present to the reader is a wispy text, needing to call on a radiant future to invest wispiness with powerful significance, visibly and audibly. One tactic these poems use is mirroring, where poems opposite each other on the page are visually similar and often chime, rhyme and echo, as though they would defeat time and achieve a synchronic compact between the poem and the often archaic language whose reorganisation produces the poem; this happens particularly at the mid-point of the sequence. Mirroring is complemented by a diachronic and extensive distribution through the sequence, whereby brief phrases recur with variation as though revenants, or like genetic code. Interest gathers round such relationships because there is little local satisfaction to be gained and no line of thought to be pursued from verse line to line when versification feels so arbitrary—blocks of verse are assembled regardless of metrics. The prosody does not lead the voice; rather, the voice has to invest the verse with sonic significance through a determined strategy, a mutter, a whisper, or an exaggerated slow savouring. Line-breaks have no sonic or semantic rationale except by accident—so the words "break" and "forget" might have been important choices at line-ends, but not so much where other end-words are insignificant, and where no particular accent falls on them other than what a reader must impart. Coding resistance to the voice in verse might bring advantages, for instance through disengaging language from individual expression, but here the sparse tract declares its recovery from the past and orientation to the future with a stilted deliberation. When each word goes exactly here but here is of no special account, the reader is left to impart life.

These tactics mean that the present of the poem is insubstantial, and has power only insofar as it echoes what has been written previously. The poems assert their dependence on prior text, not only the hitherto occluded text which has been ferreted out in the research library, but prior poetic texts. Among the poetic lineage *Souls of the Labadie Tract* summons, are the textual ghosts of the Elizabethan English songwriter and prosodic theorist Thomas Campion and of Emily Dickinson. One reason I call these textual ghosts is that they are inaudible. Given that Campion has often, and not least by Ezra Pound, been admired as a master of poetic sound, of clear yet intricate song; and given that Emily Dickinson's poems are notable for a heavily-stressed metric derived from the hymnal, the presence of these poets seems perversely disembodied. In Dickinson's case the haunting is betrayed by dashes and the visual appearance of Susan Howe's stanzas, and in Campion's by his name and by tiny fragments of Elizabethan English. In neither case are the poet's cadences discernible. This must surely represent a choice by Howe, and one consistent with her describing the earth, in a borrowed phrase, as "a mantle painted full of trees." Howe explains such a choice in 'Personal Narrative': "I wanted jerky and tedious details to oratorically bloom and bear fruit as if they had been set at liberty or ransomed by angels." But in 'Souls of the Ladabie Tract' she takes the further step of pulverising prior poetic discourse into "jerky and tedious details" as though to mark their gathering into a physical presence as illegitimate, in the same spirit as those sectarians for whom any indulgence of the senses is a satanic diversion, when all should be preparing to join the shining choir.

Hence the paradox that a discriminating, tightly focused attention to the material text, which in much of Howe's writing entails reproducing variously aged, distorted, torn and fragmented printed remnants, tends towards a poetry which is remarkably etiolated. Here is the incessant deferral of closure co-existing with a millennial conviction, and in these poems, as

Jean-Luc Nancy writes, "each existence appears in more ensembles, masses, tissues or complexes than one perceives at first, and each one is also infinitely more detached from such, and detached from itself" ('Cosmo Baselius,' *Being Singular Plural*, 186). But at the horizon these existences and ensembles must be reconciled in the "just daylight," ever-deferred.

Such a reconciliation is performed indifferently, flattening its materials and desiccating them like pressed leaves. The centrally positioned text of *Souls of the Labadie Tract* is titled '118 Westerly Terrace,' Wallace Stevens' home address. That Wallace Stevens had an address might be something of a shock to tender sensibilities; but more problematic is the suppression of Stevens' epistemological restlessness in favour of *settlement*. At all times the address is fixed:

> because beauty is what *is*
>
> What is said what this
>
> *it*—it in itself insistent is

The auditory and visual play of the final line here is welcome, but its artifice designs to settle matters, affixing them more tightly in a consonance of assertion and poetic contrivance that restricts movement. Indeed, in this extensive although sparely-scored sequence, there is scarcely a phrase which is not an assertion. These are not the fragments opening to interpretation so much beloved of contemporary poetic theorists; they are presented as gospel evidence. Neither is this the sequence that sets in play a dozen obliquities or launches a dialectical spiral; it is a part-work sermon. For all the calm and radiance characteristic of the born-again, there is discernible a passive aggression here in so extreme a traducing of Wallace Stevens, Howe's each step placed so carefully in her own footprints, almost falling over in the effort to go nowhere.

Throughout this book the anachronism of Howe's poetry is troubling. During the last half-century, the texture of life has changed profoundly. It has become a cliché to talk of the change from a modern to a postmodern world, and leaving aside the intricate debates on postmodernism within the arts, this change has been characterised as the end of grand narratives and the development of a new form of experience where time and space are radically conflated. The term 'postmodernism' has tended to merge with the technology of digitalised information and its exchange.

It seemed for many who thought about this change that infinite access had become possible; so a peasant in the Sudan equipped with a satellite dish and a cheap computer could communicate easily with a New York banker and on conditions of theoretical equality. There was some wild joyfulness in the postmodern turn, a kind of hedonism, and a real democratic impulse, a belief that an information commons had arrived, which would rattle political and economic hierarchies. What you can do with information tends however to show not that information is power but that power can use information to create greater value and to sequester it. Susan Howe's poetry is extremely intelligent within the limits of its conception of limitlessness—but it falls short of the poetry needed now, and its strengths have become its liabilities. Alas, robes of glory do not await any of us, and we can but imagine the best clothes for our continued life together, out of the immeasurable complexity that presses in. The exhibition of a wedding dress fragment will not do—"fragile serenity" will butter no parsnips. Something more motley would be becoming, something more critical, something far from reverential.

# Josh Barkan's *Blind Speed*

Josh Barkan. *Blind Speed.* Northwestern University Press. 2008.

*Peter Michelson*

The protagonist of Josh Barkan's first novel is a distinctively postmodern antihero—culturally shell shocked, marginally intelligent, precociously incapable, obsessively introspective, emotionally boxed out, hapless, white, and, as if that weren't sufficient, fat and ugly in the bargain. Mr. Barkan cites Saul Bellow in his acknowledgements, and indeed his principal character hovers somewhere between Bellow's *Dangling Man* and *The Victim.* The pace of failure in Paul Berger's life is such that he seems to be like a deer caught in the headlights of an oncoming semi. His stasis makes the ordinary world swoosh toward him at *Blind Speed,* conveniently the novel's title.

Paul is not simply a Slowski, he is a monument to what psychologists call *inadequacy*. Paul's story is a pilgrim's progress through the slough of despond, to say nothing of a slew of parodic swipes at American culture, to a last second, presumably salvific, epiphany. In the beginning Paul is unable to come to terms with the word. An instructor at a conspicuously unnamed community college, his writer's block is preventing him from starting, let alone completing, his book on something like Conspiracy-Theories-Sexual-Dysfunction-the-Porn-Industry-Gun-Collecting-Feelings-of-Inadequacy-*vis-à-vis*-the-Search-for-Nirvana-in-American-Culture. This block, understandable though it may be, will not only cost Paul his job and marriage but will precipitate a sequence of events at least as improbable as the subject of his book.

The first chapter establishes the prevailing esprit. Paul and Zoe, his fiancée, are enroute to their wedding caterers. Paul, a history buff, pulls off at Concord to see the reenactment of the shot heard round the world. His first blunder is to park the front wheels of his car—'Careful of the flowers,' Zoe says—in the red, white and blue flower bed planted by the DAR. Next he wanders off, ignoring Zoe's hints to stay with her (this will signify), recollects the recent occasion when his supercilious department chair told him it was too late to publish so he must perish, encounters his older brother, a prominent Harvard civil rights lawyer, in an open air press conference denouncing "the rotten stench in Washington"—"True, Paul thought, but what about your own crimes?"(a fortissimo signifier)—and declaring his candidacy for Congress. Apparently Paul's brother Cyrus is not only criminal but likewise not so discrete as one might expect a public figure to be, for Paul is somehow aware that Cyrus "liked to eat barbecued chicken, then have prostitutes suck the sauce off his fingers before going down on him" among other intimate peculiarities (this too will signify). Cyrus commandeers Paul into his limo, lectures him about publishing and offers to intervene with Paul's reappointment, which Paul declines. Paul, now aware of his tardiness from Zoe—"He had been late for most things in his life"-- jumps from the limo to find her as the battle of Old North Bridge commences with a comedic glitch too complex to explain. Suffice it to say that a Colonial musket's ramrod is accidentally discharged like a rocket and zings directly to Zoe, penetrating her pelvis. Since this is parody Zoe needn't meet her maker (but the pertinence of parenthetical signifiers remains). The chapter concludes with an image of Paul—"he paddled as hard as he could to reach her"—that stamps him Grade A Sad Sack.

Meanwhile, some years earlier enroute to Iowa City (Barkan is an Iowa Writers' Workshop graduate) Paul accidentally discovered the Rashna Retreat, a meditation center run by a Varanasi guru who called himself Buffalo Man, and that is where he met Zoe. Though skeptical, Paul consents to have Buffalo Man read his palm, and thereby hangs the tale. BM, as I shall designate him, tells Paul that he will meet his future romantic partner (Zoe) at the Retreat, that he "will leave" one brother (Cyrus) and a second "will leave you" (Andrew, an astronaut who dies on 9/11 at the Pentagon, another signifier), that his romance will not last, and that he will die in his forties. For reasons that are not altogether clear but to which I shall return, Paul takes BM's palmistry forecast seriously as prophecy of his fate. Understandably morose, he staggers through an adjacent cornfield to its edge overlooking I-80, where he contemplates his fate and has revelations—"Every animal…lives only to avoid death" and "Everyone makes his journey to death alone"—and epiphany number one involving "the balance between the good speed and the bad" and the first of two appearances by the afore mentioned deer (first paragraph), which adroitly evades imminent mortality via the (presumably bad) speed of the semis roaring along I 80.

Paul stiffs BM and the Rashna Retreat for the price of his room, board, yoga lessons, palmistry, to say nothing of BM's parting admonition "that it will all come to pass unless you purify yourself," and drives off to his problematic future. Accordingly, he can't shake the feeling that his future is in the hands of BM's prophecy, and it begins to look that way. His brother Andrew is killed, and Zoe does weary of the whiney static of his writer's block, which he attributes to his anxiety about the fatal prophecy. To save his job and his romance Paul adopts a bold strategem. He hires a ghost writer ("The Modern Cyrano," a blunt signifier) to write an article for him;

that is, he becomes a plagiarist. As this project is enroute to its predictable failure, Zoe's recuperation and the wedding advance toward further absurdity, featuring a crazed survivalist dropping out of a tree as the priest (preoccupied with moving the ceremony along so that he might have time for a few holes of golf) intones the oldest comedic cue in cinema history—"speak now or forever hold..."—to accuse Zoe of infidelity. It is a moment where the wedding scene in "The Graduate" meets "Dr. Strangelove." Later, by way of punctuating how infidelity in the service of pop psyche therapeutics works, Zoe lifts Paul from nuptial chaos to sexual transcendance. Still, two paragraphs later Paul can't take yes for an answer and concludes he's lost Zoe and moved that much closer to realizing BM's prophecy.

While it appears that nothing more can befall the hapless schlep, the plot has another trick or two up its sleeve. Suddenly (though the attentive reader will recall Cyrus' suspect character and be prepared for this turn of events) Paul is kidnapped by his brother Cyrus. That is, Cyrus hires an aspiring film maker from NYU film school and his crew to dress up like eco-terrorists and kidnap Paul and demand Cyrus, the political candidate, submit to their ecological program or Paul gets it, which of course Cyrus won't do so that his constituency can see he's not a liberal eco-wimp or terrorist appeaser. All of this is being filmed, of course, as an eco-politics documentary. Essentially the film crew of "eco-terrorists" is the gang that couldn't shoot straight, and Paul discovers that this is another of Cyrus's frauds. But, opportunities notwithstanding, he declines escaping, goes along with the charade, develops a kind of bond with the film maker, and continues stewing about his failure to do anything in life. Meanwhile Zoe has evicted him from their apartment in frustration, his plagiarism project with Cyrano has failed, he's lost his teaching job, and he has in effect connived with his crooked brother Cyrus to help get him elected. What's left but to expose Cyrus' fraud, which he and the film maker (who Cyrus has declined to pay, another signifier) collude to do. This is Boston, so Paul dresses as a "Native American" to confront Cyrus at a news conference, fires six shots into the ceiling from his pistola, and denounces Cyrus' perfidy before being tackled by security guards. Paul intends this to be, like the Boston Tea Party, a liberating act of choice, "demanding his freedom" (an anemic signifier). But once again Paul comes up with egg on his face. His expose` is regarded as the ravings of a man driven mad by his kidnapping.

Three of BM's four prophetic points having been realized in the loss of his two brothers and his wife, Paul, now 35, decides to return to BM's Iowa retreat to take up the fourth "curse," his own death at forty. As it turns out, Zoe has squared accounts with the retreat and even paid for this meeting with BM in order for Paul "to resolve his problems." The benevolent offstage agency of Zoe would seem to remove some of Paul's freight for the reader, but not for Paul. Appropriating a discarded shawl, he girds his loins with a "kind of red cloth diaper" and descends into BM's Kiva Hut. BM gives a plausible pop psych explanation for his dysfunctions, dating from the moment when Paul became "a wounded adult…[realizing] That you were just like everyone else in this world. That you were a mere mortal. The quest for fame gives hopes of immortality…and when you lost that… you were confronted with the shortness of life that all of us face on earth." Paul, it seems, must "purify" himself not only of his desire for immortality but also for "fame and sexual prowess and the need to be loved and for the lazy happiness…symbolized by a drug-induced stupor." This causal analysis apparently derives from a brief early side bar of the narrative, when Paul was in a rock group that had a marginal success as a warm-up act but realized it wasn't good enough for a future. The purgative requires, says BM, "an overstimulation of sex, drugs, and rock and roll."

In the "Decontamination Chamber" Paul goes to battle against his desires buck naked, sporting a kendo mask and sword of bamboo strips tied together with condoms. Though it has not been a preoccupation previously, he now nervously scrutinizes his penis—"medium to small…more of an average penis, he thought," and recounts all the size and adequacy anxieties ever documented by, say, the Kinsey Institute. He is surrounded by189 TV screens ("…as revealed by Guru Satyajit…a holy number of purification.") all showing one porn script after another, symbolic of the "pollution" he is fighting. His material opponent is one Jennifer Rashnaji, also naked and armed with a kendo sword. She displays her open vagina—"the holy grail of sexuality," says the narrator—and attacks Paul's penis. The menace makes him *act* for the second time in 277 pages (the first time 20 pages earlier, his unsuccessful Boston Tea Party), and he and the Rashnaji thrust and parry for half an hour, and then it stops, the first phase of, yes, "a twelve step decontamination process." But, notwithstanding his vague sense of Rashnaji's sex appeal, Paul has had enough. At last he figures out that BM's "wisdom" is commonplace--"Basic words about abnegation and celibacy and turning away from the feelings of inadequacy that he felt because of a lifetime of media saturated culture"—but although he "already knew all that" it has never helped. Poor guy: what now?

Foregoing the next eleven steps he wanders into the cornfield once again…and receives another epiphany. The deer (cf. paragraphs 1 and 4 above) has apparently been waiting, and this time raises the ante. Instead of evading mortality the deer now leads Paul to the center of I-80—"the center of the blind speed of the highway as it rushed toward the Pacific"—where he faces the traffic honking and swerving around him (the deer had the good sense to move out of harm's way) unflinchingly. "This is how blind speed is overcome," he realizes, "It was necessary to take risks to overcome failure." If that seems a bit anticlimactic, especially after his epic battle with "the holy pussy," there is a grace note in conclusion, "*Since the problem is from within*, he thought, *I must change myself.*"

The reader will detect a certain tonal skepticism in my survey of the plot. The plot's conclusion about risk, change and self is not really persuasive. While these and other of its themes, such as love, fate and consciousness, are certainly timeless, they are by virtue of that somewhat long in the tooth, and here they seem to bring us not so much to truth as to truism. But all the while I was reading I had the sense that Barkan was up to something other than the plot. His narrative manner frequently suggested that Barkan was as skeptical of his plot as I was. Narrative self consciousness is obligatory these days, and in itself imposes skepticism. For example, when Paul is "liberated" by the eco-terrorists Barkan arbitrarily has him be smuggled into Cyrus' election victory party by a cadre of Pakistanis through an institutional kitchen apparently so he can evoke the Bobby Kennedy assassination and ironies of post 9-11 security measures; Paul's escort says, "Given the current high-level, code-red antiterrorist standard of this building—ever since the Democratic convention this summer [2004]—it seemed the only way. It's crazy, I know, but it takes a Pakistani food worker to break legally into the system."

Such devices provide a parodic tonal energy of contemporaneousness that accompanies the narrative without exactly informing it, so that one detects the author's chuckle behind the narrative. In this instance Barkan foregrounds the chuckle by inserting a parenthetical note in his own voice, "If it seems like I'm picking on the Democrats, just imagine what a field day I could have had if I'd made the Republicans the sponsors of the ecoterrorist kidnappers," and goes on to explicate the matter. And some pages later he ends the chapter with another paragraph in his own voice, a "Coda" in which he describes the "spectacle" of "the day Michael Jackson was acquitted of getting a young boy drunk and sexually molesting him." Its function is to somehow validate Paul's psychic paralysis in the spectacle of Cyrus' election victory party, in terms of narrative, and to document the author's thematic authenticity in social terms. Barkan's description of what is in effect Michael Jackson's victory party constitutes a social parody complementing the fictive parody. At the same time, however, it upstages the narrative by making it a footnote to reality rather than an imaginative engagement of it. This narrative quizzicalness is compounded by a postscript following the coda, where Barkan notes that the Boston Tea Party perpetrators dressed as Mohawks, "who lived nowhere near Boston but rather in the Great Lakes region of New York, where they were members of the five nation Iroquois Confederacy." Paul of course got up as a Sioux, geographically farther out of synch, so the postscript is an obvious compromise of him and possibly a poke at America's ignorance of its own history. But one wonders if that rather small satiric light is worth the candle of selfconsciousness.

This sort of sometimes puzzling play is a distinct aspect of Barkan's style. It happens often enough that it seems conceptual, but the reader doesn't quite know what to do with it. Barkan's frequent parenthetical comments, which come in the voice of a narrator/author hybrid, can be informative—"(the date of this chapter is1998)"—or distracting. For example, as the reader is introduced to the Rashna Retreat the parenthetical interlocutor tells the reader that its Guru "called himself Buffalo Man. (He'd chosen the name in sympathy for the Black Hawk Indians who had lived in Iowa before they were eradicated.)" It's not clear why the reader is teased with so conspicuous a historical error (There were no "Black Hawk Indians"; Black Hawk was a notorious war chief of the Sac Indian tribe). Possibly it is to cue us to Buffalo Man's guruish fraudulence but why so coyly cast such trivia in an authorial aside? Or, again, one wonders about the narrative function of imaging the guru's followers absurdly ("...they moved their arms with one palm saluting the sky and then the other like go-go dancers trying to hail a cab to heaven") and counterpointing with stereotypical romanticism ("And Buffalo Man's arms spread slowly, slowly, so slowly they barely seemed to move; yet slowly they opened wider and wider into the sky above like a lotus exposing its delicate yet resilient petals"). These devices place the whole narrative apparatus in the shadow of an indiscriminate skepticism, which in itself may characterize the age but doesn't work so well as an aesthetic habit. Paul himself responds to an elaborated analogy by BM, "If ever there was a strained metaphor, this was it." It's a shoe that fits Barkan's narrative and invests it with an attitude that undermines the larger framework of Barkan's plot. Paul's fate, for instance, is yoked with an academic publish or perish mandate at "B________ Community College," though anyone with even the vaguest sense of academic culture knows that community colleges do not employ that mandate. Insofar as this has a satirical function it is mildly amusing, but ultimately it reduces the satire to parody and the parody to silliness. Similarly with the parodic treatment of the Rashna Retreat and its guru. At least since the sixties the word *guru* has been the punch line to manifold jokes. Put that together with an authorial skepticism deconstructing narrative credibility even as it progresses and one has to wonder why one should take BM's prophecy of Paul's fate seriously enough even for credible satire. It becomes one long shaggy guru story in which various motifs—love, fraternity, fate, failure, politics, etc.--make cameo appearances, somewhat like *Satuday Night Live*, and then dissipate into the ether of skepticism.

Barkan's m.o. revives an ongoing aesthetic question about the prospects for a contemporary rapprochment between fiction and reality. Tom Perrotta's cover blurb cites *metafiction* as one touchstone for the novel, presumably for its play with narrative and reality. Perhaps *surfiction* is a better fit because its practicioners, for example Raymond Federman, tend to ironize both narrative and reality to the end of making skepticism not simply an attitude but a metaphysics, i.e. comprehensively indiscriminate. At its most indulgent surfiction tends to induce a cartoonish allegory where even the remotest connection between fiction and reality is naïve at best. Here, when Paul dismisses BM's philosophy, as noted, and says he is caught in spirals of inadequacy "because of a lifetime of a media saturated culture" the truism punctuates a cartoonish guru motif that renders character, plot, narrative and narrator superfluous: that is, we don't need this narrative to get to that conclusion. It doesn't make us question reality or fiction or their pavanne; it just renders the issue irrelevant. Having said all that, I can also say that Barkan puts on a pretty good show, in the way that *Beyond the Fringe* puts on a good show. When it parodies Shakespeare, I don't question its critical validity, I just have some amusement at Shakespeare's expense, who can afford it. With Barkan there are times when I do question his validity, but there are also times when the question is moot, and at those times I have my amusement at the expense of reality and/or narrative. If Shakespeare can survive centuries of parody surely reality can do as much. And narrative too will no doubt take care of itself.

## Editors Select

Charles Wright, ed., *The Best American Poetry 2008*. Scribner, 2008. This annual anthology includes work by *NDR* contributor R.T. Smith and Notre Dame Creative Writing Program faculty member Cornelius Eady. There are also poems by poets who regularly show up in this series from year to year: John Ashbery, Robert Bly, Louise Gluck, Jorie Graham, Robert Hass, W.S. Merwin, Paul Muldoon, Charles Simic, et. al.

Chris Agee, ed., *The New North: Contemporary Poetry From Northern Ireland*. Wake Forest Press, 2008. Agee cleverly introduces two separate sections of younger Northern Irish poets with "classic poems" from the two literary generations—about ten years apart—preceding them: Seamus Heaney, Derek Mahon, and Michael Longley for Part One; Ciaran Carson, Medbh McGuckian, and Paul Muldoon for Part Two. The strategy provides a good sense of context and tradition for the fifteen new poets, as does Agee's introduction.

Wayne Miller and Kevin Prufer, eds., *New European Poets*. Graywolf Press, 2008. The co-editors of *Pleiades*, one of our best current journals, have co-edited a fine and rich volume of European poetry assisted by twenty-four "regional editors." Poets writing in English from England, Scotland, Wales, and Ireland take their place beside translated poets from both Western and Eastern Europe, including Russia and the former republics of the old Soviet Union. Most of the poets will be entirely unknown by most readers.

Five books by Richard Berengarten. Berengarten will be known to *NDR* readers as Richard Burns. He has recently repossessed the family name of his father and published with Salt five volumes of selected writings: *For the Living, The Manager, The Blue Butterfly, In a Time of Drought, and Under Balkan Light*. The first three books have been published in earlier editions, but the new volumes from Salt are expanded and include extensive notes by the author. It is altogether a remarkable publishing event and we hope to review the books properly in a future issue of *NDR*.

Reginald Gibbons, *Creatures of a Day*. Louisiana State University Press, 2008. Gibbons's new book includes "Fern Texts," a chapbook based on the journals of Coleridge which was noted in an earlier issue, along with a number of long-lined odes on contemporary and classical themes.

Debora Greger, *Men, Women, and Ghosts*. Penguin, 2008. Greger also derives some recent work from classical sources, particularly Horace. Following the translation of two odes, she prints a sequence of poems dedicated to each of the last five decades. As in her other books, poems dealing with her life in Florida alternate with poems about Britain, where she lives for part of each year, and Europe, especially Holland. The volume includes a moving elegy in memory of Donald Justice.

Moira Linehan, *If No Moon*. Southern Illinois, 2008. At the center of Linehan's new book is the death of her husband and her life as a newly widowed woman trying to face both the past and the future. More than once she compares her work to Penelope's: "There is no other work but starting over"…"undoing all of yesterday's work…ripping row upon endless row back to my error." Linehan has written a strong first book, and all the stronger for having waited until middle age to write it.

William Logan, *Strange Flesh*. Penguin, 2008. William Logan's new book covers some of the same territory as Debora Greger's—not surprisingly as they have been poet-companions for many years. Someday a keen graduate student will write about their influence on one another. When they both write poems about Vermeer's "Girl With a Pearl Earring" one can almost imagine a competition taking place while they stand before the painting. And Logan, like Greger, writes an elegy for Donald Justice. His work is known for its formal rigor, and is sometimes compared to Geoffrey Hill's, of which he is one of the best critics.

Elise Partridge, *Chameleon Hours*. University of Chicago Press, 2008. Stephen Burt praises this book for "the detail work that [Partridge] has learned from Elizabeth Bishop" but also for "other virtues of her own: riffs on familiar phrases that open startling vistas."

Dana Roeser, *In the Truth Room*. Northeastern University Press, 2008. *NDR* published the long and central "Fires of London" from this Morse Poetry Prize-winning volume which was selected by Rodney Jones. Jones says the book is "about a fabric of interwoven lives: four generations of family, friends, dear ones, present and departed—I would be hard pressed to name a poetry book that develops and displays affection for more characters or, for that matter, one that contains more life."

Stephanie Strickland, *Zone:Zero*. Ahsahta Press, 2008. The former Ernest Sandeen Poetry Prize-winner extends both her range and the breathtaking risks she takes in this book. *NDR* readers will be well acquainted with what Marjorie Perloff call's Strickland's "polymath knowledge and technical know-how, especially in the realm of electronic poetics.." Digital versions of "Ballad of Sand and Harry Soot" and "slippingglimpse" are included in an accompanying CD.

Carol Snow, *Placed*. Counterpath Press, 2008. Snow's book could also be called "Prepositions," like the text by Louis Zukofsky. One of the opening epigraphs quotes, in alphabetical order, "the seventy prepositions" according to Mrs. Leonore Larney, Aptos Jr. High School, ca. 1962. The book consists of a kind of oblique gloss on these prepositions, all of them used as titles, drawing on a wide range of texts and paintings for references and citations, with a few lines—not very many—written by Carol Snow. It is also meant to resemble a Japanese rock garden, and specifically the famous Karesansui in Royoan-je Temple near Kyoto. One of the sources quoted repeatedly in fragments is John Berryman's Dream Song 73, which is about a visit to that garden. The book achieves its ultimately very moving effect with great delicacy and tact.

Johannes Göransson, *Pilot: (Johann the Carousel Horse)*. Fairytale Review Press, 2008. Göransson's book might well be read beside, before, beyond, above, beneath, or after Carol Snow's, for it too is an assemblage, drawing on "a strange cast of characters abandoned from other texts, including Lilja, the Pearls of Stockholm, and assorted imperiled girls" who find in *Pilot*'s "exocity a new and beautifully stitched home," as the blurb has it. It might help to know a bit of Swedish, as Göransson writes in both languages, and translates one to the other and back again in this book. And it would also help to know that Fairytale Review Press is dedicated "to helping raise public awareness of the literary and cultural influence of fairy tales and to improve the critical understanding of new works sewn from fairy tales and celebrate their transfixing power."

Chris Viello, *Irresponsibility*. Ahsahta Press, 2008. Irresponsibility is divided into ten sections named for places, mostly in North Carolina, and given dates. There are also two parts called "interruptions," a list of the first 1000 prime numbers and a history of the meter from 1791 to 1983. The sections before and after these "interruptions" are all lyric sequences in a kind of post-Langpo journal idiom. Language is relished in its discontinuities and unexpected leaps and juxtapositions, but also kept under surveillance and subjected to all the characteristic critiques in the postmodern book. After one line referring to a recent death there is a footnote reading "Put this book down and go be with other people." The back cover is a picture of the author's young daughter smiling brightly and offering someone—the reader?—a large and very tempting pastry.

Jill McDonough, *Habeas Corpus*. Salt Publishing, 2008. McDonough's fifty sonnets are about as disorienting as Carol Snow's verbal rock garden is re-orienting. Each sonnet is a terrifying account of a legal execution in America from James Kendall's in 1601 to Michael Ross's in 2005. Along the way the obscure and the famous—Nat Turner, Sacco and Vanzetti, Julius and Ethel Rosenberg, Caryl Chessman, Perry Smith, Gary Gilmore, Timothy McVeigh—are hanged, electrocuted, gassed, and injected. The sonnets are written with enormous skill, and yet their very beauty produces a kind of nausea given their subject. This may be the most successful recent sonnet sequence since Tony Harrison's *Continuous* and David Wojahn's *Mystery Train*.

Donald Hall, *Unpacking the Boxes: A Memoir of a Life in Poetry*. Houghton Mifflin, 2008. Anyone who has read one or two of Hall's other prose books—*String Too Short to Be Saved, Their Ancient Glittering Eyes, Life Work, The Best Day and the Worst Day*—will know how good a memoirist he is. This time the 80-year-old poet remembers his childhood in Connecticut, his time at Exeter, Harvard, and Oxford, along with more recent years. Hall has now outlived most of his contemporaries, and of course also his gifted younger wife Jane Kenyon. In several respects, he was a poet of old age even before he became old. But his writing is always a pleasure even when it is sad, and his ancient, glittering eyes have always been gay.

Katherine Vaz, *Our Lady of the Artichokes and Other Portuguese-American Stories*. University of Nebraska Press, 2008. Award-winning writer Vaz (Dure Heinz prize, Barnes & Noble Discover, Library of Congress, etc.)and *NDR* contributor's new collection(which won the Prairie Schooner Book Prize)further establishes her position as one of her generation's top short story writers. These stories capture the place of Portugese Americans in California, a group with a long and varied history. Praised by Robert Olen Butler, Allegra Goodman, and Julia Glass, the Review takes personal pride in having published one of the collection's best stories, "All Riptides Roar with Sand from Opposing Shores" (Winter 2006, No. 21).

Samuel Hazo, *This Part of the World*, Syracuse University Press, 2008 and *The of the Horse: A Selection of Poems 1958-2008*. Autumn House Press, 2008. Another award-winning *NDR* contributor, Samuel Hazo, has published two capstone books, a novel and a new selection of poetry. Hazo's career has been long, indefatigable and fruitful. Though poetry is his metier, he has published a number of novels, and his latest, *This Part of the World*, is a fresh foray into geopolitical fiction. Praised by Georgie Anne Geyer, Naomi Shihab Nye and Valerie Hemingway, as well as *Publishers Weekly*, which summarizes, "poet Hazo traces the efforts of a band of guerrillas as it resists eradication by a murderous, America-backed dictator. Set in an unnamed Spanish-speaking country ruled by a premier named Caseres (who bears a resemblance to any number of autocrats in recent history), the novel moves among various points of view to set up a guerrilla ambush of government troops at the mountain village of Megiddo. The guerrillas are led by an ascetic Corsican, a veteran of wars in Algeria, Ireland and Jerusalem, and aided by embittered rebels like American Vietnam vet Hull and former priest Sabertes. As Caseres, ailing from a heart condition and in love with a singer whose brother is secretly fighting with the Corsican, prepares a crushing assault on the guerrillas, he grooms his ill-prepared son, Radames, to take over. Hazo has a convincingly bleak vision." Hazo's poetry in *The Song of the Horse* shares the "convincingly" part of that description, though his poetry is full of affirmation of humanity's indomitability. Hazo has captured many honors, though Georgie Anne Geyer's praise generated by the new novel may be the highest and most pertinent compliment, "He is one of the few moralists writing today."

Eugene Halton, *The Great Brain Suck*. University of Chicago Press, 2008. Halton, a sociology professor at Notre Dame, is known locally as Jumpin' Gene Halton, for his avocation as a blues harmonica player. *The Great Brain Suck* is his third book and his funniest and grimmest, both appropriate categories for our time. The volume is a collection of diverse essays, all acute and pointed and filled with bitter, but often hilarious, cultural criticism. A sample, from the title essay: "This strange invisible domination of American life by the alchemy of corn, brain sucking by high fructose surgaring–excess calories in, awareness out–is also mirrored in the socialization of children by advertising. Kids' TV ads communicate fantastic, magical minidramas of suguring, peopled by cartoon figures and superhero demigods, all minions of the surgaring complex." This learned book is both fun and devastating.

Lily Hoang, *Parabola: A Novel in 21 Intersections*. Chiasmus Press, 2008. Hoang, is a ND MFA and *NDR* contributor and her first novel is another award winner. Lance Olsen has this to say: "In *Parabola* Lily Hoang has created a new form of constraint writing: fractal fiction, a fragmented geometric shape subdivided in parts, each of which is a reduced-size copy of the whole, all of which are based on the Pythagorean belief in numerical magic, in unity in multiplicity. The result is a smart, ingenious, difficult, absurd, surprising, unnerving, liberating, mathematically precise, temporally crazed, impishly interactive formal rupture and rapture, a beehive of narrative nodes. Read this, and you will never see the novel in the same way again." We see it as conceptually ambitious fiction woven from the lyrical language of longing. A selection from *Parabola* appeared in the Review's last issue (Summer/Fall, 2008).

Robert Gottlieb, ed., *Reading Dance: A Gathering of Memoirs, Reportage, Criticism, Profiles, Interviews, and Some Uncategorizable Extras.* Pantheon Books, 2008. *The* dance book of the Twenty-first century (or the 20th, for that matter.) Praised universally, this volume is notable for a contribution by *NDR* contributor and ND MFA graduate Renee D'Aoust, which first won an AWP nonfiction award, "Graham Crackers," a piece dealing with D'Aoust's experience in the Martha Graham dance troupe. A splendid essay housed in a splendid collection.

Ian Pear, *The Accidental Zionist: What a Priest, a Pornographer and A Wrestler named Chainsaw taught Me about Being Jewish, Saving the World and Why Israel Matters to Both*. New Song Publishers, 2008. Part autobiography, part treatise, part scholarly exegesis, part gentle manifesto, Rabbi Pear's book offers an entirely fresh view of both the current and past Israel. Pear received his rabbinical ordination from Yeshiva University and a law degree from New York University and a degree in International Relations from Georgetown. The first half of the book focuses on the "nature of Judaism" and the second half on the state of Israel. Challenging, entertaining, full of keen religious understanding and secular wisdom, this book is must reading for anyone concerned with Catholic-Jewish relations.

Brendan Short, *Dream City*. MacAdam/Cage, 2008. Short's, an ND grad, first novel, which has been compared to Michael Chabon's *The Amazing Adventures of Kavalier and Clay*, is a Chicago book first and foremost, covering generations rooted in the city with big shoulders. The plot has old-fashioned elements, bringing up echoes of Dreiser, Algren and Farrell, its pages filled with gangsters and damsels in distress, but its sensibility is thoroughly modern. As Anthony Giardina writes, "*Dream City* cuts to the heart of our obsession with the pop cultural artifacts of the past, the solace of old things. It will sneak up on you and break your heart."

## CONTRIBUTORS

**Lisa Ampleman**'s poems have appeared in *Passages North*, *Cart Green*, *Natural Bridge*, *Center*, and *Folio*. She currently teaches at Fontbonne University. **Michael Anania**'s recent books include *In Natural Light* and *Heat Lines*. An account of his long collaboration with the artist Ed Colker appeared in *American Letters and Commentary*. **Bridgette Bates** was a winner of a 2008 "Discovery"/ *Boston Review* Poetry Contest prize, and her poetry has been published in various magazines including *Lit Magazine*, *American Letters & Commentary*, and the *Colorado Review*. **Robert Bense** is the author of *Readings in Ordinary Time*. **Joelle Biele** is the author of *White Summer*, part of the Crab Orchard Series in Poetry. New poems are appearing in *Poetry Northwest*, *Prairie Schooner* and *Yemassee*. **Sarah Bowman** received her MFA in Creative Writing from the University of Notre Dame. She currently serves as Contracts Manager at Glatting Jackson Kercher Anglin, Inc., a firm that focuses on planning and designing livable communities. **Gaylord Brewer** is a professor at Middle Tennessee State University, where he edits *Poems & Plays*. His most recent books are the poetry collection *The Martini Diet*, and the novella *Octavius the 1st*. **Ciaran Carson** is Professor of Poetry and director of the Seamus Heaney Centre at Queen's University Belfast. His *Collected Poems* is forthcoming. **Colin Cheney** teaches in the Expository Writing Program at New York University. His poems have appeared recently in, or are forthcoming from, *American Poetry Review*, *Ploughshares*, *Gulf Coast*, *Crazyhorse*, *Massachusetts Review*, and *Kenyon Review Online*. He was the receipient of a Ruth Lilly Fellowship from the Poetry Foundation in 2006. **Sean M. Conrey** is an assistant professor of English in the Saint Joseph's University in Philadelphia, where he teaches rhetorical theory and creative writing. His poetry has appeared or is forthcoming in *American Letters and Commentary*, *Aries*, *Cream City Review*, *Hiram Poetry Review*, *Midwest Quarterly*, *Notre Dame Review*, *Permafrost*, *Plainsongs*, and *Tampa Review*. **Jaclyn Dwyer** is an MFA candidate at the University of Notre Dame, where she is recipient of the Sparks Fellowship. Her work has appeared in *3 am Magazine* and the *Cortland Review*. **Chi Elliott** is pursuing two graduate degrees: a PhD in American Studies at the University of Texas at Austin, and an MFA in Poetry at Warren Wilson College. Her work has appeared or is forthcoming in the *African American Review* and *MARGIE*. **John Estes** teaches at the University of Missouri. Recent poems have appeared or are forthcoming in *Another Chicago Magazine*, *West Branch*, *Ninth Letter*, *LIT*, *Ecopoetics*, and other places. He is author of two chapbooks: *Swerve* won a 2008 National

Chapbook Fellowship from the Poetry Society of America, and *Breakfast with Blake at the Laocoön*. **Ed Falco**'s novel, *Saint John of the Five Boroughs*, is forthcoming later this year. His previous books include the novel, *Wolf Point*, the collection of short fictions, *In the Park of Culture*, and the story collection, *Sabbath Night in the Church of the Piranha: New and Selected Stories*. He is the director of the MFA Program in Creative Writing at Virginia Tech. **Helena Fitzgerald** is a writer living in New York City. The story in this publication, "Accident," is adapted from a piece of a longer novel on which she is currently at work. **Joan Frank** is the author of novels *The Great Far Away* and *Miss Kansas City*, and the story collection *Boys Keep Being Born*. **Diane Furtney**'s poems and translations have appeared recently in *Stand*, *The Marlboro Review*, *Circumference*, *Faultline*, and *Ezra*. She works in the plant biology department at The Ohio State University. **Megan Gannon**'s poems have appeared in *Ploughshares*, *Pleiades*, *Crazyhorse*, and *Best American Poetry 2006*. She is a PhD candidate at the University of Nebraska-Lincoln, where she is completing a novel entitled *Cumberland*. **Taylor Graham** is a volunteer search-and-rescue dog handler. Her poems appear *in International Poetry Review*, *The New York Quarterly*, *Southern Humanities Review*, and elsewhere. **Jarrett Haley**'s fiction has been awarded by *Playboy*. His forthcoming novel is set in New Mexico. **Jared Harel** is a graduate of Cornell's MFA program. His work has been published in over twenty literary journals such as the *New York Quarterly*, *California Quarterly*, *RATTLE*, *Rhino*, and others. He also plays drums for the NYC-based rock band, Heywood. **Henry Hart**'s most recent poetry book is *Background Radiation*. He teaches at the College of William and Mary. **Gretchen E. Henderson**'s writing has appeared in *The Iowa Review*, *The Southern Review*, *Denver Quarterly*, *Double Room*, *Alaska Quarterly Review*, and elsewhere. **Dennis Hinrichsen**'s fifth book of poems, *Kurosawa's Dog*, won the 2008 FIELD Poetry Prize and will appear this year. **Angie Hogan** received her BA from Vanderbilt University and her MFA from the University of Virginia. Her poems have appeared in *The Antioch Review*, *Bellingham Review*, *Ploughshares*, *Third Coast*, and *The Virginia Quarterly Review*, among other journals. **Elizabeth Klise von Zerneck**'s poems have recently appeared or are forthcoming in *Atlanta Review*, *Crab Orchard Review*, *Measure*, *Ninth Letter*, *The Pinch*, *Potomac Review*, *Spoon River Poetry Review*, *Water-Stone Review*, and others. **Sandra Kohler**'s second collection of poems, *The Ceremonies of Longing*, was winner of the 2002 AWP Award Series in Poetry. A first collection, *The Country of Women*, appeared in 1995. Her work has appeared in literary magazines including *Prairie Schooner*, *The Colorado Review*, and *Beloit Poetry Journal* over the past thirty years. **Hank Lazer**'s most recent books of poetry are *The New Spirit, Elegies & Vacations*, and *Days*. His *Lyric & Spirit: Selected Essays, 1996-2008* appeared in 2008. He edits the Modern and Contemporary Poetics Series for the University of Alabama Press, and he is the Associate Provost for Academic Affairs at the University of Alabama. **Jenny Malmqvist** is a doctoral candidate at The Graduate School in Language and Culture in Europe, Linköping University, Sweden. She is writing her thesis on the work of Ciaran Carson. **Peter Marcus** has had recent publications in *The Antioch Review, Boulevard*, and *The Crab Orchard Review*. He was awarded a Connecticut Commission of the Arts Fellowship for Poetry in 2001. He currently teaches psychology as an assistant professor of Social Science at Borough of Manhattan Community College/City University of New York. **Kathleen McGookey** has published over 100 poems and translations in journals including *Boston Review, Epoch, Field, The Journal, Quarterly West, Seneca Review*, and *West Branch*. Her book is *Whatever Shines*. **Bill Meissner**'s most recent poetry book is *American Compass*. His first novel—and seventh book—is *Spirits in the Grass*. He teaches creative writing at St. Cloud State University. **Peter Michelson** is the author of several books of poetry, including *When the Revolution Really*, two volumes of prose, including *Speaking the Unspeakable*, many personal and critical essays, and has edited T*he Extant Poetry and Prose of Max Michelson, Imagist.* **Derek Mong** is the 2008-2010 Axton Poetry Fellow at the University of Louisville. His poems, translations, and prose have appeared in *The Kenyon Review, Pleiades*, the *Southern Review*, and elsewhere. New work can be found in *The Cincinnati Review, Crab Orchard Review*, and the anthology *Breathe: 101 Contemporary Odes*. **Jude Nutter**'s first book-length collection, *Pictures of the Afterlife*, was published in 2002. *The Curator of Silence*, her second collection, won the Ernest Sandeen Prize from the University of Notre Dame and was awarded the 2007 Minnesota Book Award in Poetry. A third collection, *I Wish I Had A Heart Like Yours, Walt Whitman*, is forthcoming. **Michael O'Leary** edits *Flood Editions* with Devin Johnston, and works as a structural engineer in Chicago. **Deborah Pease** has published in numerous journals, including *The Paris Review* and *The New Yorker*. Her collected poems, *Another Ghost in the Doorway*, was published in 1999. She is a former publisher of *The Paris Review*, and the author of the novel, *Real Life*. **Peter Robinson** is professor of English and American Literature at the University of Reading, UK. His most recent collection of poetry is *The Look of Goodbye: Poems 2001-2006. The Greener Meadow: Selected Poems of Luciano Erba* won the John Florio Prize. Forthcoming are *Poetry & Translation: The Art of the Impossible* and *Spirits of the Stair:*

*Selected Aphorisms*. **Steven Rood** is a trial lawyer in Oakland, California. **Anis Shivani**'s short fiction collection, *Anatolia and Other Stories*, is being published later this year, and a novel, *Intrusion*, is in progress. **John Shoptaw** teaches poetry reading and writing at UC, Berkeley. *Times Beach*, his first book of poems, is nearing completion. **R.D. Skillings**'s story "The Dude" belongs to a collection called *The Washashores*, which takes place in Provincetown 1963-1985. A washashore is a non-native resident. **Frederick Smock** chairs the English Department at Bellarmine University, Louisville. His most recent book is *Craft-talk: On Writing Poetry*. **Marjorie Stelmach**'s third volume of poems, *For Now, For Love*, will be published later this year. **Lars-Håkan Svensson** is professor of Language and Culture at Linköping University. His current projects include *Translation as Intervention in the Poetry of Paul Muldoon*, and *Imitation and Cultural Memory in Edmund Spenser's* The Faerie Queene. **Brian Swann** has published collections of poetry and short fiction, has translated volumes of poetry and edited books on Native American literatures. **Leslie Ullman** is the author of three poetry collections, most recently *Slow Work Through Sand*, winner of the Iowa Poetry Prize. Now Professor Emerita at University of Texas-El Paso, she teaches in the low-residency MFA program at Vermont College of the Fine Arts and does freelance manuscript consultations. **Stephanie Magdalena White** is an MFA candidate in poetry at the University of Notre Dame. She is a regular attendee of Calvin College's Festival of Faith and Writing. **John Wilkinson** is research professor in the Department of English at Notre Dame. His recent publications include a book of criticism, *The Lyric Touch: Essays on the poetry of excess*, and a book of poetry, *Down to Earth*. **James Matthew Wilson** is Assistant Professor of Humanities at Villanova University. His work appears regularly in *Contemporary Poetry Review*, *Modern Age*, *Christianity and Literature*, *The Dark Horse*, and elsewhere. **William Wolak** is a poet whose work has appeared in many literary magazines. He also is the author of a collection of poetry, *Pale As An Explosion*. He has translated Joyce Mansour, Stuart Merrill, and Francis Vielé-Griffin. He is adjunct professor in the English Department at William Paterson University. **Ryo Yamaguchi**'s poems have appeared most recently in *Tin House*, *Sonoma Review*, *The Louisville Review*, and *Ninth Letter*, among others.

# Sustainers

*Anonymous* [Two]

*Nancy & Warren Bryant*

*Kevin DiCamillo*

*Gary & Elizabeth Gutchess*

*John F. Hayward*

*Samuel Hazo*

*Tim Kilroy*

*Richard Landry*

*Steve Lazar*

*Carol A. Losi*

*Jessica Maich*

*Vincent J. O'Brien*

*Kevin T. O'Connor*

*Daniel O'Donnell*

*Beth Haverkamp Powers*

*Mark W. Roche*

*In Honor of Ernest Sandeen*

*John Sitter*

*In Honor of James Whitehead*

*Kenneth L. Woodword*

Sustainers are lifetime subscribers to the *Notre Dame Review.* You can become a sustainer by making a one-time donation of $250 or more. (See subscription information enclosed.)

# santa clara review

poetry • fiction • nonfiction • drama • art

The santa clara review showcases the work of new and established writers and artists. Issues have featured such figures as Neil Gaiman, Ron Hansen, Bo Caldwell, Katharine Noel, and Frank Warren.

The review is published biannually. Submit to the address below or on www.santaclarareview.com/submit. All submissions are eligible for the $100 Editor's Choice Prize awarded to one contributor in each

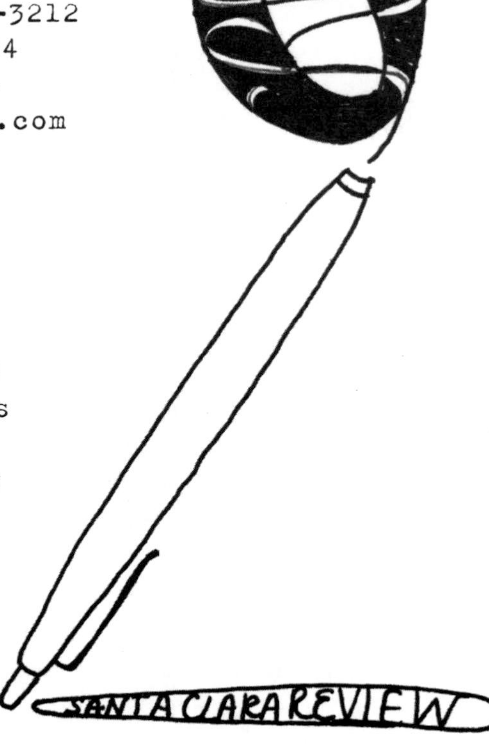


santa clara review
500 El Camino Real
Santa Clara, CA 95053-3212
phone: 408.554.4484
fax: 408.554.5544
www.santaclarareview.com

Subscriptions:
One Year: $10.00
Two Years: $19.00
(Postage Included)
*Please make chacks
payable to the
santa clara review

# NORTH AMERICAN REVIEW

First published in 1815, The *North American Review* is among the country's oldest literary magazines. As a writer, you can have a subscription to the *North American Review* at the reduced price of $18. The *North American Review* is located at the University of Northern Iowa and has published such well-known artists and writers as Walt Whitman, Louise Erdrich, Mark Twain, Maxine Hong Kingston, and Rita Dove.

**Subscribe today and enjoy a 20% savings as well as contemporary literature at its best.**

Subscriptions$22.00 per year US

**E-mail** nar@uni.edu

**Web** http://webdelsol.com/ NorthAmReview/NAR

# CREAM CITY REVIEW

ISSUE 32.1
SPRING
2008

FEATURING
LITERARY PRIZE WINNERS

AND INTRODUCING
COMICS FROM EUROPE

ALSO AVAILABLE
SIBLINGHOOD FALL 2007

BEN PERCY, ARIELLE GREENBERG, YANNICK MURPHY,
AND AN INTERVIEW WITH JONATHAN LETHEM

VISIT OUR NEW WEBSITE FOR EXCERPTS
AND INFORMATION ON OUR
ANNUAL LITERARY PRIZES

creamcityreview.org

$22 ONE-YEAR SUBSCRIPTION
$12 SINGLE ISSUE

# Found

creamcityreview

FALL 2008 ISSUE

AVAILABLE IN NOVEMBER

Annual Literary Prizes: $1,000.00
and Spring 2009 publication

Judges: Kelly Link (Fiction)
Arielle Greenberg (Poetry)
Lee Martin (Nonfiction)

Submissions and $15 entrance fee
accepted through December 1, 2008

$12/single issue
$22/one-year subscription
$41/two-year subscription

creamcityreview.org

Annual Non-Fiction Contest*

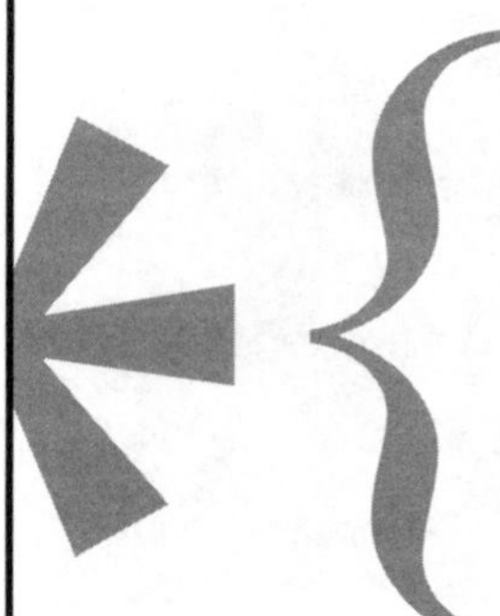

**Three winners will receive $500 each plus publication!**

**$29.95 entry fee includes 1 year of EVENT**

**5,000 word limit**

**Deadline April 15**

Visit **http://event.douglas.bc.ca** for more information

Canada Council for the Arts
Conseil des Arts du Canada

Douglas College

# GREEN MOUNTAINS REVIEW

Nin Andrews
Antler
Ellen Bass
Marvin Bell
Michael Blumenthal
Christopher Buckley
Matthew Cooperman
Jim Daniels
Tracy Daugherty
Greg Delanty
Denise Duhamel
B.H. Fairchild
Gary Fincke
Patricia Goedicke
Lola Haskins
Brian Henry
Bob Hicok
H.L. Hix
David Huddle
Peter Johnson
Timothy Liu
Robert Hill Long
T.M. McNally
Sandra Meek
Benjamin Percy
William Pitt Root
Stephen Sandy
Maureen Seaton
Reginald Shepherd
Betsy Sholl
Alexander Theroux
Daniel Tobin
William Trowbridge
Charles Harper Webb
Walter Wetherell
Jay White

Neil Shepard, Editor and Poetry Editor • Leslie Daniels, Fiction Editor

*Best American Poetry* • *Pushcart Prize* • *Poetry Daily* • *Verse Daily*

"A strong record of quality work… many exciting new voices."
–*Library Journal*

"Character, vision and energy…The production is beautiful and the space crisp and clear."
–*Magazine Rack*

"Solid, handsome, comprehensive."
–*Literary Magazine Review*

Subscriptions: $15/year
Send check to: Green Mountains Review
Johnson State College, Johnson, VT 05656

Contact us by email: gmr@jsc.edu
Visit http://greenmountainsreview.jsc.vsc.edu for submission and subscription information

*Celebrating a decade of literary excellence!*

# Notre Dame review

THE FIRST TEN YEARS

EDITED WITH AN INTRODUCTION BY

**John Matthias** AND **William O'Rourke**

". . . a lively, engaging, unpredictable literary journal."

—ROBERT PINSKY
author of
*Gulf Music* and
former Poet Laureate
of the United States

$30.00 paper • 584 pages
ISBN 978-0-268-03512-9

Contributors to this anthology represent a wide range of styles and aesthetic orientations. This collection includes over 100 poems and nearly 30 short stories that challenge, surprise, comfort, discomfort, and delight—each in its own unique way.

Available at bookstores, or order online at: *www.undpress.nd.edu*

**University of Notre Dame Press**

# PUSHCART PRIZE 2009

## THE PREFERRED LITERARY & CLASSROOM COMPANION

☆ *"The 33rd Pushcart anthology demonstrates that independent presses still publish much of the world's most engaging literature … a must-have book for contemporary literature lovers."*

FROM THE PUBLISHERS WEEKLY STARRED REVIEW

---

**63 brilliant stories, poems, essays and memoirs selected from hundreds of small presses**

618 PAGES ■ HARDBOUND $35.00 ■ PAPERBACK $16.95

PUSHCART PRESS ■ P.O. BOX 380 ■ WAINSCOTT, NEW YORK 11975

ORDER FROM W. W. NORTON CO. ■ 800 223-2584

WWW.PUSHCARTPRIZE.COM

60th ANNIVERSARY / The Hudson Review / CELEBRATING SIXTY YEARS OF LITERATURE AND THE ARTS

For the final installment of our 60th Anniversary Year,
The Hudson Review announces the publication of a special

**TRANSLATION ISSUE** *Volume LXI, Number 4 (January 2009)*

---

Featuring literary essays, fiction, and poetry translated from French, Russian, Portuguese, Japanese, Romanesco, Middle English, and Ancient Greek.

*In which . . .*
RICHARD PEVEAR translates Swiss critic JEAN STAROBINSKI
EMILY GROSHOLZ translates French poet YVES BONNEFOY
ALFRED MACADAM translates Brazilian novelist MACHADO DE ASSIS
RICHARD WILBUR translates French tragedian PIERRE CORNEILLE
JOHN RIDLAND translates the fourteenth-century epic *Sir Gawain and the Green Knight*

By encouraging excellence in literary translation, we strive to provide a gateway to international literatures. More than a special issue, this will be an anthology of world literature to be treasured.

---

*Order online at www.hudsonreview.com*

**The Pinch** seeks previously unpublished work in **fiction, creative nonfiction, poetry, art,** and **photography.** We publish a broad spectrum of established and emerging writers and artists. Contributors include Naomi Shihab Nye, Dinty W. Moore, Steven Wingate, Stephen Dunn, Bobbie Ann Mason, George Singleton, Mark Doty and many others. www.thepinchjournal.com

**Subscriptions:**
-Individual $10/copy or $18/year
-Institutions $20/year

**The Pinch Literary Awards**
*$1500 Fiction Prize -- $1000 Poetry Prize plus publication
*Postmark submissions between January 15 and March 15
*No electronic submissions
*See website for details*

Study writing in the land of blues, barbecue, and Elvis. Concentrations in Fiction, Creative Nonfiction, and Poetry. Faculty includes Richard Bausch, John Bensko, Cary Holladay, Kristen Iversen, Tom Russell, and Rebecca Skloot. For more information, call (901) 678-4692 or visit our website www.MFAinMemphis.com

THE UNIVERSITY OF
MEMPHIS
Dreamers. Thinkers. Doers.

**www.thepinchjournal.com** The Pinch - Department of English,
Phone: (901) 678-4591, Fax: (901) 678-2226
The University of Memphis, Memphis, TN 38152

# PLEIADES

a journal of new writing

stories

essays

reviews

poetry

www.ucmo.edu/englphil/pleiades

*New from Notre Dame Press . . .*

$25.00 cl • ISBN 978-0-268-03513-6

## Spirits in the Grass
## Bill Meissner

"Bill Meissner's *Spirits in the Grass* is nothing short of stunning, his mastery of the prose is evident in virtually every sentence as it intensifies and heightens the intrigue of the wonderful story being told. This is a vibrant and original novel, a triumph, and Meissner's linguistic veracity places him among the finest prose stylists writing today."

—Jack Driscoll,
author of *How Like an Angel*

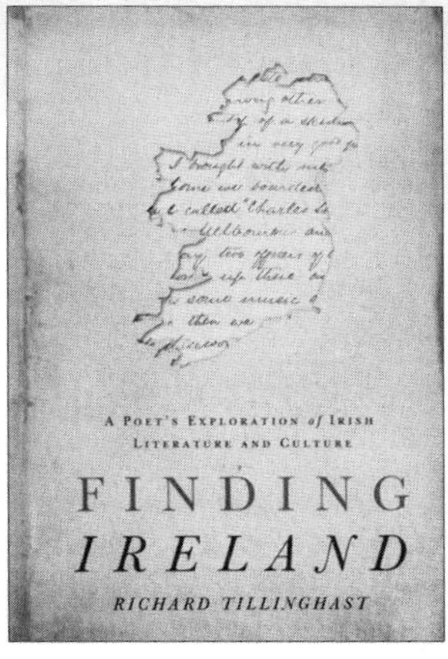


$25.00 pa • ISBN 978-0-268-04232-5
*October*

## Finding Ireland
### A Poet's Explorations of Irish Literature and Culture
## Richard Tillinghast

"*Finding Ireland* offers a welcome gathering of perceptive pieces by the poet-critic Richard Tillinghast. An American who has lived on and off in Ireland, Tillinghast brings a refreshingly clear-eyed perspective to his subjects. Whether riffing on the aftermath of the Celtic Tiger, Nobel laureates like Yeats and Heaney, or Irish traditional music and gardens, he writes with grace, aplomb, and unflagging insight. A joy to read."

—George Bornstein,
University of Michigan

Available at bookstores, or order online at: *www.undpress.nd.edu*

**UNIVERSITY OF NOTRE DAME PRESS**
Tel: 800-621-2736 • Fax: 800-621-8476

SURVIVORS & TESTIMONY

# TORTURE

HEALING & RECUPERATION

A Three-Part Series with Inge Genefke,
Founder of Copenhagen's Center for Rehabilitation
and Counsel for Torture Victims.

GLOBAL ACTIVISM AGAINST TORTURE.

Volume 74 nos. 1, 2, 3 (2007 & 2008)
Set of three issues: $28 ppd.
Inge Genefke speaks, based on interviews by renowned
journalist Thomas Larsen, translated from Danish
to English by Thomas E. Kennedy.

*New Letters* a journal of writing and art,
University of Missouri-Kansas City, Kansas City, Mo. 64110
www.newletters.org
(816) 235-1168 / newletters@umkc.edu